Two Down, Bun to Go

Oxford Tearoom Mysteries

Book Three

H.Y. Hanna

Copyright © 2016 H.Y. HANNA
All rights reserved.
ISBN-13: 978-09945272-3-3

This book is a work of fiction. Names, characters, places and incidents are the product of the author's imagination or are used fictitiously. Any resemblance to actual events, locales, business establishments, persons or animals, living or dead, is entirely coincidental.

This book is licensed for your personal enjoyment only. No part of this publication may be reproduced, stored in a retrieval system or transmitted in any form or by any means, electronic or mechanical, including photocopying, recording or otherwise, without written permission from the author. Thank you for respecting the hard work of this author

DEDICATION

For Jean, Ron, Ferdie, Jimmy, Roger—and all the other college staff who made me feel so welcome during my time at Oxford.

CONTENTS

CHAPTER ONE

When you're jolted awake by the shrill ringing of the phone at two in the morning, somehow you always know it's going to be bad news.

Groaning, I dragged myself out of the depths of sleep and heaved up on one elbow, reaching for my phone on the bedside table. It slipped from my fingers and fell to the floor. *Argh!* I leaned over the side of the bed, groping frantically in the dark until my hand found something flat and hard. I scooped it up, fumbling to answer.

"Gemma?"

It was my friend, Seth Browning, and the fear in his voice jarred me instantly wide awake.

"Seth? What's the matter?" I sat up in bed.

"Gemma—" His voice was low and strained. "I need you to do something for me."

"What? What's happened?"

"You need to go to Wadsworth College. Now. And—
"

"Wadsworth? But it's the middle of the night!"

He ignored me and kept on speaking, "Go to the Porter's Lodge and look in Professor Barrow's pigeonhole. There's a note from me in there—God, I hope it's still there!—I need you to remove it." He paused, then added urgently, "And don't let the police see you."

"The *police*?" Seth, what on earth is going on?"

"I can't explain now, Gemma," he said desperately. "Just trust me and do what I say, please?"

He was scaring me. "But Seth—"

"Gemma!"

"Okay, okay, but how am I going to get in? The college gates will be locked at this time of the night and I'm not one of the students. I don't have the keys."

"You can get in from my side. There's a connecting gate through from Gloucester."

"There is? I never knew about that."

"It's not public knowledge, but those of us in the two colleges know about the shortcut. There's a wooden door leading from the rear wall by the Master's House in Gloucester into the Walled Garden on Wadsworth's side. You've still got my spare keys, right?"

I did. Like the typical absent-minded academic,

Seth had a tendency to be so wrapped up in his books and research that he forgot practical everyday things. After yet another expensive visit to the locksmith for a new set of keys, Seth had finally asked me to keep a spare set for him.

"Yeah, I've got them. But aren't you at Gloucester yourself? Seth, you've got to tell me what's going on! Where are you? And why are the police involved?"

"Just get the note quickly. *Please.*"

Then the line went dead.

I lowered the phone and stared at the screen glowing blankly in the dark, as if it would give me the answers. I brought up the call register and noticed that it didn't show Seth's name. It was an unregistered number. So he hadn't been calling from his own phone. What on earth was going on?

I can't explain... trust me... please. Seth's desperate voice echoed in my mind. I'd never known him to sound like that. Brilliantly clever but very shy, Seth had chosen a life of academia and remained at Oxford after he'd completed his Chemistry degree and graduate studies. He had been one of the youngest post-doctoral scientists to get the Senior Research Fellow position at Gloucester College, and divided his days between research and giving lectures and tutorials to students. He was usually the calmest, most precise and methodical person you could meet. What on earth could have happened to make him so rattled?

I pushed back my duvet. It didn't matter. Seth was

one of my oldest friends—we'd known each other since that first week when we'd started as Freshers in Oxford together. I didn't know what was going on but just the fact that he was asking for my help was enough.

I switched on the bedside lamp and scrambled out of bed, shivering in the chill of the room. I dressed quickly, putting on several layers for warmth. It was mid-January and Oxford was deep in the grip of a harsh winter, with icy winds and ominous grey skies dominating the days. Going out now, in the middle of the night, would be freezing. I pulled a woolly sweater over my head, then added an extra fleece top for warmth, zipping it snugly up to my chin.

"*Meorrw?*"

I glanced back at the bed where my little tabby cat, Muesli, was sitting amongst the rumpled blankets. She tilted her head to one side as she regarded me with her bright green eyes, then she jumped off the bed and trotted to the bedroom door.

"*Meorrw?*" She looked over her shoulder at me expectantly.

"No, Muesli," I whispered. "It's still the middle of the night. You can't go out now."

"*Meorrw!*" Muesli gave a petulant twitch of her tail.

"Sorry..." I muttered, easing her gently away from the door.

I opened it and slipped out, shutting it quickly behind me before Muesli could follow. Then I tiptoed downstairs, going slowly as I didn't dare switch on any lights. In the hallway, I hesitated, wondering if I should leave my parents a note. They'd be worried if they awoke and found my bed empty, with no idea where I'd gone. On the other hand, I didn't know what I should say; how could I explain why I was going out to Wadsworth College at this time of the night? Not without mentioning Seth's phone call and something—some instinct—held me back from doing that.

I sighed. This was another problem with moving back to live with your parents. I wasn't used to having to account for myself to anybody anymore—after eight years of living and working in Sydney, freedom and independence were things I took for granted. Now it was weird to be back in a position where you had somebody *worrying* about you.

I'll be back in less than an hour, I thought. No need to leave a note. Least said, soonest mended. Not exactly the right proverb for the situation but close enough.

I let myself out of the house and inhaled sharply as the cold hit me. It was frigid and a light fog lay on the street, turning the glow of the streetlights into pale halos in the night sky. I pulled my scarf up to cover my mouth, then unchained my bike from the railing at the front of my parents' house, climbed astride, and pushed off.

At least the streets were empty at this time of the night. I pedalled as fast as I could, the cold air biting my cheeks as I peered ahead into the mist. My parents lived in the leafy suburb of North Oxford and I followed the main artery of Banbury Road into the centre of the city. The bike sailed silently past rows of elegant Victorian townhouses, past the various University departments and colleges, until it merged into the junction at St Giles'. Normally swarming with hordes of tourists in the day, it was now eerily empty and silent. The Martyrs' Memorial loomed out of the mist ahead of me and I let the bicycle freewheel past, skimming down Magdalen Street and then curving around into the wide boulevard of Broad Street.

Filled with many of Oxford's most iconic buildings—those "dreaming spires", Gothic towers and grand college quadrangles that you saw on all the postcards—Broad Street was the symbolic heart of the University, the closest thing to the "campus" that tourists were always searching in bewilderment for. It was difficult for them to understand the collegiate system and that "Oxford University" was really spread out across the whole city, made up of nearly forty colleges and an assortment of department buildings, research laboratories, and libraries—all interspersed with the original houses, markets, and buildings of the historic town of Oxford itself. There was no campus—the entire city *was* the campus.

Wadsworth College was one of the member colleges, tucked in amongst the cluster of ancient buildings that occupied the end of Broad Street. I cycled down the lane, past Wadsworth itself, and pulled up in front of Gloucester College next door. At least the brisk pedalling had warmed me up. Clouds of steam billowed from my lips as I got off the bike and paused to catch my breath.

Like many Oxford colleges, Gloucester had a pair of giant medieval wooden doors guarding its entrance, their thick surface reinforced with iron bands and studs. College gates were usually shut in the evenings but all students (and college staff) were given keys to the wicket door—a small, narrow door cut into the wooden surface of the gate—so that they could come and go at any time.

Seth's keys worked easily and I swung the wicket inwards, stepping into the main quadrangle. It was deathly quiet. Quickly, I began to make my way across the college grounds to the south side, where its wall abutted that of Wadsworth's. I was fairly familiar with Gloucester—not only had I been here several times in my undergraduate days but it was now Seth's affiliated college, and it had also been involved in a murder case which I got embroiled in recently. I located the Master's residence and, after a bit of searching, found the small wooden door embedded in the stone wall alongside. Funny how I had walked past it so many times without even noticing.

A few minutes later, I was stepping noiselessly into the Walled Garden of Wadsworth College. Wadsworth was one of the slightly smaller Oxford colleges (though what's considered "small" in Oxford is still spectacular everywhere else) and one I wasn't so familiar with. If I remembered rightly, the Walled Garden was at the rear of the college. To get to the Porter's Lodge, where the pigeonholes were located, I would have to find my way to the front gate. I looked around, trying to decide which was the quickest way there.

Facing the Walled Garden was a large imposing Georgian building, all tall grid windows and classical columns, which I guessed was the college library. To the left of the library building was an archway. I walked over and peered in. A long, narrow passageway—almost like a tunnel—cut through to a courtyard beyond the library. *No, wait, it wasn't a courtyard*, I realised, as I caught a glimpse of multiple Gothic arches and ornately carved pillars at the end of the tunnel. I remembered now—this was the Wadsworth College Cloisters. Many Oxford colleges had cloisters, a remnant of their monastic roots, usually situated around the college chapel.

To my surprise, I saw lights at the other end of the tunnel. And movement. Lots of movement. Why all the activity? The Cloisters were in an isolated corner of the college, away from the student dormitory quads, the dining hall, and the main quads. It should have been dark and empty at this time of night but I could see beams of torchlight scanning the area, the powerful flashes of a camera, and the crackle of a radio... a *police radio?*

Suddenly I remembered Seth's warning about not letting the police see me. What was going on? Why were the police here? I hesitated, fighting my natural instinct to go towards the activity and ask someone for an explanation. I remembered the urgency in Seth's voice and turned instead in the other direction.

On the other side of the library building, the Walled Garden opened up into a wide path which led towards the front of the college. I hurried down this now, passing through a smaller quad and then the main quadrangle of Wadsworth College. I quickened my steps, crossing the flagstones of the quad as fast as I could without actually running; I didn't want to draw too much attention to myself.

A high medieval gate tower was situated at the far corner of the main quad. The front gate of Wadsworth College led into the tower, so that all visitors had to pass through the tower to enter the college. Situated next to the front gate was the traditional Porter's Lodge, where the college porters—who provided a combination of security and concierge services—had their desk and office. It was also where the pigeonholes were located.

I slowed as I approached the tower. A group of students were gathered around the doorway to the Lodge and, from their drunken laughter and rowdy behaviour, I guessed that they'd probably just left a party. Most parties in college rooms were usually shut down after midnight and these were probably the last stragglers who had been kicked out. They were still in high spirits, monkeying around, laughing and teasing each other. The girls were wearing short dresses with flimsy cardigans for warmth and many of the boys had only a shirt, with no jacket or coat.

My God, aren't they cold? Then I felt a wry smile tug my lips. *I'm sounding like an old granny.* It wasn't that long ago that I had been part of a crowd like that, with nothing more than a skimpy dress and high spirits to keep me warm. It seemed like a lifetime away. In a way, it *was* a lifetime away. Though it had only been eight years since I'd left Oxford for that graduate fast-track executive position in Australia, it felt much longer. Maybe it was because I'd changed so much since then and come to realise that all the things which had seemed so important to me, meant so little now. For one thing, I'd never thought I would give up that prestigious high-flying career to come back to Oxford and open a village tearoom...

Then a figure stepped out of the Lodge into the quad and cut short my reminiscing instantly. I saw the black uniform, the peaked cap.

Police.

Quickly, I ducked my head and shoved my hands into my pockets, assuming the slouching gait of a typical student. I sidled over and joined the edge of the rowdy group, hoping desperately that the constable wouldn't look this way. Wrapped up in my multiple layers of wool and fleece, it would be obvious that I didn't belong to the group if he really looked.

I risked a glance in his direction. He wasn't looking. In fact, he had his head down, talking into a radio. He drifted past the group, walking down the quad towards the rear of the college.

I breathed a sigh of relief. I waited until he was a good distance away, then turned hesitantly towards the Lodge entrance. Would there be another constable inside? Did I dare risk it? The memory of Seth's voice flashed through my mind and, taking a deep breath, I went up the steps into the Porter's Lodge.

To my surprise, it was empty. Even the porter's desk was unmanned. I frowned but didn't waste time trying to figure it out. That constable could return any moment.

I hurried across to the far wall, which was covered by rows upon rows of wooden cubbyholes. These were the pigeonholes, the University's internal mail system and yet another charming quirk of Oxford life. It might seem an archaic way to communicate but it was surprisingly effective. Each morning, the porters received mail for the students at their college address and carefully distributed the items into the correct pigeonholes. You could also leave messages for a fellow student or college tutor in their pigeonholes, as well as small items that were borrowed and returned. If you wanted to send a message to someone at another college or one of the University departments, there was the handy "pigeon post"—a free service which operated between all University buildings. Just label your envelope "By internal mail", drop it into the wooden post box in the Porter's Lodge, and it would be delivered by the next day.

In the "old days", notes left in people's pigeonholes were the quickest ways of reaching them, better even than leaving a note under their bedroom door. After all, you might not return to your room during the day, especially if it was situated at the top of four flights of stairs at the far end of college, but you always passed by the front entrance several times a day and it became routine to pop into the Porter's Lodge and check your pigeonhole regularly.

I'd always thought that this quaint old system would be killed off—what with instant messaging apps and emails—but looking at the wads of paper and envelopes bursting from several pigeonholes, I was pleased to see that it hadn't been abandoned. I scanned the wooden compartments, reading the names on each label. They were arranged in alphabetical order and I found "Prof Q. Barrow" easily—one of the pigeonholes on the top row. I glanced quickly around, then stretched up on tiptoe and pulled the sheaf of papers out of the compartment.

There were two stamped envelopes, a photocopy of a journal article, a flyer from the Oxford Past Times Society, and a folded piece of notepaper. I unfolded the latter and instantly recognised Seth's illegible scrawl. I shoved it into my pocket, returned the rest to the pigeonhole, and hurried back out of the Lodge.

And not a moment too soon. I saw that familiar figure in the peaked cap coming back across the quad. Quickly, I stepped behind the group of students, keeping them between me and the policeman as he walked past. I slipped around to the other side and began to walk away as nonchalantly as I could. I had just begun to relax when I heard the voice behind me.

"Excuse me, miss..."

I faltered and turned slowly around to find the constable walking towards me.

"Yes?" My voice came out in a squeak and I hastily cleared my throat.

"You a student here?" he said, coming closer.

I swallowed. Should I lie to the police? The answer was out before I realised it.

"Yes, I am."

I held my breath. If he asked me to produce my university card, I was stuffed. I did actually have my old university card in my wallet but a quick glance would show that I wasn't a member of Wadsworth and even wishful thinking couldn't make me look like the photo of my fresh-faced, eighteen-year-old self.

"Can you tell me if there's another way into the Cloisters from here?"

I relaxed slightly. "No, there's only one way in and out of the Cloisters. You have to go through this quad and the smaller Yardley Quad, around the Walled

Garden and then through a tunnel at the back of the library."

The constable scratched his head and gestured to the side of the quad we were standing in. "But... aren't the Cloisters just on the other side of this wall here? So aren't you doubling back on yourself? Isn't there a cut through?"

I shrugged. "Not that I know of. It *is* a bit of a roundabout route but that's the way the college was built."

"Righto," he said, making some notes on his pad. "And aside from the back gate by the student staircases, is there another way out of the college?"

I hesitated. I couldn't lie about this. "Yes, there is another gate. It's in the Walled Garden. It's a wooden door that leads into Gloucester College."

"Ah..." He wrote busily in his notebook, then gave me a nod. "Cheers."

He turned away and headed back into the Lodge. I hesitated. I should have taken this opportunity to escape, but curiosity was killing me now. What on earth had happened?

I drifted towards the student group again and gently tapped the arm of a freckle-faced youth.

"What's going on? Why are the police here?" I asked.

"Oh, hadn't you heard?" He giggled drunkenly. "There's been a murder in the Cloisters!"

I stared at him incredulously. "A what?"

"Old Barrow's come to a sticky end," said another

boy next to him, with more glee than sorrow. I guess Professor Barrow hadn't been particularly popular with the students.

The first boy nodded, his eyes bright with excitement. "And they got the killer too! Caught him red-handed, apparently. Some young don over from Gloucester—"

"No..." I said faintly, a horrible suspicion beginning to dawn on me.

"Oh, there's no doubt," said the boy with relish. "The head porter found him standing over the prof's body, holding the knife and covered in blood."

A girl squealed in the group and leaned over to join the conversation. "Is it true? Is it Dr Browning over at Gloucester? Fancy that! I've had tutorials with him. I never thought he'd be the type."

"Wait... No... this can't be right," I said desperately. "There must have been some mistake."

The freckle-faced boy looked at me solemnly. "There's no mistake. Professor Barrow was stabbed through the neck and killed. The police have arrested Seth Browning for murder."

CHAPTER TWO

The little Cotswolds village of Meadowford-on-Smythe looked picturesque and welcoming despite the grey wintry morning. The rows of thatched cottages, huddled together against the sharp wind, were silhouetted gently against the rolling hills in the distance and a flock of geese flew slowly past the church steeple, an elegant V in the grey skies.

In fact, everything looked so reassuringly normal—from the groups of tourists already bustling down the village high street, peering eagerly into the antique shops and craft stores, to old Mrs Stanton going past on her bicycle, her little Scottie dog riding proudly in the front wicker basket as usual—that I wondered if I might have dreamt everything the night before. It seemed too incredible to believe that I had spent an hour creeping about an Oxford college in the middle of the night, only to discover that my friend, Seth, had been arrested for murder.

Then I stepped away from my tearoom window and glanced down at the mobile phone I held in my hands. It was there on the screen, the record of Seth's call at 2:03 a.m., sharp and clear in the cold light of day. I hadn't imagined it. And of course, there was that note I had removed from Professor Barrow's pigeonhole...

I had read the note as soon as I got home but the contents had left me none the wiser. Seth had seemed to be referring to some project by the Domus Trust... I vaguely remembered hearing of them— weren't they a charity that helped the homeless?— and his tone had been uncharacteristically aggressive. One line in particular jumped out at me: "*You had better change your mind about things or I'll make sure you're sorry.*" *He must have been joking*, I thought, but you could almost take that the wrong way. I wondered what had happened to prompt Seth to write a note like that.

It didn't take a genius, though, to work out why he had asked me to get hold of the note. It was the worst kind of incriminating evidence. The one time you don't want to be writing a threatening message to a man is when he turns up dead, brutally murdered.

And what about me? By helping Seth remove the note so the police couldn't find it, wasn't I breaking the law too? Being an accessory to murder or something like that?

I set my lips. *I don't care.* Seth was my friend; I knew he hadn't murdered anyone and I'd have done anything to help him. Besides, if it came out, I could always argue that I hadn't known about the note's relevance when I was sent to get it—which was the truth.

But it wasn't going to come out.

No one had seen me remove the note and no one need ever know. Carefully, I cleared my call register and deleted all records of Seth's call.

I was so immersed in my thoughts that I almost missed the tinkling of the bells attached to the front door, announcing the arrival of new customers to the tearoom. It was a group of Japanese tourists, jabbering excitedly, cameras at the ready as they stared around in admiration. One Japanese lady pointed at the exposed dark wooden beams and the whitewashed walls, and said something to the others, who all smiled in delight.

"Hello! Welcome to the Little Stables Tearoom!" I hurried over to seat them. "Would you like some morning tea?"

"*Hai!*" Five pairs of almond eyes looked at me and they bowed.

I hesitated, then made a bow in return.

They bowed again.

"Uh... why don't you sit down?" I said hastily, ushering them to a nearby table.

"*Hai! Arigato!*" They chattered excitedly as they

settled themselves. Then one of them saw the inglenook fireplace in the corner and gave a cry of delight. Instantly, five cameras began clicking away like machine guns.

The first lady turned to me and said slowly, "Is... Old Engulish? King Henry?" She pointed around the tearoom's interior.

I was puzzled for a moment, then my face brightened. "Oh! Oh yes, this was a Tudor inn. Yes, that's right. A bit older than Henry VIII, actually. I believe it was built in 1489 or something like that."

"Ahhh..." She turned to the others and let out a stream of rapid Japanese.

I laid the menus on the table in front of them and said with a smile, "Everything we serve is also 'old English'—traditional cakes and buns which are made the same way they have always been for hundreds of years."

They examined the menu eagerly. Then the first lady turned back to me and said, "*Ano...* Engulish scone... and jam? *Daisuki desu!*" She beamed at me.

"You would like scones with jam?"

The others nodded eagerly.

"And would you like some clotted cream as well? That's how we eat proper English scones—with home-made jam and lovely clotted cream."

They furrowed their brows. "Clot cream?"

"It's a type of thick cream that's made by heating milk using steam and then leaving it to cool. You get this lovely rich cream which rises to the top and clings together and that's what you skim off..." I could see that they weren't following me so I tried again: "It's like whipped cream meets butter... very delicious!"

"Ahh!" Smiles spread around the table.

One of the women nearest me tugged my sleeve and said shyly, "Earl Grey, *onegaishimasu*?"

I smiled. "Of course. Earl Grey's my favourite tea too."

I took their orders for a plate of warm scones with jam and clotted cream, some hot buttered crumpets, a few slices of Madeira cake, and a large pot of Earl Grey tea to share. Then I was rushing to seat the next lot of tourists who walked wide-eyed into the tearoom, sniffing appreciatively.

It looked like it was going to be another busy day. It was barely ten minutes since we opened, but already tourists and locals alike were beating a path to the door. I felt a swell of pride. I might have only started four months ago but my tearoom was gaining a reputation as *the* place to go for delicious traditional British baking and proper English tea. It made my crazy impulse to give up my high-flying job and come back to run a tearoom in this little village seem worthwhile after all.

Oh, things had been tough at first, especially when an American tourist was found murdered within a few weeks of the tearoom's opening, with one of my scones shoved down his throat. I still winced when I thought about it. But since that mystery had been solved, things had gone from strength to strength. The Christmas season had been happily hectic and now, even though we were well into January, it didn't look like business was slowing down.

I felt a hopeful excitement stir in me. Even after increasing my friend Cassie's wages and dealing with the tearoom's expenses, I was starting to save up a nice little nest egg from the profits—which might have a chance of becoming a real "nest" at last! I'd been forced to move back with my parents when I returned to England, so I could pour all my savings into the tearoom, but after four months of living back home again, I was ready to put my head in the tearoom oven. Oh, don't get me wrong—I'm really thankful to have a place to stay—but there *is* such a thing as living *too* close to your parents. Especially when your mother was like my mother.

So I'd been looking at my bank account recently and eyeing the rental listings in the local papers with anticipation. If things continued like this...

Then I remembered something and came back down to earth with a thump. When I had lost my first chef, my mother had kindly stepped into the breach, and while her baking was absolutely divine, I'd always known that this was only a temporary solution. It wasn't fair to expect my mother to slave away in a tearoom kitchen all day, no matter how much she claimed to enjoy it. I would have to start looking for a permanent baking chef sooner or later.

In fact, I'd put an advert into the papers last week and had a few interviews lined up.

Of course, there was always the option of me or Cassie putting on the chef's hat and giving it a try... I glanced doubtfully across the room at the pretty, raven-haired girl serving at the tables. My best friend, Cassie, was a struggling artist who had happily dumped her other part-time jobs to join me full-time in the tearoom when I started. But while she could paint like a dream, charm customers with a smile, and wait on tables with a skill and grace that was mesmerising to watch, baking was one talent Cassie didn't possess.

As for me, I *had* been trying to learn but my efforts were hit-and-miss at best. Ask me to coordinate a multi-media global marketing campaign for an international corporation and I'll do it with ease, but producing an edible cheesecake was something else entirely. Besides, someone had to remain out here in the dining room, manning the cash register and looking after the customers...

I sighed. I knew in my heart that the extra money should really go towards hiring a full-time chef. Didn't they say you should always re-invest profits back into your business first? I gave another wistful sigh. My little nest would have to wait.

The front door's bells tinkled again and I glanced up automatically. Four little old ladies bustled in, taking off their scarves and mittens. There was a time when my heart would have sunk at seeing Mabel

Cooke and her friends, Glenda Bailey, Florence Doyle, and Ethel Webb, come into the tearoom. Known affectionately as the "Old Biddies", they were your typical meddling old ladies with far too much time on their hands and far too much interest in other people's business. All retired and in their eighties now, they also had a taste for detective novels and were all too ready to jump orthotics-first into any murder investigation they could find.

So far, their efforts at amateur sleuthing had been more hassle than help and usually got me embroiled in all sorts of trouble, but I had to admit that their network of community intel—otherwise known as local gossip—was pretty impressive. There was very little that didn't reach Mabel Cooke's ears and the police would have done well to have her as an informant.

Still, in spite of their meddling, I'd come to appreciate the Old Biddies. They were like the bossy, eccentric, exasperating great aunts I had never had. I knew they meant well and, to be honest, it was nice to feel someone cared about you. I was incredibly touched recently when they stepped in to help me wait at the tables during a really busy time, and since then, we had evolved a sort of unofficial arrangement where they helped out whenever they were free.

They wouldn't take any payment for their efforts, no matter how much I begged—insisting that they had spare time and enjoyed "feeling useful"—so in the end, all I could offer in return was a table at the tearoom any time they liked and to help themselves from the menu.

To be honest, I think the Old Biddies secretly enjoyed serving customers and having the chance to gossip with locals and tourists alike. They treated the tearoom as *their* little headquarters in Meadowford-on-Smythe and hardly a day passed without them popping in. Now, they helped themselves to a few things from the kitchen, then settled at their usual table by the windows. A few minutes later, however, they waved me frantically over. I arrived to find a plate of dainty finger sandwiches in front of them. They were examining the fillings like archaeologists poring over an excavation.

"Have you been changing the tearoom menu?" Mabel eyed me suspiciously.

"Yes, I've made some new additions," I admitted.

Mabel's chest swelled indignantly. "When you re-opened this tearoom, Gemma, we thought you would be serving good, wholesome, English food. It's about time somebody showed an appreciation for proper British cooking. But then we come in this morning and we see this!" She jabbed a finger to the menu in front of her.

I looked down. She was pointing to the "Tea Sandwiches" section of the menu, which listed a selection of traditional finger sandwiches such as English cucumber, smoked salmon, watercress, and creamy egg salad.

"Fresh dill and crème fraiche? Multigrain bread?

In a cucumber sandwich?" Mabel's voice rose with added outrage at each word. She wagged her finger at me. "I'll have you know, miss, that a proper English cucumber sandwich is made with plain butter on white bread with the crusts cut off and nothing else! What on earth were you thinking?"

"Well... I thought it would be nice to have a modern variation with more flavour..." My voice trailed off under that incredulous glare.

"I suppose you learned this sort of nonsense in Australia?" Mabel gave a contemptuous sniff. "I hear that the cafés and restaurants there are full of fused cooking."

I hid a smile. "I think you mean fusion cuisine."

Mabel sniffed again. "I suppose one can't expect much from a nation of convicts."

I think in Mabel's mind, everyone in Australia still walked around in striped pyjamas, dragging a ball and chain attached to their ankles.

I started to protest, then had a better idea. Now that I knew the Old Biddies better, I had my own ammunition. I looked at her slyly. "The Queen's Birthday is a public holiday there, you know," I said.

Mabel gave a gratified smile. "Is it really? Well! It's good to know that these colonies still show proper respect for the monarchy. Hmm... perhaps there is hope for them after all." She looked back down at the plate of sandwiches and her scowl returned. "But these modern monstrosities have to go."

She looked to the others for agreement. Ethel and

Glenda nodded but Florence, who was plump and loved her food, took a bite of the offending sandwich and chewed thoughtfully, then said:

"Well, actually, I think it's jolly delicious. Not like a proper, old-fashioned cucumber sandwich, mind, but Gemma is right—the herbs and crème fraiche do give it a lovely flavour and the cucumber is just so crisp and fresh against the buttered bread..."

Mabel glared at her but Florence remained stubbornly unmoved, helping herself to another dainty rectangle of thinly sliced bread and cucumbers. Mabel looked as if she would say something else, then she paused as if remembering something and turned suddenly to me.

"Now, Gemma, what's this I hear about your friend, Seth, being arrested for murder?"

I stared at her. Mabel's ability to always know things never failed to astound me.

"How did you know about that? It only happened in the early hours of this morning—it's not even on the internet yet."

Mabel waved a dismissive hand. "Pah, internet. Susan Bromley, who is on the church floral committee with me, has a neighbour whose niece works part-time in the kitchens at Wadsworth, and she told her aunt who told Susan who told Mrs Sutton down at the post office while she was having her hair done—Susan, I mean, not Mrs Sutton—and Mrs Sutton told me when we popped into the post office this morning to collect our pensions."

I blinked. I'd lost her somewhere between Susan Bromley's neighbour and Mrs Sutton's hair.

"Yes, but it's all a terrible mistake," I said. "Seth would never murder anybody!"

"Have you spoken to Seth himself?" asked Ethel, her eyes wide with concern. The quietest of the Old Biddies, Ethel was a lovely gentle soul who used to be the librarian at the village library.

"No, I haven't managed to speak to him. He's in custody, the police have confiscated his mobile, and they wouldn't let me talk to him."

I wondered if the police knew that Seth *had* managed to speak to me last night. He must have somehow convinced them that he was ringing his solicitor—you were entitled to a private call for legal advice. I hoped that meant that no one had eavesdropped on our conversation or checked the number he'd called. The last thing I needed was for the police to arrive on my doorstep demanding to know what Seth had asked me to do for him at 2 a.m. in the morning.

"We heard it was a very brutal murder," said Glenda with a shiver. "One of the Oxford college dons, wasn't it? What was his name—Professor Burrows or something like that?"

I almost corrected her, then I remembered that I wasn't supposed to know the details. The only reason I knew so much was because I had been at Wadsworth myself and had spoken to those students.

"Is that what happened?" I said, opening my eyes wide. "How horrible!"

Mabel looked at me shrewdly and I wondered if my show of surprise had been a bit overdone.

I rushed on, "How was he killed?"

"He was stabbed," said Glenda. "With an ice pick!"

"No, I heard it was a bread knife," said Florence.

"Oh no, it was a knitting needle!" said Ethel.

"No, no, you've all got it wrong," said Mabel impatiently. "It was a dagger. An Egyptian dagger. I know because Susan Bromley told me herself when I saw her outside the post office. Her neighbour's niece said the police were questioning all the staff about it, asking if any of them had seen it before."

"Well, Seth certainly doesn't own any Egyptian daggers," I declared. "So if that was the murder weapon, it's proof that it can't have been him—"

"Ah, but it could have been borrowed or stolen from its owner," Mabel pointed out. "And Seth was the one found holding it."

"He must have had a good reason for that," I said quickly. "Do they know who owns the dagger? An Egyptian dagger is pretty unusual. Surely, it would be fairly easy to find the owner."

They shook their heads.

"Do *you* know why Seth was in Wadsworth last night?" asked Glenda.

"No, I... I didn't speak to him last night. I knew nothing about this, really, until you told me."

"If you didn't know all this, how did you know

that Seth was arrested?" said Mabel suddenly.

"Oh, um…" I scrambled for an answer. "His… his solicitor rang me this morning and told me."

"Ah, we thought… since you have a special friend in the CID…" Glenda gave me a coy smile. "Perhaps Detective Inspector O'Connor might have told you."

I blushed slightly and was annoyed with myself. "No, Devlin doesn't talk about his work. And besides, I've hardly seen him," I said, trying not to sound petulant.

It was actually a bit of a sore point with me. Devlin O'Connor and I went back a long way—all the way back to our student days, when we had been at Oxford together. Devlin had been the first man I ever loved—okay, he might have been the *only* man I ever loved—but he was also the man whose marriage proposal I'd turned down. What can I say? I was young and impressionable at the time and I'd believed everyone when they told me that the rebellious youth with his fierce blue eyes and working-class background was the wrong man for a nice girl from a proper, upper-middle-class family like me. We were too different, they said. We could never be happy. Those kinds of crazy romances only worked in novels, not in reality. And I'd always been the dutiful type, brought up to "do the right thing"…

Except that eight years of doing "the right thing" and fulfilling society's expectations had left me miserable and frustrated. And lonely. Sometimes, when my defences were down, I'd let myself look back and wonder how things might have been different if I had only said "Yes" that day when Devlin had presented me with that simple engagement ring he had worked so hard to afford...

When I'd come back to England and discovered that Devlin was now a top detective with the Oxfordshire CID, it had been a shock to say the least. A shock to see those piercing blue eyes and lean handsome face again, to feel that special, silent bond that had always existed between us. He had matured into a cool, enigmatic man, the wild, rebellious spirit now carefully contained, but still I had caught glimpses of the boy I had once loved. And somehow, despite the hurt and years that had built a wall between us, working on two murder cases together had brought us close again and I had found myself wondering if we might have a second chance...

Well, I was still wondering.

After the last case had been solved, Devlin had asked me out on a date and I'd tentatively agreed. Dinner and a night at the ballet had seemed like the perfect way to test the relationship waters again—but a rape out in Cowley had brought that to a grinding halt. Devlin had had to cancel that date, plus the three others afterwards. Homicide, serious assault, aggravated robbery... honestly, it was as if every bloody criminal in Oxford conspired to keep us apart by planning their crimes for our date nights! And then, just as Christmas was approaching, a cold case was re-opened in Devlin's old department up in

Yorkshire and he was called back north. That was the last I'd seen of him in three weeks.

I know, I know, it's the nature of his work and if I was going to fall in love with a detective, this came with the territory. These men were dedicated and driven, working crazy hours in the quest for justice. I knew the last few months had probably been unusually bad and, in any case, I'd been madly busy myself with holiday season at the tearoom, but still, I couldn't help feeling just a little bit peeved.

So when Devlin had finally come back to Oxfordshire last week and rung me up, I'd been pretty cool in my reception. I was wary now of getting too excited over any idea of a date with him. In fact, we were supposed to meet up tonight, but I wasn't holding my breath.

"So will you be seeing Inspector O'Connor any time soon?" said Mabel, breaking into my thoughts.

"Yes, tonight—" I broke off. *Bugger.* I'd answered without thinking. Now Mabel would be pumping me for information on the murder tomorrow. As far she was concerned, I was an unofficial channel into the secrets of the Oxfordshire CID.

Well, maybe she was right. What was the point of having a detective boyfriend if you didn't get some perks?

CHAPTER THREE

The bells tinkled again and I glanced over to see an elegant middle-aged woman step into the tearoom. I recognised her instantly as my mother's closest friend: Helen Green. I hurried towards her.

"Gemma! Lovely to see you, dear." She came towards me and gave me a light peck on the cheek, enveloping me in a cloud of discreet perfume.

Like my mother, Helen Green always looked as if she was on her way to an audience with the Queen, her grey hair carefully coiffured, an elegant necklace of pearls around her neck, and a cream cashmere twinset peeking out from beneath her classic camel coat. She pulled off her leather gloves and said to me, "I was hoping to have a word with your mother, dear. Is she in the kitchen?"

As if hearing her name, the door to the kitchen swung open and my mother sailed out, resplendent in a wool crepe dress with a large sterling silver brooch and a 1950s-style frilly apron. How she managed to stay looking so glamorous and immaculate while baking in the kitchen was a mystery to me.

"Oh Helen, I've just booked it! We leave on Monday!" my mother beamed at her friend.

I looked at my mother in confusion. "Booked what, Mother? Where are you going?"

"To Borobudur, darling."

I stared at her. "To where?"

"Borobudur! It's a Mahayana Buddhist Temple in Magelang."

"Where on earth is that?"

My mother looked smug. "In Central Java, darling."

"Central Java... you mean, Indonesia?"

"Yes, Borobudur is the world's largest Buddhist monument and one of the original Seven Wonders of the World!" my mother said excitedly. "You can climb all the way to the top and watch the sun rise over the stupas and there are five hundred and four Buddha statues across the hilltop. Or was it five hundred and five? Anyway, it's really just the most marvellous design! Only imagine, they built it 1,200 years ago without any cement or mortar—it's just like a set of giant interlocking Lego blocks held together without any glue!"

"Uh... that sounds wonderful," I said warily. "But why all this sudden interest in Buddhist temples,

Mother? You've never said anything about wanting to visit Indonesia before."

"Oh, it's the deal of the week on Lastminute.com, darling!" my mother said. "And if you book by this weekend, they'll throw in a trip to a *batik* factory for half price!"

Oh God. My mother's recent passion for online shopping had mutated into an obsessive interest in travel sites. I'd thought that it was mostly window shopping—you know, we all do that: look longingly at places we'd love to travel to and check out airfares and hotel options just for fun—but I never thought that she'd seriously book anything. After all, my parents' idea of travel usually involved sedate weekends visiting art galleries and museums in Paris or Rome, not traipsing off to the outer wilds of Southeast Asia. I guess I was wrong.

"What about Dad?" I said. "Are you sure he's happy for you to go?"

"Well, I did try to persuade your father to come with but he's only interested in his silly cricket," my mother complained. "Besides, he left for Cape Town this morning with some of his old Eton chums to watch the South Africa vs. England test match and you know he won't be back for a week at least. So I thought... why not just go by ourselves? Like that film, you know, *Thelma & Linda*—"

"Louise," I muttered.

"—Helen thought it was a wonderful idea!"

Helen Green nodded and said eagerly, "We can

even visit Krakatoa! You can do it as a day trip from Jakarta. It's still active, you know, and they say it can blow at any time! And the water in the sea around is boiling hot and the sand too hot to even stand on."

My mother gave a delicious shudder. "Oh, how absolutely frightful! I can hardly wait, Helen!"

I stared at the two of them in bewilderment. Was this some kind of weird mid-life crisis thing? Maybe my mother shouldn't have stopped her HRT. Since when had two conservative British middle-class housewives become so bloodthirsty for danger and excitement?

"Er... Mother, you know Krakatoa is a volcanic island in the sea off the coast of Java?" I said. "And nobody wants to go to Jakarta now if they can help it! There was that warning on the BBC saying it's officially an area of 'high threat for terrorist attacks' and they think—"

"Oh, nonsense, darling," my mother said. "You're worrying too much. I'm sure we'll be fine. We're not going anywhere political—we're just going to take a boat out to see a volcano."

"But Mother—"

"Do you think our Samsonite cases will do, Helen? Perhaps we should get one of those 'knapsack' affairs," said my mother, frowning.

"They would fit better on the fishing boat," agreed Helen. "I read that you can carry a third of your body weight in your knapsack."

"Really?" said my mother in delight. "That would be so helpful. I have to take my electric toothbrush and my Crabtree & Evelyn soap, of course. Oh, and a pair of nice shoes. And maybe some Tupperware containers just in case? The memory foam neck pillow for the plane—but that should squash down, I think. And what about some lavender sachets to keep things smelling fresh?"

I had a sudden vision of my mother and Helen Green staggering around Indonesia with matching Harrods knapsacks on their shoulders.

"Mother, I really don't think this is a good idea. I mean, you've never done 'independent travel' before—it's very different, you know. It's rougher and dirtier and much harder work. I don't think you really understand... and besides, Southeast Asia probably isn't the best place to start for two... uh... mature ladies like you and Aunt Helen. Aren't there any Lastminute.com deals for Paris?" I asked desperately.

"Oh, Paris is boring." My mother gave a disdainful sniff. "Who wants to go to Paris when you can go to Jakarta?"

Lots of people. People who don't want to be killed in terrorist bombings or blown up in a volcano, I thought.

"Now, darling," my mother continued blithely. "Don't you worry about the tearoom. I'll make up several batches of scone dough and put them in the fridge. That should keep you going for a day or two.

And some shortbread and Chelsea buns too. And I'll leave the recipes for the other things. It's very easy. You just have to follow the instructions."

I sighed and gave up. "Okay, Mother. Thanks for doing that. Shall I drop you and Aunt Helen at the airport? The tearoom's closed on Mondays, so I'll be free."

"Oh no, we're taking the express coach from the bus station! Just like all the other 'real' travellers," my mother said proudly.

"Besides, you'll probably be busy getting your hair done or something for Monday night," said Helen with a smile. "I'm so delighted that you're going with Lincoln to the Oxford Society of Medicine dinner, Gemma."

"I... I am?" I stared at her in surprise. It was the first I'd heard of it. I gave my mother a suspicious look.

"Oh yes, darling, remember I told you?" said my mother airily. "I was chatting with Helen the other day and she told me that Lincoln is the keynote speaker at the Oxford Society of Medicine dinner this term. Isn't that such an honour? I knew you'd want to be there."

Grrr. She had told me nothing of the kind. My mother was obviously up to her match-making tricks again. Lincoln was Helen's son and if betrothal contracts were still in place, my mother would have had us engaged from birth. Ever since I'd returned to England, she had been doing everything in her power to throw us together. I suppose she thought if she pretended that I'd already accepted Lincoln's invitation, I couldn't back out.

It was on the tip of my tongue to snap a refusal, then I saw the expression on Helen's face. Irritation warred with compassion in my heart and compassion won.

"Oh... er... yes, that's right... I... er... I'd forgotten," I said. I gave Helen a wan smile. "I'm really looking forward to it."

"You know, he's *so* fond of you, Gemma," said Helen with a meaningful look.

My smile felt frozen on my face. "Um... yes, I... I'm very fond of Lincoln too."

Thankfully, my mother suddenly remembered a new recipe she wanted to show Helen and the two of them disappeared into the kitchen. I took a deep breath and tried to lower my blood pressure again. Cassie joined me at the counter and I started to complain about my mother's meddling, but paused as I saw the strained expression on her face.

"Have you heard back from that lawyer yet?" she asked.

"No." I frowned. I'd called Seth's family solicitor this morning and he had given me the name of the criminal lawyer that he had passed Seth on to. According to him, the man was the best in Oxford and I'd felt a childlike hope that the whole nightmare would be over soon. But when I'd rung the number, it was to find a frustratingly indifferent receptionist at the other end of the line, who informed me in a cool, blank voice that Mr Sexton was out at a meeting and unavailable. I had hoped that meant he was at the police station sorting things out for Seth and had to be content with leaving him a message. It was a bit worrying that he hadn't rung me back yet...

"I'll try him again now," I said.

I managed to get through to Mr Sexton this time but if I'd been hoping for some reassurance, I was sorely disappointed. In fact, I felt a prickle of annoyance at the lawyer's off-hand manner.

"Yes, I went to see Mr Browning at the station this morning." He made a tutting sound. "Really, a very bad state of affairs..."

My heart sank at his tone. Somehow, I had still been clinging to the hope that he would say it was all a misunderstanding, something easily fixed.

"How bad?" I asked.

"Well, considering that Mr Browning was found holding the murder weapon, covered in the victim's blood, and there are witness reports of a violent confrontation earlier that evening..."

"A what? What violent confrontation? What are you talking about?"

"Apparently Mr Browning and Professor Barrow were involved in a heated argument over dinner and things became quite unpleasant. Threats were made, a glass of wine was thrown in Professor Barrow's face, I believe, and they had to be separated. There were further altercations in the S.C.R.—the Senior

Common Room—afterwards... It seems that they almost came to blows." He made that irritating tutting sound again. "I have advised Mr Browning that in a case such as this, pleading guilty might be the best option. I would then be able to direct my efforts towards negotiating a more lenient sentence. Perhaps manslaughter or—"

"*What?* You can't be serious! You know Seth didn't murder anyone! You're his lawyer! You're supposed to be helping to release him, not helping the police convict him!"

Too late, I realised that I was shouting in my indignation. The entire tearoom was staring at me, including the Old Biddies with beady-eyed interest. Cassie looked horrified. I flushed and turned my back to the room, lowering my voice and saying urgently, "Surely there must be other suspects? I mean, there will be a proper investigation, won't there?"

"Well, naturally... The inquest is being held on Monday but it will be immediately adjourned, of course, and I believe the police are pursuing several lines of enquiry. But I must tell you, young lady, that very few cases look as incriminating as this." He cleared his throat. "Now if you'll excuse me, I have a lot of work still to attend to."

"But what about Seth? What are you doing for him?"

"I am preparing a case for his defence," he said testily. "I shall be in touch with Mr Browning again as soon as I have something more concrete to discuss. At this juncture, there is little else I can do but wait for the police to proceed with their investigation. The date for the court trial has not yet been set. However, I have managed to persuade the police to agree to release Seth on bail. Pending any other new developments, he should be released tomorrow afternoon. And now, I really must bid you good day."

I hung up and lowered the phone. "Miserable old git," I muttered.

"What?" said Cassie, her eyes wide with concern. "What did he say?"

I glanced back at the tables, where several customers were still eyeing us curiously, and dragged Cassie into the little shop area adjoining the tearoom, where we sold English tea paraphernalia and Oxford souvenirs. I shut the glass door behind us. We could talk in private here.

I turned to my friend and said with a shrug, "Nothing much. To be honest with you, he doesn't seem that interested in helping Seth. He sounds like some stuffy old solicitor who just wants the easiest way out. He wants Seth to plead guilty so he can negotiate a lesser charge."

"But that's bollocks!" Cassie cried. "Why should Seth plead guilty when he's innocent? Besides, even if he gets a lesser conviction, it's still years in jail and a criminal record that will dog him for the rest of his life. Seth's career at Oxford, his whole life, will be destroyed!"

I was surprised by her passionate reaction. Cassie had the typical artist's fiery, volatile temperament, but this seemed excessive, even for her. She looked almost close to tears. I put a hand gently on her shoulder.

"The police will be conducting an investigation," I said. "I'm sure they'll find other suspects... and eventually they'll find the real murderer."

"Eventually isn't good enough for Seth," said Cassie fiercely. "And you know what the police are like! That solicitor isn't the only one who wants the easy way out. They've got the perfect culprit handed to them on a plate: a suspect with a previous history of aggression towards the victim, found holding the murder weapon next to the body... why would they bother trying to find anyone else?"

"I'm sure they'll investigate thoroughly," I said lamely.

"No, they won't! They don't really care about Seth, like we do. He's just a statistic to them." Cassie gripped my arm. "You have to do it, Gemma!"

"Me? Do what?"

"Find the real killer!" Cassie's grip tightened. "You've done it twice already. Both times, you put together the pieces and solved the mystery well ahead of the police—"

"Well, that's not really true," I protested. "Devlin is a shrewd investigator. He would have worked things out—"

"Devlin! That's it! You're seeing him tonight, aren't you?"

"Yes, but—"

"You need to find out everything about the case from him!"

"He might not be assigned to the case."

"He's CID! Even if he's not the lead officer on the case, he'll be able to get all the intel on the investigation."

I stared at her. "You mean... you want him to feed us information?"

"Why not? He knows Seth is innocent, just as we do! He's just helping to prevent an innocent man from being wrongfully convicted." Cassie gave me a look. "Besides, Gemma, you know he has a soft spot for you... he'll do it for *you*..."

"Well... uh..." I shifted uncomfortably. "I'm not sure Devlin would see it like that. He can't just share confidential information with me because we... uh... um... and the suspect is my friend."

"Why not?" demanded Cassie. "What's the point of having a boyfriend in the CID if you can't use him when you need it?"

Okay, so I'd had the same thought myself earlier, but I'd been joking, really. Somehow, the way Cassie said it now made me uncomfortable. For one thing, Devlin wasn't the kind of man you could ever imagine "using" in any way.

"Cassie, what you're suggesting is sort of like nepotism," I said uneasily. "Devlin is bound by a code of ethics and—"

"Rubbish! Do you think everybody is all high and noble and just follows the rules? Don't be a bloody idiot!" Cassie's dark eyes flashed. "It's all still an 'old boys club' and it's all about who you know. People doing each other favours behind closed doors, people giving special treatment to those they have a connection with—"

"Yes, but—"

"Look, Gemma, do you care about Seth or not?" she demanded.

"Of course, I care! But—"

"Well, if you really cared, then you'll do whatever it takes. You wouldn't give a toss about being all bloody ethical and noble. And you'd make Devlin help you."

"I—" I stared into Cassie's pleading eyes. "Okay, I'll speak to him tonight."

Cassie is right, I thought. We should have been using every advantage we had to help Seth—and besides, I'm sure the whole ethics thing wouldn't be an issue. Devlin knew as well as I did that Seth was innocent and I was sure he would jump to help him.

I thought of our date tonight with eager anticipation. Aside from getting to spend some time together at last (would we finally have our first kiss?), I knew Devlin would fix everything for Seth.

CHAPTER FOUR

After a hectic day, the crowds finally started to thin out towards the end of the afternoon. I could see that my mother was desperate to get back home and start packing for her trip, so I suggested that she leave early. We had all the baking we needed for the day anyway.

As the hands of the clock ticked towards five o'clock and closing time, I began drifting around the tables, making sure that they were clean and resetting them for the next day. Cassie was serving one of our few remaining customers over in the corner and I didn't think we'd get any more before closing. The fog was returning, draping like a damp, cold blanket over the village high street, and most people were eager to head for the dry warmth of their home or hotel rooms.

As I was clearing the table by the front window, I glanced out and saw a middle-aged woman standing on the street outside the tearoom. She seemed to be reading the menu outside of the door, her eyes lingering wistfully over the entries. I hurried to the front door and pushed it open, leaning out to greet her.

"We're not closed yet," I said with a smile. "Why don't you come in and look at the menu inside so you're not out in the cold?"

She flushed and her eyes slid away from mine. "Don't have enough cash on me," she said gruffly.

"Oh, that's no problem. We take credit cards and debit cards too..." I started to say, then trailed off as I realised what she was *really* saying.

My eyes took in the shabby tweed fabric of her coat, the thin cheeks and hollow eyes. There was a button missing from her coat and her shoes were faded and scuffed. She was clutching the edges of the coat tight around her, shivering slightly in the gathering mist.

"You can have a scone and a cup of tea for £2," I said impulsively.

She stiffened and raised her chin. "I don't need your charity."

"Oh, it's not charity! We're having a special at the moment," I said blithely. "'Tea for Two', see? It's a... a sort of end-of-day special, so that we can clear our supplies for the day."

"Oh..." I saw her eyes go hungrily to the menu

46

again.

I pushed the door of the tearoom open wider and a gust of warm air carrying the fragrant smell of fresh baking wafted out.

"Come on in," I urged her. "It'll be nice to get out of the cold for a bit."

Almost against her will, the woman let me escort her into the tearoom and settle her at one of the smaller tables by the far wall. Cassie saw us and started towards us with a menu but I waved her away, saying casually, "Oh, the lady has already decided what she's having. You know, that special we're doing—'Tea for Two'—the scone and cuppa for two quid."

Cassie stopped in her tracks. "We are?"

"Yes, don't you remember?" I said quickly. "Never mind, I'll go and fix it up myself."

I hurried into the kitchen and looked for the tray that held our signature scones. I was relieved to see that there were still a few left. Some days we sold out completely. I picked the largest I could find and quickly warmed it in the microwave, then placed it on a plate, together with a generous spoon of our home-made strawberry jam and a dollop of rich clotted cream. I put the plate on a tray and added a Royal Crown Derby bone china teapot filled to the brim with hot English tea, a matching teacup, a little jug of fresh milk, and a pot of old-fashioned sugar lumps. I glanced around and hastily scooped two shortbread biscuits out of the tin on the sideboard.

These I arranged on the edge of the saucer, then I carried the whole thing out to the woman at the table. Her eyes widened as the food was placed in front of her.

"No, no… I didn't ask for the shortbread as well. I can't afford—"

"Those are compliments of the house," I said quickly. "We're trying out a new shortbread recipe so we've been giving all customers a free trial to see what they think." I gestured towards the food. "Go on, have a taste. I'd love to know your opinion—it would be really helpful to us."

She hesitated, obviously torn between hunger and pride. I turned discreetly away but as I walked back to the counter, I glanced over my shoulder. The woman was biting into a scone, heavily slathered with jam and cream, and her eyes were closed blissfully. She chewed and swallowed, then took a sip of the hot tea and I saw her shoulders relax under the threadbare coat and colour come into her haggard face. A wave of gladness spread through me.

I got back to the counter and observed her surreptitiously. She looked vaguely familiar—had I seen her around the village? Yes, that's right… in the village post shop, I think. Unlike most of the residents of Meadowford-on-Smythe who were keen to chat and ask nosy questions, she had kept mostly to herself. A severe-looking woman with wispy grey hair pulled back in a bun and a haughty tilt to her chin. I wondered what her story was. She looked to be in her late fifties or early sixties and she moved with a certain stiffness. Arthritis? An old injury perhaps? Maybe one that prevented her from working?

One of the remaining customers came over to pay, interrupting my thoughts, and then I was kept busy by a trio of Swedish tourists who wanted to buy souvenirs from the shop. By the time they left, the woman had finished. She approached the counter with her old leather handbag.

"Thank you," she said formally. "It was delicious."

I was glad to see the spots of colour in her cheeks and hear the energy in her voice. I wanted desperately to do something else for her but I didn't know what else I could do, without offending her pride. I stood awkwardly behind the counter, trying not to look as she laboriously counted out loose change from a small faded purse. I was almost more nervous than she was that there wouldn't be enough to make up the full amount and breathed a silent sigh of relief as she finally pushed the motley collection of coins across the counter.

"There... that's £2... and another pound for the shortbread."

"Oh, no, I told you, that was complimentary—"

"And I told you, I'm not taking charity," she snapped.

I hesitated, then reluctantly took the money. "Any time you're passing by, don't hesitate to come in. We often have specials at the end of the day..."

"Do you?" She looked at me sharply. "Funny how it's not advertised. Most places can't hang signs big enough to shout about their specials."

"Oh... um... well..." I stammered.

She leaned across the counter and fixed me with a ferocious glare. "Don't think I didn't realise what you were doing." She paused, then added stiffly, "But I appreciate your kindness."

I gave her a hesitant smile. "I think I might have seen you around the village. My name is Gemma. Gemma Rose. I'm the owner of the Little Stables Tearoom."

"I'm Dora Kempton," she said.

She held a hand out and I shook it. Her hands were warm now but terribly thin. I glanced down. The skin on her fingers was calloused and worn.

"I meant what I said." I smiled at her again. "You're welcome any time."

She gave a slight nod. "I will be back... when I can pay for my own meal."

Turning, she walked stiff-backed towards the front door and I watched her open it and disappear into the mist.

CHAPTER FIVE

I was relieved when I got home to find that my mother had already gone out for her dinner with friends. Things were complicated enough with Devlin without adding my mother into the mix. I wasn't sure I wanted to brave the awkwardness of a confrontation between them. I knew that Devlin blamed my mother for breaking us apart eight years ago and, in a way, he was right.

She meant well, but my mother was a bit of a snob and although he was a fellow Oxford graduate, Devlin—with his working-class roots and his lack of the "right connections"—had seemed a poor match for her only daughter. How ironic that now, eight years later, Devlin should be one of the top investigators in the CID and the owner of a beautiful converted farmhouse in the Cotswolds, whilst I—with my brilliant Oxford education and middle-class privileges—was living back with my parents, trying to keep a tearoom business afloat.

Muesli met me at the front door, loudly demanding to know when her dinner was going to be served. My mother had offered to feed the little cat before she left, but I liked to save this bit of daily ritual for myself. After a long hectic day, it was lovely to return to the familiar evening routine in the cosy kitchen, humming a tune and preparing Muesli's food as she wove herself between my legs and told me impatiently to hurry up.

"*Meorrw*," she grumbled, rubbing against my shin. "*Meorrrrrw!*"

"All right, all right," I said, as I portioned the food into her little ceramic bowl. I bent down and placed it on the tiles, underneath the breakfast counter. "Here you go, madam."

Muesli scampered over and put her face eagerly into the bowl. A loud rumbling sound began to fill the kitchen and I smiled in spite of myself. There was just something wonderful about the sound of a contented cat purring.

I glanced at the clock on the wall. *Yikes. I'd better hurry if I want to have a shower before Devlin arrives to pick me up.* Twenty minutes later, I was just putting the finishing touches to my makeup when the doorbell rang. I hurried downstairs, trying to ignore the rapid beating of my heart. Why did I always feel like a teenage girl going out on her first date when Devlin was around?

The door swung open to reveal a tall figure standing on the front doorstep. The mist swirled around him and, for a moment, he looked just like those Celtic warriors you see in ancient mythology—all fierce blue eyes, wavy dark hair, and strong, aquiline profile—then he stepped into the hall and the impression was gone, to be replaced by a tall, handsome man in beautifully tailored coat. He must have come straight from work as he was dressed in a charcoal grey three-piece suit, with an Italian silk tie and crisp white shirt. On any other man, it might have come across a bit dandyish, but with his dark good looks, Devlin wore it all with a suave sophistication worthy of James Bond.

"Hi," I breathed, not quite meeting his eyes. It was stupid but I hadn't seen him since before Christmas and suddenly, I don't know why, I felt shy.

"Hi." The corner of his lips quirked in a smile. "I was going to bring roses again but I decided I'd better not tempt Fate. Maybe if we don't act like it's a date, we might actually get there."

I laughed and the tension was broken. "Come in... I just need to grab my coat from the living room..."

Devlin followed me but as he entered the living room, he stumbled and tripped. "What the—?"

A streak of grey fur had shot out from behind the sofa and across the room towards him. It was Muesli. She twined herself around Devlin's legs, purring like a little engine and looking up at him adoringly.

"Oh... uh... hi, Muesli," said Devlin, hobbling slightly.

I laughed. "I think she likes you."

Devlin looked as if he didn't know whether to be relieved or horrified at this suggestion and the expression on his face made me want to laugh even more. I *was* a bit surprised at Muesli's reaction, though. It wasn't as if she had met Devlin many times—in fact, the last time was when she had helped him save my life. But it looked like he was firmly on her list of "Most Favourite Persons". She wouldn't leave him alone. When Devlin finally managed to free his legs enough to walk across the room and sit down on the couch, she promptly hopped up and made herself comfortable on his lap, shedding grey and white fur all over his Italian wool trousers.

"Oh, sorry about that—" I leaned over to pick her up but Devlin waved me away awkwardly.

"No, no, it's okay. Leave her. She... er... looks comfortable."

Muesli certainly looked comfortable, her eyes half shut as she began kneading ecstatically in Devlin's groin. He drew in a sharp breath and stiffened.

"Er... what's she doing?" he said, trying to maintain the image of manly calm.

I stifled a laugh. "It's called kneading. Cats do that when they like you."

Devlin winced as Muesli's claws dug into the fine fabric of his trousers but he didn't try to move her.

"I thought you said you're not a cat person," I teased, coming over to sit next to him on the couch.

"I'm not," said Devlin, with some surprise. "I've always preferred dogs. But there's something about her..." He gestured helplessly as the little tabby stopped kneading and rested her chin on his stomach. She closed her eyes and began to purr even louder than before.

I bit back a laugh and wished I dared to pick up my phone to take a photo. The sight of Devlin O'Connor, CID detective extraordinaire, pinned to my parents' sofa by a little tabby cat was something to behold.

"What time's the table booked for?" I asked. "Shouldn't we get going?"

"Yeah, but..." Devlin looked down at the sleeping cat on his lap. "She looks so comfortable... I hate to disturb her."

I rolled my eyes. It looked like Muesli had made another conquest. How was it that cats always managed to worm their way into your affections, even when you didn't want to like them?

Devlin was shuffling awkwardly around on the couch, trying to slide Muesli off his lap, but she clung to him like a limpet.

"You'll have to push her off," I said.

He looked horrified at the suggestion. "Won't that hurt her?"

I burst out laughing. "No, I think it'll hurt you more than it'll hurt her."

Devlin didn't look convinced but he reached a hesitant hand towards Muesli's rump and gave a gentle push.

"*Meorrw!*" she cried mournfully.

Devlin jerked his hand back. "Oh, bloody hell—sorry!"

I gave Muesli a stern look. She blinked at me innocently but I could see the gleam of mischief in her green eyes. The little minx was putting it on—she knew Devlin was a soft touch and she was milking it for everything she was worth.

"She's fine," I said. "She's just having you on. You've got to be firm otherwise she'll walk all over you."

Devlin hesitated, then tried again, pushing Muesli gingerly off his lap. She gave another indignant *meorrw* but allowed herself to be shifted onto the couch cushion. Devlin looked torn as he stood up.

"She's fine," I assured him.

"*Meorrrrw...*" said Muesli in her most pitiful voice.

"Maybe we should give her a little something before we go?" said Devlin. "Like a treat?"

I rolled my eyes again but went obligingly into the kitchen to get some of Muesli's favourite dried duck jerky treats. Devlin gave her a generous handful and she tucked into them with a smug expression.

"Little minx," I muttered, giving Muesli a sour look as I herded Devlin out of the living room.

We went to a new Italian restaurant that I wasn't familiar with, on Little Clarendon Street. It had the clichéd red chequered tablecloths, pictures of the Leaning Tower of Pisa on the walls, and melted stubs of candles stuck in wine bottles on each table, but somehow, the overall effect was charming rather than cheesy. We sat down and tried to decipher the menu in the flickering candlelight. Finally, we took a gamble and just randomly chose two pizzas and an *insalata verde mista* to share.

The waitress took our order and brought us each a glass of *Chianti*. Devlin took a sip of the red wine, then leaned back with a sigh. I cast him a covert look. He was looking tired, I noticed, with lines of fatigue around his eyes and mouth.

"Tough day?" I asked.

He let out another sigh. "Yeah, one of several. And we had a new murder come in last night." His eyes flicked to mine. "Your friend, Seth, is in custody."

"Are you working the case?" I asked eagerly.

Devlin hesitated. "Yes."

Hope surged in my chest. "You're going to release him, right? You know he can't possibly be the murderer!"

"Gemma..." said Devlin gently. "I don't know anything of the kind. You can't ask me to ignore the evidence in front of me and..." His mouth twisted. "At the moment, the evidence against Seth is very strong. He was discovered holding the murder weapon, standing over the body, and covered in the victim's blood."

"Who found them?"

"The head porter of Wadsworth College, Clyde Peters. He was doing a round of the college and came upon Seth with Barrow's body. It's easy to see why it looked like murder."

"But... but that's just ridiculous and you know it!" I said. "You know Seth! You've known him since we were all here at Oxford together! You know there's no way he could murder anyone!"

"We don't know how anyone can react when under stress."

I stared at Devlin in angry disbelief. "Are you telling me you're seriously considering him a suspect?"

"I'm telling you I have to do my job."

"What about the murder weapon? I heard that it was an Egyptian dagger. Seth doesn't own anything like that."

"How do you know about the murder weapon?" Devlin asked sharply.

"The Old Biddies told me."

Devlin cursed under his breath. "Is there anything those meddling busybodies don't know?"

"But it is, isn't it? You must have checked that, first thing. It's such an unusual weapon to use. Who does it belong to?"

He was silent for a moment, as if considering whether to tell me, then finally said, "It isn't actually a real dagger—the Old Biddies were getting a bit carried away, I think. It's a paper knife—a letter opener—that's shaped like a replica Egyptian dagger.

But with a pretty sharp point and lethal nonetheless if stabbed with enough force. It's one of those souvenirs you can buy in tourist shops in Cairo. It belongs to a don at Wadsworth—a colleague of Professor Barrow's actually—called Dr Leila Gaber. She brought it with her when she came from Egypt. But—" he said, forestalling my protest, "I interviewed Dr Gaber myself today and she says that she had been using it as a paperknife and Seth asked to borrow it the day before."

"And Seth confirmed this?"

"Yes. He admitted that he did borrow the 'dagger'. His prints are all over it, which would be expected if he was the last person to handle it. But *he* claims that he returned it to Leila Gaber's pigeonhole before dinner last night and that that was the last time he saw it before finding it lodged in Professor Barrow's neck."

"Well, in that case, anyone could have got hold of this dagger letter opener," I said. "You know as well as I do—pigeonholes aren't like lockers. They're just open compartments. Anything put into them can be easily taken out by someone else. And they could have worn gloves."

"I'm aware of that," said Devlin. "But the fact remains that Seth is the last known person to be in possession of that dagger."

"Did you check Leila Gaber's alibi, though?"

"Of course," said Devlin impatiently. "She says she was working late in the library."

I frowned. "That can't be true. The library wouldn't still be open at midnight."

"Not normally, but Dr Gaber was given special dispensation. She's working on a research project at the moment which requires access to some valuable old manuscripts held at the Wadsworth College library. She managed to get permission from the college to gain an extra set of keys so that she could use the library out of hours."

"Was anyone else in there with her?"

"Earlier in the evening, yes."

"But not around midnight," I said quickly.

"No," Devlin admitted. "Although she says she was in the library until 12:45 a.m. when she heard the commotion outside and went out to see what was going on. That tallies with the police report from last night."

"Yes, but still, you've only got her word that she was in the library the whole time. That's not a proper alibi! The library overlooks the Cloisters on one side. The main entrance of the library is from Walled Garden but I'll bet there's a back door leading into the Cloisters. She could have easily slipped out, killed Barrow, and then slipped back into the library without anyone seeing her."

"She could have—but the question remains: why? Why would she kill Barrow? She had little motive."

I had no comeback for that. Irritated, I said, "What about any strangers lurking around the college? Maybe the murder wasn't committed by someone from the college at all. Don't you have footage from security cameras, so you can see who'd been in the Cloisters around the time of the murder?"

"This is Oxford, Gemma. You should know better than anyone else what it's like. Half the buildings here are heritage-listed treasures from the 13th century. You can barely get a phone line put in without special permission and there is no way the colleges are going to rig up ugly security cameras in the quadrangle walls. No, we have no footage from within the college to work with." He paused, then added, "There is a CCTV on the street opposite the front gate and the back gate, and we have been looking through the footage from those."

"And?" I looked at him eagerly.

"Nothing suspicious outside the back gate but on the side of the street opposite the front gate, there is someone—a man—who can be seen lurking around."

"What time?"

"12:23 a.m."

"Who is it? Have you identified him?"

"It's hard to tell exactly because of the dim light but it appears to be a tramp. Big fellow, red hair, we think, though that might be due to the glare from the street lights... My sergeant is trying to track him down at the moment so we can question him. It won't be easy, though, because if he really is a member of the homeless community in Oxford, he probably won't be recorded in the usual systems and databases. Things like credit cards, bank accounts, employer records, and drivers' licences won't help us much."

"Can I see the footage?"

"No." Devlin's brows drew together. "I can't believe you just asked me that."

I flushed.

Devlin took a deep breath. "Gemma, look... I know you want to help Seth but you can't get involved. It's not that I don't trust you with confidential information but this case is different. It's one of your closest friends who's been charged with murder. You aren't able to act dispassionately or consider things unemotionally." He leaned forwards. "If you really want to help Seth, the best thing you can do is stay out of it and leave the investigation to the police."

CHAPTER SIX

I stared at Devlin mutinously. "You can't expect me to just sit back and do nothing!"

"That's exactly what I expect you to do."

I opened my mouth to argue, then I had a better idea. Forcing myself to sound calm and reasonable, I gave Devlin a smile and said, "Okay, can you at least tell me everything else you know about the case? Just so I feel like the police are really following up every lead," I added hastily. "I promise not to get involved after this."

He eyed me sceptically.

"I mean, what about any enemies that Barrow might have had? And who stands to gain by his death?"

Devlin hesitated and I gave him a pleading look.

He sighed and relented. "We're looking into his

relationships with colleagues and students. As for gain, Barrow was an old bachelor and his estate goes to his next of kin: a sister called Joan and a younger brother, Richard."

"Have you questioned them?"

"We haven't been able to trace the brother yet but Joan Barrow lives in Reading. She's coming to Oxford tomorrow to see me at the station."

"She's coming here?" I looked at him in surprise. I would have thought that the police would go to her home to interview her.

"She insisted. I did offer to go down there but she seemed reluctant to let the CID invade her home. I gather that her partner is an invalid and a bit of a nervous type and she didn't want to upset him."

"Does she stand to inherit a lot of money?"

Devlin inclined his head. "Barrow was a pretty wealthy man."

"Money is a strong motive."

"So is anger."

"Aw, come on!" I said scornfully. "I can't believe that they're accusing Seth of murder just because he had some philosophical debate with another don at High Table! You know what these college fellows are like in the Senior Common Room, especially when they've had a couple of drinks! Everyone's obsessed with their pet subject in some obscure area of academia and they'll argue for hours over the origin of genius during the Italian Renaissance or whether sub-atomic particles really do exist or are just *thought* to exist... Bloody hell, if having a heated argument with another don made you guilty, half the academics in Oxford should be put behind bars!"

"This wasn't some academic debate," said Devlin. "There were several witnesses, including other dons and students in the dining hall, who say they saw Seth and Barrow having a loud, aggressive argument and Seth throw a glass of wine in Barrow's face, then reach across the table as if to harm him. The two men had to be forcibly separated by the Steward. And then they had further words later in the S.C.R.— which is situated alongside the Cloisters, by the way. In fact, Clyde Peters, the head porter, reported seeing the two of them arguing outside the S.C.R. entrance and almost coming to blows. His account was backed up by a witness statement from a student who was returning from the college chapel at the time. Both of them claim to have heard Seth threatening Barrow and the latter laughing at him."

"But people say all sorts of things they don't mean in the heat of an argument! They didn't actually see Seth strike Barrow or anything, did they?"

"No," Devlin admitted. "The two men seemed to calm down eventually and go their separate ways. Barrow went back into the S.C.R. and Seth was last seen heading towards the Walled Garden. I suppose he was making for the shortcut back into Gloucester."

"What time was this?"

"Around a quarter to twelve."

"Was that the last time anyone saw Barrow alive?"

"No, a student reported seeing him at around 12:10 a.m. coming out of the SCR. He was lighting his pipe—it was well known that Barrow liked to have a walk around the Cloisters and a smoke last thing at night before turning in. He had bachelor rooms in college."

"So anyone familiar with his habits could have lain in wait for him there."

"Yes," Devlin conceded. "But it would probably have to be someone fairly close to him—or at least a regular visitor to Wadsworth College."

He didn't add *"as Seth was"* but it hung in the air between us. I ignored it and continued doggedly on.

"And when was his body found?"

"Well, Seth claims to have stumbled across it just before half past twelve, and the head porter found them at around 12:30 a.m. So that leaves a twenty-minute gap from when Barrow was last seen alive, during which the murder must have taken place."

I was almost afraid to ask but I had to know. "What was Seth doing in the Cloisters at that time?"

Devlin shrugged. "He said that he had gone back to his room in Gloucester, then realised that he didn't have his mobile phone. He thought that he must have dropped it in Wadsworth, perhaps even during the last argument with Barrow outside the SCR, so he retraced his steps and found Barrow's body. The thing is, Gemma..." Devlin gave me a hard look. "It's not just a case of being in the wrong place at the wrong time. Seth had a motive."

"What do you mean?"

"I told you—they weren't just having some academic debate. They were arguing over the work of the Domus Trust and specifically over the college-sponsored housing project."

The Domus Trust? Where had I heard that name before? I remembered suddenly: the note I'd removed from Professor Barrow's pigeonhole. The note from Seth. It had mentioned something about the Domus Trust. But that wasn't the only time... it was coming back to me now... Seth had been heavily involved with a charity in recent months. I remembered him talking enthusiastically about their efforts to help the homeless in Oxford. He'd been an active volunteer, spending time helping out in the mobile soup kitchens around the city. I wished I'd paid more attention to him now when he had talked of them but I was pretty sure the charity was the Domus Trust.

As if reading my thoughts, Devlin said, "Seth is a volunteer and an active member of the Domus Trust. In fact, he's been campaigning for the use of college-donated land to provide accommodation for those in need. Wadsworth and Gloucester have joint ownership over a piece of land on the outskirts of the city, and as part of the University's efforts to tackle the homeless problem in Oxford, the two colleges have been considering the donation of this piece of land to the Trust, for them to build some affordable housing. In fact, Seth was the official representative for Gloucester College and Quentin Barrow happened to be the Wadsworth committee member elected to represent the college's interests."

I frowned. "Barrow supported the charity too?"

Devlin shook his head. "No, that was just it. He didn't support it—or the housing project—at all. And as one of the longest-standing members of the college, Barrow wielded a lot of power and influence over the rest of the college committee. It seemed that his vote was crucial in deciding whether Wadsworth would approve the proposal. The final decision was to take place next week. And since the land is jointly owned by the two colleges, they needed both sides on board before the donation could be approved. If Barrow had vetoed the donation, then the whole project would have fallen apart. On the other hand, with Barrow out of the way..."

"But it's ludicrous to think that Seth would murder someone just to ensure that the project goes ahead!"

"Is it?" said Devlin challengingly. "People have been known to kill for their causes. If you believe in something passionately and think that you're doing something for the greater good, you often feel that the end justifies the means."

"Yes, but *murder...*?" I shook my head. "Seth might join a protest in the street or something, but it's a big jump from that to murder! You'd have to be a really cold-blooded, ruthless person to even entertain the idea and I can tell you for a fact that

Seth isn't that kind of person!"

"I'm not saying that he's capable of killing someone in cold blood," said Devlin. "In fact, this murder has all the hallmarks of someone experiencing great anger and loss of control. The attack on Barrow was extremely violent—according to the forensic pathologist, the force with which he was stabbed was three times greater than that necessary to kill him. And think about the risks the murderer took! Anyone could have come upon them in the Cloisters. No, this wasn't a carefully planned murder, but more like someone overcome by a strong emotion and unable to contain their fury."

"I still can't believe anyone would feel like that for the sake of a cause," I said. "For the death of a loved one, perhaps, or an insult to yourself but…"

"You might change your mind if you've met some of the animal rights activists that I've put behind bars," said Devlin dryly. "People will do crazy things for causes because they feel like they're part of something greater than themselves. Think of all the suicide bombers."

I sat back, feeling despair wash over me. I realised now what the solicitor had meant. It did look very bad for Seth. With no alibi for the time of the murder, a strong motive, the last sighting of him being in an aggressive situation with the victim, and then being "caught red-handed" holding the murder weapon… it was no wonder that the police were focusing on him as the prime suspect. I had to admit that if Seth hadn't been my friend, even I would have found it hard to ignore the evidence in front of me.

I gave Devlin a beseeching look. "Devlin, please... I know the evidence is stacked against him but we both know that Seth is really innocent. Can't you just... 'massage' the investigation a bit, so that he's given a chance? I know there are ways the police can... um... present evidence in a different light and—"

Devlin's face darkened. "Are you asking me to compromise my ethics and professionalism for your friend?"

"I..."

I didn't know what to say. Then Cassie's words in the tearoom that afternoon came back to me and I felt a surge of indignation and resentment.

"And what if I am?" I said. "What's wrong with bending the rules a bit when you *know* what you're doing is the right thing? You're the one who always used to say—back when we were students—that the end justifies the means. Everyone uses the advantages they can get; it's how the world works. The secret handshake. The old boys' club. You can't deny that it doesn't exist! It's no use being all ethical and noble, when nobody else follows those rules." I looked at him reproachfully. "Even if you don't care about Seth... I thought you'd do it for *me*—"

I broke off at the expression on Devlin's face. There was a dangerous glitter in his eyes.

"Gemma," he said in a low, furious voice. "Don't

think you can use my feelings for you to influence an investigation. I'm not some kind of tame pet policeman for you to direct and manipulate. I am an officer of the law and I am sworn to uphold justice, including..." he paused significantly, "... doing everything in my power to convict your friend if he's really committed a murder."

I drew back as if he had slapped me. The waitress arrived at that moment with our pizzas: great round slabs of thin crispy base, with the cheese still bubbling on top and a medley of pepperoni, juicy mushrooms, fresh tomatoes, and bright peppers scattered across the slices. It looked delicious but I found that I had lost my appetite.

We ate in silence, neither looking at the other, and I felt a pang of loss and regret. This wasn't how I imagined our first date to be. I'd waited so long for tonight, daydreamed about it, looked forward to it, wondering how he'd look and what we'd talk about, whether we'd still laugh together at the same jokes as we once did, whether he'd walk me to my door at the end of the evening and what his lips would feel like on mine...

When Devlin finally escorted me to the front of my parents' house, it was not in the warm glow of romantic anticipation but in the tense hostility of cold anger and resentment.

"I'll see you to the door," he said stiffly as we paused outside the front gate.

"There's no need," I said, just as coldly. "I can

manage fine by myself. Thank you for dinner. Good night." I drew away from him.

He seemed about to say something else, then gave me a curt nod. "Good night."

I went up the path and the front steps of the house, conscious of him standing there in the street, shrouded in the mist, watching as I let myself into the house and shut the door behind me.

CHAPTER SEVEN

I was still simmering with anger and resentment the next morning when I arrived in the tearoom and it didn't help that I had to recount the whole evening again to Cassie.

"You didn't try hard enough!" she said angrily. "He would have helped if you really talked to him—"

"I did!" I cried, hurt and angry at the injustice of her accusation. I'd practically sacrificed my relationship with Devlin for Seth's sake. "He's just—"

"I'm going to talk to Devlin myself," said Cassie, setting her mouth in a sullen line.

"Cassie, I—"

We were interrupted by the tinkling of the front bells, signalling our first customer for the day. But when I looked up, it wasn't a group of tourists or a local pensioner I saw standing on the threshold, but a familiar male figure. Lincoln Green.

He looked diffidently around, then his brown eyes lit up as he saw me and he came rapidly across the room. He was dressed, as always, in a well-cut, conservative suit, with an Argyle sweater vest peeking out from beneath the jacket and a Burberry trench coat over one arm. The wind had ruffled his light brown hair but otherwise he was the perfect well-groomed English gentleman. You could almost see Lincoln as a hero in an Austen novel—oh, not Mr Darcy but one of the quieter, gentler heroes: Edmund from *Mansfield Park*, perhaps, or Edward Ferrars who loved Elinor in *Sense and Sensibility*—solid, respectable, and quietly attractive.

As he came towards me, I had to admit that my mother wasn't wrong in her praise of him. Lincoln was good-looking and a nice guy to boot and I enjoyed his company very much. So he didn't make my heart race the way Devlin did... so what? I thought of the disastrous dinner last night and pressed my mouth into a thin line. Maybe I needed to think twice about being with a man who always raised your blood pressure—and not always in a good way.

"Hi, Gemma, I just came in to..." Lincoln trailed off as he caught sight of the enormous purple elephant water feature next to the counter. "Er... What on earth is *that*?"

I rolled my eyes. "Long story. Involving my mother. You don't really want to know."

"Ah." Lincoln gave me an understanding smile.

As Helen Green's son, he had come in for his fair share of embarrassments. *His* mother had been my mother's keenest accomplice when it came to throwing the two of us together. Not that Lincoln seemed to mind their efforts – in fact, he had made it quite clear to me that he would like to turn our friendship into something else. I hadn't encouraged him but I had to admit, I hadn't exactly rebuffed him, either. I had thought that maybe... after last night and a "proper" date with Devlin... my feelings would be clearer and I'd know what I really wanted. Instead, I felt in more of a turmoil than ever.

I sighed inwardly. Why was life always so complicated? Here was a man who was simple and straightforward, an eminent doctor, attractive, dependable, and kind—and a long-time family friend too. Why couldn't he be the one who made my heart skip a beat every time I saw him?

Not that I didn't feel a different kind of pleasure when I saw Lincoln, I reminded myself. Maybe he was the kind of man who grew on you more slowly. I knew that choosing Lincoln would make my mother very happy, but I was long past the age now of making life decisions just to make my mother happy. I had done that once, eight years ago, and regretted it bitterly.

Though sometimes I did wonder if it had been the right choice after all. Would Devlin and I have been happy, would we have remained together if I had said yes to his proposal eight years ago? We had both been so young then—so hot-headed and impulsive and full of romantic ideals. Now that I was older and wiser, I was aware that we were both very different, strong personalities, neither willing to budge for the other. Last night had shown me that. Life with Devlin would always be full of challenges and conflict, although full of passion and joy too. Could a relationship built on that kind of turbulent foundation last?

Maybe the person you loved the most wasn't the person you were most suited to spend your life with...

I shook away my thoughts as Lincoln stepped up to the counter.

"Um... Gemma..." He looked uncomfortable. "I was actually just popping by to ask you... that is, to check... um..."

I looked at him in puzzlement. Lincoln was normally the epitome of polite, social aplomb, always knowing the right thing to say on any occasion. It was unusual for him to be so tongue-tied.

I gave him an encouraging smile. "Yes?"

"It's about the Oxford Society of Medicine dinner," he blurted out suddenly. "My mother said that you were coming with me ..."

"Oh! Oh, God, yes..." I said, feeling a wave of embarrassment wash over me. In all the drama with Seth and Devlin, it had completely slipped my mind. "I'm sorry, I know you didn't ask me, Lincoln. I think it was just my mother interfering again and... I didn't want to refuse in front of your mother and hurt her feelings... but... but please don't feel obliged... I mean, I don't want to force myself on you—" I broke off, flushing as I realised my unfortunate choice of words.

"Oh no, no, don't apologise. I'd love to... Please force yourself on me any time you like—I mean... er..." he stammered, his cheeks reddening as he also realised what he had said. He took a deep breath and tried again. "What I mean is, it would be a pleasure to take you as my guest. I just didn't want you to feel like you had been forced into it out of politeness."

I smiled at him. "No, Lincoln. Not at all. I would be honoured to go as your guest."

He looked delighted. "Great! I had been meaning to ask you but I wasn't sure..." He hesitated. "I thought you might have had other plans..." He didn't say it but I knew he was referring to Devlin.

"No," I said firmly. "No other plans."

He beamed.

"Is it black-tie?" I asked.

"Yes, usual guest dinner dress code. Black-tie for the men, cocktail dress for the ladies. Dinner starts at seven but there will be drinks first at 6 p.m., in the Buttery at Wadsworth."

I froze. "Did you say Wadsworth?"

He looked at me, puzzled. "Yes, why? There's a tradition for the Society of Medicine dinner to circulate around the different colleges, a different one each term. It just so happens that Wadsworth College was chosen for this term."

What a fantastic coincidence, I thought to myself with a smile. It would give me the perfect chance to snoop around Wadsworth, without needing an excuse to get in there.

"Gemma? Is something the matter?"

I came back to the present. "No, not really... It's just... you know about the murder at Wadsworth?"

Lincoln frowned. "Yes. I read about it in the papers this morning. They said they had a suspect in custody."

I winced. "Yes, that's my friend, Seth. He's been arrested for the murder of Professor Barrow."

Lincoln's eyes widened. "But surely there's a mistake? Seth couldn't have committed the murder."

I felt a rush of liking for him. "Oh, I'm so glad you think that too! Seth was just in the wrong place at the wrong time. But there's a lot of circumstantial evidence against him and... well, he's the strongest suspect the police have at the moment."

"I'm very sorry to hear that," said Lincoln. "If there's anything I can do to help..."

I felt an even greater wave of affection and gratitude. I gave him a warm smile. "Thanks, Lincoln... that's really nice of you."

"Lincoln!" trilled a voice behind us.

My heart sank. I turned to see my mother standing in the doorway of the kitchen, surveying us with delight. She came forwards, holding her arms out to Lincoln.

"You naughty boy—you never told me that you were coming to visit!" She gave him a kiss on the cheek, then stood back and looked him up and down. "I think you get taller every time I see you! And don't you look dashing in that suit? Doesn't Lincoln look handsome, Gemma?" She gave me a suggestive smile.

I saw Lincoln flush with embarrassment and I squirmed, wanting to throttle my mother. I had been hoping that she wouldn't realise Lincoln was here—she had been so busy this morning, since we arrived, rushing around the kitchen, preparing and baking some last-minute cakes and buns.

"Now, Lincoln, you must come and have a taste of these Chelsea buns," said my mother, grabbing his arm and dragging him to the hatch from the kitchen.

She picked up a plate of the plump swirls, scented with cinnamon and lemon zest, filled with dried raisins and sultanas, and the tops shining with a rich sugar glaze. I had tried one earlier and knew they were delicious—full of melting buttery sweetness and sticky satisfaction.

My mother stuck the plate under Lincoln's nose. "Gemma made these herself and they're divine!" She simpered. "She's going to make some lucky man a wonderful wife some day!"

I gasped, not only at her outrageous matchmaking but also at the blatant lie. I couldn't bake a decent bun to save my life. I started to protest, then sighed and gave up. It was pointless. My mother was like a force of nature—like a tsunami or a tornado or something—it was easier to seek shelter and wait for her to pass, than to try and fight against her.

After Lincoln had duly consumed a plate of Chelsea buns, a bowl of gooseberry trifle, a slice of blueberry cheesecake, and a custard pie (and was starting to look slightly sick), my mother finally let him go—mainly because the smell of burning began drifting out from the kitchen and she threw up her hands with a squeal of: "Oh! My carrot cake!" and disappeared. Lincoln and I both breathed an audible sigh of relief.

"I think I'd better go now while I can still walk," said Lincoln with a rueful grin at me. "So I'll see you tomorrow night at quarter to six?"

I returned his smile. "I'm looking forward to it."

CHAPTER EIGHT

The rest of the morning passed uneventfully and I was glad to have a moment to catch my breath when the lunchtime rush was over. I was just sitting down to rest my weary feet when the front door opened and a middle-aged woman in a tweed coat stepped into the tearoom. For a moment, I thought it might have been Dora Kempton, then I saw that this woman was younger and taller, with a tight pursed mouth and small, close-set eyes. I rose and reached automatically for the menus from the rack.

"Is it just for one?" I said with my standard welcoming smile.

"My name is Abby Finch. I'm here for the interview," she said.

"Oh! Of course, that's right..."

In fact, I had completely forgotten that I had

scheduled some chef interviews for this afternoon. I had organised these last week—well before I had known about my mother's sudden desire to see the darkest corners of Southeast Asia—but I was glad now that I had. The need to find a replacement baking chef was greater than ever.

I went forwards, holding out my hand. "I'm Gemma Rose, the owner of the tearoom. Would you like to come into the kitchen?"

Leaving Cassie to look after the customers, I escorted the woman into the kitchen, which was still warm with the smell of freshly baked buns and crumpets. My mother had finally finished her frantic last-minute baking and had left early to do some shopping with Helen Green. I was pleased to have a quiet place for the interview.

The woman looked around with a critical eye and sniffed disapprovingly. Her gaze fell on the packet of sliced toast bread on the sideboard and she turned an outraged face to me. "You use white bread?"

"Well, yes..." I faltered. "That is how traditional English tea sandwiches are made... with white bread..."

Her mouth, if possible, grew even more puckered. "I won't use anything that's not gluten-free, soy-free, nut-free, lactose-free, organic, and non-genetically modified. Most pantries are filled with processed products full of the most dreadful toxins and chemicals and preservatives! They can give you migraines, Irritable Bowel Syndrome, hyperactivity—

even cancer!"

Slightly taken aback by her rant, I gestured weakly towards the large wooden table in the centre of the kitchen. "Yes... Well... um... would you like to sit down?"

She plonked herself down on a chair by the table and reached out a finger to touch the white flour smeared across the worn, brown surface, then made a sound of derision.

"Disgusting. Did you know that processed white flour is one of the unhealthiest foods you can eat? It's been completely stripped of all nutritious components, like bran and fibre, and what's more, has been chemically bleached to appear whiter, and is one of the greatest risk factors for diabetes."

"Oh... er... right. I'm glad you told me."

I had a bad feeling about this interview already. Nevertheless, I sat down opposite her and began asking her some questions. It was soon obvious, however, that Abby Finch had come not so much to answer my questions as to tell me her requirements.

"I won't bake with refined white sugar; I only use stevia or honey—or raw brown sugar, at a pinch, organic, mind... and I will only use organic butter in my baking... and what is more, I think that all heavy cream should be replaced by evaporated skimmed milk..."

I nodded and listened and bit my tongue. Finally, when she paused for a breath, I said smoothly, "I'm not sure we're a good fit for each other, Ms Finch—

I'm afraid my pantry is too corrupted now and I would hate for you to... er... suffer emotional stress while working here. But thank you very much for coming."

She gave a nod and rose, then walked stiffly out of the kitchen. I followed her to the door and drew a sigh of relief as I shut it after her. Cassie gave me a questioning look and I had to refrain from saying what I really wanted to say as I was aware of the customers still in the tearoom. Before I had time to do more than make a face at her, the next candidate had arrived and I found myself back in the kitchen, this time facing a smartly-dressed woman with very glamorous hair who was overflowing with enthusiasm.

"Oh, this is simply marvellous! Marvellous! There is so much potential here—we could add a laminated resin counter by the window with stainless steel stools—bring in a bit of that industrial chic that's all the rage at the moment—and some geometric pendant lamps, very Scandinavian, and of course, the menu must be revamped—can't have all these stodgy old cakes and breads and things—"

"But we're a traditional English tearoom... Those are the kinds of things that people expect to eat when they come in here," I protested.

"Nonsense!" she cried. "Gastropubs are so 'in' right now! And they're providing customers with fresh, innovative options—we don't want boring old cucumber sandwiches with butter and white bread!

We want zucchini ribbons and truffle butter in French brioche or honeydew melon with mascarpone on soy and linseed loaf!"

I thought back to the Old Biddies' outraged reaction to my *slightly* "different" cucumber sandwiches. Somehow, I had a feeling that this woman didn't understand how much people loved and embraced the "boring old menu options".

"I'm sorry, I think you might have misunderstood my advertisement," I said. "I'm looking for a traditional English baking chef—someone who can recreate the old-fashioned British favourites, to the highest quality. Of course, we don't want stodgy baking, but we want to preserve the traditional qualities that's made these cakes and puddings and buns such firm favourites for centuries. And the tourists who come here want to know that they are tasting real, old-fashioned English baking, not some modern concoction."

She waved a contemptuous hand. "They don't know what they're missing until they try it. Once they've tasted my modern alternatives, they'll never want to go back."

Her presumptive attitude was beginning to annoy me. "Well, it's very interesting to hear your thoughts on the subject and I will bear that in mind. However, for the time being, I am happy with the identity of the tearoom and with what we serve on the menu. In fact, our traditional English scones are one of the things we're gaining a reputation for, with people coming from miles away just to sample our scones. I wouldn't want to change that."

"Oh, don't worry—once I make the changes, everyone will wonder what they had been missing. When I'm chef, I'll take over everything for you."

Over my dead body, I thought. Aloud, I said with a pleasant smile, "Thank you for coming, Miss Reynolds."

"So when shall I start?" she said. "I'm free at the moment, so if you're busy, I can start this weekend if you like."

"I haven't made a decision yet—I have several other candidates to see," I said quickly. "I'll let you know soon if your application has been successful."

She stared at me, her mouth slightly open. I don't think it ever occurred to her that she might not get the position.

"Oh. Oh, right..." She stood up reluctantly. Casting a look around the rustic, cosy kitchen, she said, "You could really do with some modernising in here too. Well, I'm sure I'll be discussing it with you next week."

I'm sure you won't, I thought grimly but I kept my smile in place and escorted her to the door.

"Well?" said Cassie as soon as I returned to the counter.

I shook my head with a sigh. "So far, between the gluten Nazi and the modern décor maniac who wants to turn our tearoom into a gastropub, I don't know which is the worse choice."

"Don't worry, there'll be other candidates. In fact, it looks like someone else is arriving right now..."

I glanced out of the windows and my spirits lifted. A plump, jolly-looking woman with rosy apple cheeks was coming up the path. She looked exactly like what you expected a baking chef to look like. A moment later she let herself into the tearoom and I went forwards eagerly to meet her.

"Are you here for the chef interview?" I asked.

She nodded and sniffed appreciatively. "Yes, my name's Emily Tucker. My, what is that wonderful smell?"

I showed her into the kitchen and as we passed the latest batch of scones that my mother had baked, I saw her eye the tray hungrily.

"Would you like to try one?" I said, thinking that it was probably a good idea to let the chef sample the items they would have to recreate.

"Sure, I'd love to!" Without waiting for me to offer, she grabbed a plate from the sideboard and helped herself to two scones from the tray, adding a large dollop of clotted cream and some home-made jam from the jar. I was slightly taken aback but told myself that it was good that she felt so at home already.

That was an understatement. In the next half hour, as I tried to take her through the interview questions, Emily Tucker felt so at home that she managed to consume six jam tarts, a plate of rhubarb crumble, two mini muffins, a slice of lemon meringue pie, and a sticky toffee pudding, all while I watched her in alarm. Politeness and astonishment at her audacity had prevented me from stopping her.

I stared at her, thinking: *Never mind how good a chef she might be—if I hired her, she would probably eat me out of house and home!* The tearoom would have to double its food supply bill, just to keep up with her appetite!

"Oh and I don't like to work weekends much, so I usually just bake an extra batch in advance on Fridays," she said with her mouth full. She swallowed and looked around the kitchen. "You got any coffee and walnut cake? I saw that on the menu and it sounded fabulous."

"Yes, but I'm keeping it for the customers," I said pointedly.

I was feeling annoyed. My poor mother had come in early this morning to get some extra baking done so that we would be stocked up as much as possible while she was away and this woman had just single-handedly consumed a quarter of them.

"I'm afraid the next candidate will be arriving soon," I lied, rising and hoping she would take the hint. "Thank you for coming. I'll be in touch soon."

She got up reluctantly and left, though not before asking if she could take a Chelsea bun to go. I shut the door behind her and sagged against it.

"That bad, huh?" said Cassie, grinning from behind the counter.

I shook my head in despair. "We're never going to

find another chef!"

"You've only just started looking," Cassie consoled me. "I'm sure it's like any job—you probably have to interview quite a few candidates before you find the right one. Don't worry, I'm sure you'll find the perfect person."

I sighed and hoped that she was right. It was just after four-thirty but the tearoom was already empty of customers, which was quite unusual. I glanced out of the window—we were well past the shortest day of the year now but it was still getting dark by mid-afternoon. It was depressing and something that I had really struggled with in the past few weeks. Coming back to England had seemed exciting and romantic after eight years of continuous sunshine in Sydney but now that I'd been here a few months and we were stuck in the dismal darkness of winter, the novelty was wearing off quickly. I walked to the tearoom windows and peered out. The skies were an ominous grey-black and that heavy fog was coming in again. I wasn't surprised that there weren't many people and tourists about.

"Think we'll get any more customers?" said Cassie, coming to join me at the windows and looking out doubtfully. "Maybe we can close a bit earlier today." She glanced at the clock on the wall. "Seth's being released from the police station soon. I was hoping to pop home and change before we went to pick him up."

The tearoom door opened and we both turned

from the windows. A middle-aged woman peered in.

"Are you still serving?" she asked hesitantly.

"You go on," I said to Cassie in an undertone. "I'll look after her and lock up here. I'll meet you at the police station." Then, turning to the woman, I gave her a smile and said, "Yes, of course, would you like a table by the window?"

I settled her and quickly brought her order: a pot of English breakfast tea with scones, jam, and clotted cream. She took her time, sipping the tea and gazing out the window, as if lost in thought, and I chafed a bit under the delay. When she finally rose and approached the counter to pay, I breathed a sigh of relief and rang up her bill with alacrity.

"This is a lovely establishment," she said. "And your scones were delicious."

I smiled. Praise for my tearoom always gave me a warm glow. "I'm glad you like it. Are you local or just visiting?"

"I live in Reading, actually, although I'm familiar with Oxford and the Cotswolds. But I hadn't heard of this tearoom before. In fact, I only came because I got a recommendation."

I was only half-listening as I took her credit card and started to put it through the machine. Then I froze as I saw the name printed on the card. *Joan Barrow.*

I looked up at her. "You're Professor Barrow's sister!"

CHAPTER NINE

The woman looked at me with mild surprise. "Yes, I am... Did you know my brother?"

"Um... well, not personally. It's just that... I heard about the murder," I said awkwardly. "I'm very sorry."

She nodded, although I didn't discern any particular signs of grief on her face. "Yes, it was a great shock," she said in a colourless voice.

I looked at her in surprise. She might as well have been discussing the weather. But perhaps it was just her way. I knew that not everyone wailed and sobbed or even wanted to express their sorrow openly; some withdrew, became distant and grieved privately. Perhaps she was that type.

I looked at her with more interest. Her features were plain and strangely colourless, like her voice.

Her clothes were the typical combination of Marks & Spencer's cardigan and beige tapered trousers, her eyes a watery blue, her face showing some signs of make-up. She looked like a dozen other British suburban housewives you'd probably pass in a shopping centre or supermarket and never look at twice.

"It's the reason I'm in Oxford," she explained. "The police wanted to see me; I've just been to the Oxfordshire police headquarters. It was actually the detective who questioned me—a Detective O'Connor—who recommended that I come here. He said you had the best scones in Oxfordshire."

A warm feeling filled my chest, in spite of myself and my recent anger with Devlin, and I felt slightly mollified. It was nice of him to recommend the tearoom and send me some business.

"Your brother's death is a huge loss to the University, I'm sure," I said. "I believe he's a great expert in his field."

"Yes, he's great man," she said but my ears pricked at something in her voice. At last, a bit of emotion had flickered in that colourless tone and, if I wasn't wrong, it was bitterness. I was surprised.

I hesitated, then tossed caution to the wind and said, "Were you and your brother close?"

"No," she said shortly.

I waited, knowing that sometimes silence was more powerful than any question. It was human nature to feel compelled to explain, to justify—

especially when you did the socially inappropriate thing of expressing dislike for your own sibling.

I was rewarded for my patience. Joan Barrow glanced away, then back at me and said:

"My brother, Quentin, might have been top of his field and respected in Oxford, but he was also a pompous, overbearing, elitist snob who thought he knew best for everyone, including me. He didn't like the fact that I 'married beneath me', as he called it—actually, Steve and I aren't even married—we just live together—which made it even worse in Quentin's eyes. He said I was throwing myself away, living in sin, when I should have married a nice, respectable Oxbridge man. And even though Quentin knew that we needed financial help and he was well able to afford it, he wouldn't help us when we desperately needed it." The bitterness was thick in her voice now and there was colour coming into her cheeks.

"Oh, I'm sorry..." I murmured.

But she went on as if she hadn't heard me. "My partner, Steve, is sick. He suffers from anxiety and nerves and a terrible sort of lethargy. Quentin thought he was just playing the invalid but it's not true! You don't know what poor Steve suffers. And he can be treated—I know there are special treatments which would help him—but they're expensive. You have to go to the United States... but it wouldn't have been much to Quentin! He was rich! And he had no family of his own. Why shouldn't he have spent a bit to help his sister?" Her mouth twisted and her pale blue eyes simmered with anger. "But he refused. So we're having to scrimp and save and hope that maybe eventually we might save up enough to afford the treatment..."

"Do you have any other brothers and sisters who can help you?" I asked, hoping that she might mention Richard Barrow.

Her expression softened. "Yes, I have a younger brother, Richard. Now he's completely different from Quentin. He understands how difficult it is for Steve and he's always so generous! Not that he has much to give, unfortunately. Of course, he can't help it if he gets into a bit of trouble now and then. He's had a run of bad luck. He was invited to join several schemes and things which somehow turned out badly and he ended up owing people money or losing everything he invested." She sighed, shaking her head. "He's got too much of a good nature, Richard, and trusts people too easily. Quentin used to say that Richard's just a gambler who didn't want to work but he never understood that Richard is a dreamer, with big ideas—much bigger than Quentin's stupid research in the closed world of Oxford."

"Have you told Richard about Professor Barrow's death?"

Her expression closed suddenly. "No," she said. "I haven't spoken to Richard at all recently. He travels a lot and I'm not quite sure where he is at present. He's not very good about keeping in touch."

She reached out and took her credit card, sliding

it back into her wallet, then shouldered her handbag. "Well, I must hurry now or I'll miss the train back to Reading. There's a bus going from here back into Oxford town centre, isn't there?"

"Yes, you can pick it up from the bus stop in front of the village school," I said.

She nodded and thanked me, then left. I watched her stout figure through the windows, retreating into the distance, and thought about what she had told me. There had certainly been little love lost between her and her dead brother. Could that bitterness and anger have translated into something more? With Barrow dead now, Joan was due to inherit a lot of money—more than enough for her precious partner to have his treatment in America. Reading was only about thirty minutes from Oxford by train and there were frequent services, with the last one well after midnight...

And what about her brother, Richard? Had she been telling the truth about not contacting him? He sounded like he could have done with a big injection of funds too. Was it possible that the brother and sister had hatched a plan for murder between them?

I sighed and began shutting up the tearoom. There were just too many unanswered questions. Then I thought of Seth. He might have some of the answers. I began to move faster, eager to get back to Oxford and see him.

***

Seth looked terrible when he stepped out of the police station. He was unshaven, his clothes dishevelled, and his eyes were slightly bloodshot behind his glasses. But most of all, it was the look of haggard despair on his face that got to me.

"Seth!"

Cassie and I went towards him. She beat me to it, rushing up to him as if she was going to throw herself into his arms, but just as she reached him, she faltered. Cassie fumbled, as if suddenly trying not to touch him, and turned her head quickly so that her lips brushed his cheek instead. Seth flushed and looked intensely embarrassed. He pushed his glasses up his nose and turned hastily to me, catching me in a careless hug, whilst Cassie stepped back and fiddled with her hair. I looked at her in surprise but she wouldn't meet my eyes.

"Thanks for coming. You have no idea how glad I am to see you guys," Seth said. "I was having nightmares of seeing my parents out here and wondering how I was going to explain things to them..."

I'd been wondering about Seth's parents myself—I'd assumed that his family solicitor would have contacted them. "Where *are* your parents?"

"On a cruise," said Seth with some relief. "It's their ruby wedding anniversary and they're supposed to be gone for two weeks. I asked Mr Sexton not to inform them of what happened. My father had a heart attack a few months back and the doctors warned against any kind of stress. The last thing I want to do is to have them worried about me and cutting their trip short to come back." He took a deep breath. "I'm still hoping that the police might find the real killer and drop the charges against me before they return."

"Seth, what happened last Friday night? How did you end up mixed up in this whole thing?" demanded Cassie.

He threw a glance at the police station behind him and hunched his shoulders. "Let's not talk here. I'm desperate to get back and have a hot shower—wash the feel of this place off me."

"Have you eaten?" I said.

"Not since lunchtime. And to be honest with you, I didn't have much of an appetite."

"Come on, we'll drop you back at Gloucester College and then we'll leave you to have a wash while we go pick up some takeaway—how does that sound?"

Seth gave me a tired smile. "Sounds fantastic."

By the time we saw Seth again he was looking a lot more like his usual self. He had showered and shaved, and got a bit of colour back into his cheeks. We dished out the boxes of Indian curry and basmati rice, then hunkered down cross-legged around the coffee table in his spacious college room and tucked into the meal.

For a moment, I was transported back to the time

when Seth, Cassie and I were all students here at Oxford and we had had many a night like this, sharing a takeaway curry while discussing the latest college gossip or moaning about our looming essay crisis. Well, okay, not Seth. He wasn't the type to have an essay crisis—far too organised and conscientious—but for me and especially Cassie, lurching from one essay crisis to another had been our default state for most of the term.

Oxford was one of the few universities to still follow the quaint old "tutorial system" which meant that rather than classroom teaching, tests, and assessments, students were taught in private sessions of two or three by individual tutors who would assign a weekly essay. You were expected to research the topic thoroughly and then write a well-thought-out summary of the ideas on the subject, presenting the arguments for and against and analysing them critically. The idea was that it was better learning because you weren't just being lectured to and fed information—you were being taught to think for yourself and question everything.

I suppose it was a great way to challenge you to use your own mind. Of course, it was also a great way to encourage you to procrastinate. I spent many a night when I was a student staying up till dawn, frantically scribbling, trying to complete the essay in time before the tutorial the next morning. Still, moaning about your essay crisis was part of student life at Oxford and, in a way, I almost missed it.

Then I heard Cassie ask Seth about last Friday night again and I came back to the present with a thump. I wasn't just a student sitting around without a care in the world any more—I was here with my friend who had been accused of murder.

"Seth, you have to tell us everything!" Cassie was insisting.

"Yeah," I said. "Why did you and Professor Barrow get into a fight at High Table? And what's all this about the Domus Trust project? And what's that note I removed from Barrow's pigeonho—*OWW*!"

I stared at Seth in surprise. He had kicked me viciously under the table.

"What note?" said Cassie. "What are you talking about?"

I realised suddenly that I'd never mentioned the note to Cassie. Somehow, in all the fuss on Saturday morning with the solicitor and the Old Biddies and my mother's sudden travel plans and the dinner with Devlin... and then Lincoln and the interviews this morning, it had slipped my mind. Which might have been a good thing since it was obvious that Seth didn't want Cassie to know.

"What note?" Cassie said again, looking from me to Seth suspiciously. "What are you keeping from me?"

"It was nothing," said Seth quickly. "Just some silly... uh... joke."

"If it was just a joke, why can't you tell me?"

Seth looked torn. Finally, he looked down,

flushing, and said, "I... I did something a bit stupid."

"*What?*" Cassie demanded.

Seth swallowed. "You know how after a fight, you always think of all the things you wish you had said? Well, when I got back to my room on Friday night, I was still really fuming. I kept thinking of all the things I hadn't said to Barrow and how I wished I'd had the last word. I guess I should have just waited until morning and let things cool off... but I was too worked up. So I decided to write him a note with what I wanted to say and go back to leave it in his pigeonhole. I'd been planning to go back to search for my phone anyway, so it was like killing two birds with one stone." He winced as he realised his choice of proverb. "Sorry, no pun intended."

"I read the note," I said.

Seth winced again and said hastily, with a glance at Cassie, "You see, it was just silly stuff, right, Gemma? No big deal, really."

Actually, it had been closer to a death threat, but I realised suddenly that Seth didn't want Cassie to know about the note's contents. I'd long suspected that Seth harboured a secret crush on Cassie and it was obvious that he was embarrassed about her seeing him in a bad light. He gave me an urgent look and I took the hint.

"Uh... yeah, it was a bit childish, really. I just chucked it," I said, much to Seth's relief.

However, Cassie was no fool. She frowned. "If it was that silly and unimportant, why would you have called Gemma in the middle of the night to go and get it?"

"I… I just didn't want the police to find it and jump to conclusions," said Seth lamely. "You know what they can be like. Anyway, forget the note—it's not important."

Cassie didn't look convinced but Seth rushed on before she could say anything else. "I don't even know where to begin telling you both what happened. The whole thing just seems so surreal. I felt like I was standing there watching everything happen to me from afar, you know? I mean, you never expect to be arrested for murder!"

"What was going on between you and Barrow?" I said. "Why do the police think that you have a motive to want him dead?"

Seth set his jaw. "Barrow and I didn't see eye to eye on the Domus Trust housing project. The man was a tosser! He had no pity for the homeless and was really opposed to the college donating the land to the Domus Trust to build affordable housing. He was one of those pompous, elitist misogynist types who thinks that Oxford should still be an exclusive men's club where women aren't allowed and only sons from certain families can be admitted! Bloody hell, which century did he think he was living in?" He shook his head in disgust. "Can you believe it—he actually told me that charitable giving is a waste of time! That it's just a waste of money and resources and teaches people to beg or rely on welfare—"

"Was this what you were arguing about at High Table?"

Seth blew out a breath of irritation and nodded. "I got invited over to Wadsworth for dinner by Ron Bertram—he's the Tutor for Admissions there; we play squash together and we often go over to each other's colleges for dinner afterwards—and I ended up sitting opposite Barrow at High Table. He was being really obnoxious and I just couldn't keep quiet any longer. We got into an argument and I guess it just sort of snowballed. He wasn't willing to back down and neither was I." He gave us a sheepish look. "I suppose we both had a bit too much to drink... I probably said a few things I shouldn't have. The thing is, Barrow was being such a prat! I mean, he actually said homeless people are all lazy drug-addicts and criminals, who deserved to be chucked out in the streets! It made me livid. I threw a glass of wine at him, just to wipe that smirk off his face, and I guess I must have got up and reached across the table without thinking..."

"Devlin said the Steward separated you," I said.

"Yeah. But then I saw him again in the S.C.R. after dinner and we got going again. I was trying to keep it civil this time—you know, have an academic debate about it—but it's like trying to reason with a pig! In fact, calling Barrow a pig would be an insult to swine! We ended up outside the SCR, really yelling at each other, and then that head porter fellow—Clyde Peters—came up and separated us."

"What time was that?"

Seth shrugged. "Dunno... about 11:40? Maybe a quarter to twelve?"

"And you went back to Gloucester after that?"

"Yeah... I got back to my room but I was still pretty worked up... and then I realised that I didn't have my mobile phone. I thought I must have dropped it when Barrow and I were having that last argument outside the SCR, so I went back... Of course, I'd barely stepped into the Cloisters when I stumbled across Barrow's body."

He passed a hand over his face at the memory.

"Was he still alive?" asked Cassie, her eyes round.

Seth grimaced. "No. But he was still warm. And I didn't realise that he was dead. I could barely see anything—those old lamps in the Cloisters hardly give off any proper light—and I didn't even realise that it was Barrow. I thought it was someone who had passed out or something; I mean, you just don't expect to come across a dead body! So I was groping around and then I felt the hilt of a knife and I just pulled it out without thinking... and the next minute, there was this light in my face and the head porter, Peters, was there staring at me like he'd seen a ghost... and I looked down and saw all this blood on me and Barrow lying there dead on the ground... and then Peters was saying something to me but I couldn't think... I just kept staring at the dagger and the blood on my hands... and then... and then I started yelling back at Peters, telling him to call for an ambulance..." Seth drew a shuddering breath. "I guess, even then, I didn't really want to believe that Barrow was dead."

He leaned back against the couch, looking exhausted from his narrative. "It wasn't until later—when the police arrived and started asking me questions, and then said they were taking me down to the station—that I realised how it looked, that I was being arrested for murder..."

CHAPTER TEN

I sat back and pondered what Seth had recounted so far. There was something he had said—something that seemed odd—but I couldn't grasp the thought and then it was gone, like smoke dispersing into the air.

"What about the murder weapon?" Cassie was asking. "Gemma told me that it belonged to some female don at Wadsworth?"

"Yeah, Dr Gaber—Leila. She's an Associate Professor at the Department of Ethnoarchaeology and a colleague of Barrow's. Actually, an enemy of Barrow's would be a better description."

I raised my eyebrows. "Enemy?"

Seth laughed. "Well, maybe that's too strong a word but she's been gunning for him ever since she arrived in Oxford. She's been trying to get him to step down as head of the Ethnoarchaeology Department."

"With her taking over the position instead?" I said.

"Well, she never said that... but now that you mention it, I wouldn't be surprised," said Seth. "She would be so much better than him too. She's a real powerhouse and I think she'd be exactly what the department needs. Breathe some life into the place, have some vision for the future... not like Barrow, who's one of those types that just wants to uphold the 'old boys' club' and get the glory of being the leader without actually getting off his arse to do anything," said Seth disgustedly.

"So was Leila Gaber actually trying to discredit Barrow?" I said.

"Well, I don't know if she'd mounted a public campaign against him or anything; I think it was more that she was gathering evidence to put a case together. It was how I got to know her, actually—she asked to speak to me because I'd had dealings with Barrow. I think she was planning eventually to take the case to the University authorities to show them that Barrow was unfit for the role."

"Did she have a case?"

Seth shrugged. "Well, if all she needed to prove was that Barrow was a major plonker, there would have been no problem. Plenty of people happy to stand up and support that. But I think she was actually going for something more concrete." He paused, then said, "There were a lot of rumours going around that Barrow was an alcoholic."

Cassie chuckled. "You could probably say that about a lot of academics, based on the amount they drink!"

Seth laughed as well. "Yeah, I know. But I don't mean a glass of sherry before dinner or port in the S.C.R. afterwards—I think in Barrow's case, it was getting out of control. My friend, Ron, told me stories of Barrow turning up drunk to tutorials and even getting into a drunken brawl in a couple of the town pubs."

Cassie made a tutting sound. "So if Leila Gaber could prove that Barrow's drinking problem was impinging on his work and his judgement, she might have been able to force him to step down as head of department."

"Ambitious woman, isn't she?" I said.

Seth gave a laugh. "You have no idea. I'm actually glad I'm not in her department—I'd hate to get on her wrong side."

"Well, now that Barrow is dead, she won't even have to worry about gathering a case against him, will she?" said Cassie. "How can the police not be treating her as a suspect? After all, the murder weapon actually *belonged* to her!"

"Devlin said that he questioned her about that and she claimed that you borrowed it...?" I looked at Seth questioningly.

"Yes, I did borrow it. I was giving a tutorial on T-shaped molecular geometry on Friday and I happened to see the dagger letter opener on her desk and I thought—with the hilt across the blade like that—it was the perfect way to demonstrate T-shaped geometry and its relation to the trigonal bipyramidal molecular geometry for AX5 molecules with three equatorial and two axial ligands. And you know they think that trifluoroacetate anion is possibly the first example of an AX3E3 molecule, which is really exciting because—"

"Seth...!" I interrupted him

He stopped and gave a sheepish grin. "Sorry. Got carried away... Yeah, about the dagger... I finished the tutorial and put it back in Leila's pigeonhole, just like we'd agreed, and that was the last I saw of it."

"If it was in her pigeonhole, anyone could have got hold of it," said Cassie.

"That's what I told Devlin," I said. "I mean, for all you know, Leila could have retrieved it herself and was simply lying when she said she never got it back."

"Does she have an alibi for the time of the murder?" asked Seth. "I tried to find out from the police but they wouldn't tell me."

"She was supposed to be in the college library," I said. "Which adjoins the Cloister... I know the main library entrance opens onto the Walled Garden—is there a door on the other side of the library, which opens into the Cloisters?"

Seth frowned. "Yeah, actually there is. Not a public door, mind you, but a sort of service entrance at the back, leading from the library storage room out into the Cloisters. Ron mentioned it to me once. It's really more for the librarians to use if they want to bring something in or out of the storage room and don't want to have to lug it through the front of the library."

"Well, apparently Leila had been given special dispensation for a set of keys to the library, so that she could work in there after the official closing time. Maybe the librarians gave her a tour and showed her the back door."

Cassie sat forwards suddenly. "Maybe she framed you, Seth! She knew that you and Barrow were at loggerheads with each other—maybe she wanted a way to get rid of him and she saw an opportunity when you asked to borrow the dagger—she knew then that the murder weapon could be linked to you."

"I guess..." said Seth, looking a bit uncomfortable.

I realised that he didn't really want to consider Leila a serious suspect. He *liked* her. Oh, not romantically—but obviously as a person and a friend. I found myself suddenly curious to meet this woman who possessed so much charm that others were willing to overlook her possible ruthlessness.

"Maybe it's not anyone from the college," suggested Seth. "That head porter's been going on lately about college security and suspicious types lurking about. He's a bit of a gossipy old woman but he might be right. And didn't Kent College have a burglary last week? Some things were stolen from one of the undergraduate rooms, I heard. Maybe this was also an attempted robbery or a mugging gone wrong."

"Funny place to lie in wait to mug someone, in the cloisters of an Oxford college," I said dryly. "Not exactly a lot of foot traffic, is there? Unless students are going to the college chapel. Although, being serious, Devlin did tell me that the CCTV footage in front of the college picked up a strange man lurking on the street opposite the front gate."

"They never told me that!" said Seth, sitting up straighter. "Have they identified him?"

"They think it might be a tramp." I described the figure caught on camera.

"Hmm... tall... red hair... sounds like Jim..." mused Seth.

"Jim?" I looked at him.

"Yeah, he's one of those living rough on the streets. I actually met him through the Domus Trust; he's been acting as a sort of... well, 'consultant', I guess, to the architects and designers, and also as a liaison between the charity and the homeless community in the city—you know, canvassing the other street persons for their opinions on the project. He's only come to Oxford recently and the charity are delighted to have him because he's literate and better educated than a lot of the other drifters; probably had a white-collar job at one time, poor sod, and lost it."

"So if this housing project got approved, Jim would have the chance to have a roof over his head?"

I said

Seth nodded. "He would have had first dibs, especially given his work on the project."

"That would be a big deal for someone like him—a chance to get off the streets at last. And Barrow was going to block it..." I looked at Seth. "Does Jim have a history of violence? Any arrests?"

Seth shrugged. "I don't know. That's not the kind of thing you'd ask a man, is it? I have to admit, Jim doesn't make much attempt to be pleasant and I've seen him get pretty surly, especially with figures of authority. He's got a temper. But that's pretty understandable. A lot of the homeless have had awful things happen in their past—you know, domestic abuse, mental illness, terrible tragedies... I know one girl who was being used by her stepfather as a prostitute for his friends and another young man who lost everything he owned in a fire; Jim lost his family in an accident, I think, and then his job, like another tramp down by Carfax who was framed by his boss for fraud and lost his job and his credit rating too... it's terrible what some of these homeless people have suffered. It's not surprising that they end up going into a downward spiral. And then with all the disadvantages and frustrations they have to deal with now, living rough on the streets, it's hardly surprising that they feel resentful!"

"Still, you have to admit, it gives Jim a very good motive," I said gently.

"Oh yeah, let's just all jump on the homeless guy!

Why not?" snapped Seth. "Because they're always criminals anyway, right? Because all homeless people are just drunks and drug addicts and losers!"

Cassie gave me a startled look. I put my hands up soothingly. "It was just a thought, Seth. I mean, you have to consider all possible suspects in a situation like this..."

Seth passed a hand over his face. "Sorry... sorry, Gemma. It just makes me so mad... If you've spoken with some of these people like I have and heard their stories... A lot of them are just unlucky and have been kicked to the gutter and now they're trying their best to climb out—but they're struggling because of the system and other people's prejudices... It's just incredibly unfair! And now with something like this, I can just see the police honing in on the first homeless man in the neighbourhood."

"Well, actually, they're honing in on *you*," I said dryly. "And I'm just trying to find out who the real murderer is so you can be released from the charges."

Seth look shamefaced. "I know. Sorry. I didn't mean to snap. I just... the last forty-eight hours have been pretty rough and it's all getting to me a bit."

"We'll let you get some rest now," said Cassie, standing up. "Come on, Gemma."

Giving Seth a pat on the shoulder, I turned and followed Cassie out of the room. We walked slowly back towards the college entrance, our breaths coming out in clouds of steam in the chilly night air.

"I've never seen Seth like that before, have you?" said Cassie, breaking the silence.

I glanced at her. "What do you mean?"

"Well, he's usually so mild and sweet and patient," said Cassie. "I've never seen him get so passionate and even... *aggressive* about something. I mean, I thought his chamber music obsession was bad but this is something else...

"Do you remember," she continued, "that one time in college when he found a bunch of students teasing one of the first years who had a stammer? They were being pretty cruel and making fun of the poor fresher. Seth really lost it. Punched one of the other students. They had to call the porters to come and calm him down. He just can't bear to see people abusing the weak and disadvantaged." She looked at me. "And now, this is the same thing. It's like this charity taps into what he believes in and he's taking it so personally."

I walked silently, deep in thought. Cassie was right. It had been bothering me too. I had always thought that I knew Seth but tonight I'd seen a new side to him. I thought back to that dinner with Devlin and the way I had insisted I knew Seth and what he was capable of. I felt a flicker of unease. Maybe I was wrong?

CHAPTER ELEVEN

I usually had a lie-in and a bit of a lazy morning lounging around in my pyjamas on Mondays—it was my one day off from the tearoom—but this Monday, I was up and dressed early as I'd offered to drop my mother and Helen Green at the bus station for the start of their big adventure. I stood waiting patiently in the hall as my mother flitted around, fussing over her luggage and giving last-minute instructions.

"And don't forget to water the herb pots in the kitchen window... and the palm here in the hallway needs some water too... and remember to put out the rubbish on Wednesday... oh, and if your father rings, tell him I found his reading glasses by the bathroom sink—he is so dreadfully forgetful—he must have forgotten to pack them..."

A clatter in the living room made us turn around.

"What's that?" I said.

"Oh, it must be that naughty Muesli again!" said my mother in exasperation. "She's developed some sort of a fixation with one of the floor vents in the living room. She won't leave it alone."

I peeked into the living room. In the far corner, Muesli was huddled over the floor vent, which was covered with an ornate Victorian cast iron grille. Her head was cocked to one side and she was batting at the grille, which made a clatter each time it shifted in its frame.

"I wonder if she can smell something in the crawl space beneath the house and she wants to get down there to investigate," said my mother, coming to peer over my shoulder.

I went over to the little cat and waved my hand. "Leave that alone, Muesli... Shoo!"

"*Meorrw*!" said Muesli indignantly. She gave me a baleful look, then turned and stalked off.

I tapped the grille with my toe. It shifted slightly in its frame—probably a bit loose—but it seemed okay. I'd ask my father about it when he got back from South Africa.

"Oh heavens—is that the time?" my mother gasped, looking at the clock in the hallway. "I'm going to miss the ten o'clock coach, Gemma!"

We bundled ourselves into the car and—pausing only long enough to pick up Helen—I drove to Gloucester Green, where Oxford's central bus station was located. Parking was a bit of a nightmare and I had to park a fair distance away, then help my mother and her friend with their bags. I was glad they had decided to forgo the knapsack option although I wasn't too sure about their choice of luggage. They couldn't have picked anything else that screamed "Rich, naïve Western tourist!" more loudly. In fact, Helen's fancy wheeled case looked like a cousin of R2-D2, complete with 180-degree spinner wheels, impact resistant polycarbonate casing, and slick aluminium frame.

"Oh, I'm so worried I might have forgotten something... I've got my ticket and passport, haven't I?" fretted Helen as we stood next to the airport express coach, waiting for the luggage to be loaded into the belly of the vehicle. She began rummaging through her handbag for the twentieth time. "I've got my passport here but... where's the ticket?" she gasped.

"Oh, I told you, remember? We're using *e-tickets* now," said my mother loftily. "It's all in their computers. You just give them your passport and they scan it and find your ticket attached."

I hid a smile of amusement. For someone who had only entered the online world properly four months ago, my mother was acting like a top authority on the subject.

"Well, I still wish there was some sort of ticket," grumbled Helen. "I feel so naked travelling this way."

"Don't forget to send me a text or email when you arrive in Jakarta," I said to my mother. "Just so I know you got there and everything is okay."

"Oh, stop fussing, darling... I'm sure we'll be fine," said my mother, busily thumbing through a brochure on *Treasures in Jakarta*. "Oh, Helen, listen to this! There's a market in Jakarta where you can see and touch live *eels*!"

"Mother—did you hear me? Don't forget! I'll be worrying otherwise... and remember that you need to haggle in Asia. Don't just pay the asking price—make sure you bargain. They expect Westerners to be easy game so they'll probably try to rip you off, especially in the tourist areas."

"Yes, yes, darling," said my mother distractedly. "We'll be fine. Oh, they're boarding! Come on, Helen! Krakatoa, here we come!"

She gave me a hurried kiss on the cheek, then joined the line of people scrambling up the coach steps. I stood and watched until the coach had rumbled out of the bus station. It was a bit weird— like some kind of strange role reversal—me standing there watching my mother go off on some independent travel and worrying about her. I turned away at last, then paused. The parking on the car was still good for some time and my stomach was growling. I hadn't had breakfast yet. Rather than go home to a boring bowl of cereal, I decided to be indulgent and treat myself to breakfast in town.

Besides, after days of gloomy skies and heavy fog, there seemed to be a welcome break in the winter weather today. The skies were a watery blue and there was even a peek of sunshine from behind the clouds. It was a pale, weak sunshine but sunshine nonetheless. I smiled to myself, feeling my spirits lift, and decided that a brisk walk in the fresh air was just what I needed.

I wandered from the bus depot area into the main square of Gloucester Green. Despite its name, it actually bore no resemblance to the typical village green with the patch of grass and the duck pond. It was more in the style of an Italian *piazza*, with a row of tall, elegant red brick apartment blocks fronting two sides of the square, and cafés and boutique stores on the ground floor. The other side of the square backed onto George Street, which was a bit like Oxford's version of the West End—filled with cinemas, theatres, and eateries.

I bypassed the restaurants on George Street, heading for the junction with Cornmarket, the main pedestrianised thoroughfare through the centre of town. There was a McDonald's on Cornmarket—a place I knew well from my student days—and I was heading for the guilty pleasure of an Egg McMuffin. I smiled wryly as I imagined Abby Finch's face—she'd probably have an apoplexy, as they said in the olden days, if she knew about the *non*-gluten-free-full-of-white-flour-high-fructose-cholesterol-laden meal I was heading for.

As I was about to enter the Golden Arches, I passed a tall, thin man in an old anorak and faded jogging pants, with a lanyard around his neck. He was holding a bunch of what looked like thin, non-glossy magazines and I realised that he was a *Big Issue* vendor. They'd become a common sight in cities around the U.K.: selling the street newspaper gave the homeless a chance to earn a legitimate income and meant that they could have a better chance of reintegrating back into society too.

I smiled at him and was automatically reaching for my purse when I saw that, like many of the homeless in Oxford, he was accompanied by a dog: a stocky little Staffordshire bull terrier, its mouth wide open in a typical "Staffie smile" and its tail wagging wildly. It jumped up as I approached them and shoved its nose into my crotch.

"Whoa! Sorry 'bout that! Ruby can be a bit enthusiastic, like," said her owner with a grin.

I grinned back, rubbing her ears. "Don't worry. I like dogs. She is gorgeous! How old is she?"

"Nearly six, I reckon," he said. "Though you'd never know it from the way she be'aves. Still like a pup, she is."

I crouched down to give Ruby a belly rub. The Staffie rolled onto her back, closing her eyes as one back leg twitched whilst I stroked her exposed stomach. I laughed at the expression of utter bliss on her face.

"She looks very well," I said.

He drew himself up proudly. "Always look out for 'er first, I do. Always make sure that Ruby's fed and got a warm place to sleep. And there's kind charities that provide free vet care for dogs that are livin' on the streets with us."

"She seems really happy," I said, rising to my feet and rubbing her ears again. I thought of all the dogs belonging to wealthy families who languished alone and neglected in homes and gardens all day. This dog may never have known the luxury of a faux fur bed or organic dog food, but it had constant love and companionship, and I wondered if it was happier than a lot of "pampered" pets out there.

"I'm Owen," said the man, offering his hand with a smile. "Can I interest you in a copy of the latest *Big Issue*?"

"Oh yes, of course... that's what I came over for, actually. I got side-tracked by Ruby." I chuckled as I gave him the money. I flicked through the magazine, then said casually, "I see that the murder at Wadsworth College didn't make it into this issue."

His face darkened. "Bad business, that," he said grimly. "Police were 'ere yesterday, questioning a bunch of us street people..."

"Why? It happened in a college, didn't it?" I said. "Why would the police think you know anything about it? Surely they're not immediately assuming that the homeless are involved?" I said with exaggerated indignation.

It worked. I could see that I had gained his sympathy. And loosened his tongue.

"It's always easy to blame the 'omeless," said Owen, making a face. "But fair's fair—in this case, seems they 'ad a good reason. Some bloke caught on the camera outside the college—looked like a tramp—so they were showin' us a picture taken from the footage and askin' us if we knew 'im."

"Did you?" I asked, trying to conceal my eager interest.

He shrugged again. "Could be. 'ard to tell—real grainy picture, it was. But I reckon it looked like Jim. Same red 'air and 'e's a big bloke, real tall."

"Do you think he could be involved? I mean, do you know him well? Does he seem like the type who could... um... you know, hurt someone?"

"Who knows? You can never tell, can you? I learned long ago to stop askin' people 'bout their past. Some of us 'ave 'ad it real rough."

"Yes, I can imagine," I said with genuine sympathy. I thought of Seth's words from the night before. "I suppose it's understandable that a homeless person might react violently to something—"

"Didn't say that," Owen said quickly. "Don't think you can ever justify violence. Take Ruby 'ere—she was beaten by 'er previous owner 'cos 'e was pissed off that she'd chewed up 'is shoes. There en't ever any call for that! No matter 'ow angry you are."

I looked up at him—at this thin, balding man with his tattered clothes and stubbled chin—and yet who had more integrity and natural dignity than a member of the House of Lords. I felt something tighten at the back of my throat.

"You're right," I said, leaning down to rub Ruby's ears again. "But sadly I don't think many people share your view."

"Ah, well, more's their loss," he said with a smile.

I smiled back. "By the way, are you familiar with the Domus Trust?"

His face brightened. "Oh, yeah. Great charity, they are. New but doin' a lot o' good work. They've got this scheme to build affordable 'ousing, so us 'omeless 'ave a chance to get off the streets. Actually, that bloke, Jim, was involved with 'em—it's 'ow I got chattin' to 'im. 'E came down here from the north a few weeks ago and I'd seen 'im around, but 'e's not real friendly, like, so we didn't speak much. Then 'e came and asked me if I'd be interested in applyin' for a unit if they approved the project."

I looked at Owen in surprise. "But surely... wouldn't everyone want a place? Why would you even need to ask?"

"Ah, well... Not everyone wants to get off the streets, you know. Some of us are used to the freedom of livin' rough." He looked down and gave Ruby a pat. "And there's those of us with pets. I mean, would they let Ruby come stay with me in this 'ousing? I en't goin' nowhere without Ruby. I'd rather sleep on the streets than 'ave 'em take 'er away from me and put 'er in a shelter."

"I hope they can work it out," I said sincerely. "Hey, listen—I was just going into McDonald's. Can I get you anything? A burger and a cup of hot coffee?

And I'll get something for Ruby too."

His face split in a toothy grin. "That's real kind of you, miss. 'ot drink wouldn't go amiss in this weather..." He rubbed his chapped hands together. "I'm partial to a 'ot coffee. And a burger would be real nice."

"Okay, I'll be right back."

I had just missed the breakfast menu but I didn't mind as this meant I could pick up a bigger meal for Owen. I ordered him a Big Mac meal with all the trimmings, together with a chocolate muffin, an apple pie, and a hot cup of coffee. And a side order of chicken nuggets for Ruby. The smell of the thin, crispy fries was making my mouth water and I had to resist pinching a few on my way out.

"Cor! This 'ere's a real treat!" said Owen, grabbing the paper bag when I returned to him.

Ruby looked up hopefully, her nose working overtime. Owen put his hand in the bag and drew out a chicken nugget, holding it above the dog's nose.

"Look at this, Ruby girl! Chicken nuggets, eh? Now, you show the nice lady your manners. *Sit.*"

The Staffie dropped her bum on the ground, squirming in place, barely able to contain herself. Owen laughed and gave her the nugget. It was gone in less than a second and the dog licked her chops and looked up eagerly for more.

I laughed as well. "Maybe I should have got her two boxes. Well, I hope you enjoy them." I bent down to give Ruby a final pat, then as I was turning to leave, a thought occurred to me.

"By the way, you wouldn't happen to know where I could find Jim?"

I wondered if he would ask why I wanted to know, but luckily Owen was busily tucking into his burger, too distracted to wonder at my question.

"'E likes the patch down by the canal," he said with his mouth full. "Down near Jericho, I think. Might find 'im there." He paused and gave me a look. "But I'd go carefully, if I were you. Jim don't like strangers much."

CHAPTER TWELVE

The Oxford canal started from Hythe Bridge Street, which was at the bottom of George Street, near Gloucester Green. This was handy as my watch told me that my time was nearly up for the parking. I could swing by the bus station, add more money to the parking meter, and then head on down to the canal.

The whole thing shouldn't have been more than an extra five-minute detour but as I was crossing the wide expanse of the *piazza* square, I suddenly heard the most dreadful noise. It was somebody singing, I realised. No, squawking would have been a better word. I looked around with a mixture of disbelief and annoyance, trying to see who was making that terrible racket. Gloucester Green was popular with many of the homeless folk and buskers, and you could usually find a few huddled against the buildings at the sides of the square, but the street musicians I'd come across here before were usually pretty good. This singer was so awful, on the other hand, you almost wanted to pay her to stop.

I scanned the space around me, then did a double take as I saw the four small figures swaying by the side of the cinema. They were dressed in some kind of outlandish hippy outfit—all tie-dyed head scarves and long fringed skirts, which clashed badly with the M&S woolly cardigans they had kept on for warmth—but I would have known them anywhere. The Old Biddies.

I marched over to them. "Mabel! Glenda! Florence! Ethel! What on *earth* are you doing?"

Glenda, who was the one singing—no, make that *trying* to sing—paused long enough to give me a bright smile, then continued warbling on. I winced as she hit a particularly high note with a loud screech. Next to her, Ethel and Florence shook tambourines with great enthusiasm but absolutely no rhythm, whilst Mabel hopped from foot to foot in some grotesque parody of a tap dance and thrust a cap under the nose of an unfortunate passer-by, who reeled back in fright, stuffed a pound coin into the cap, and hurried away.

Mabel turned and shoved the cap at me. "Donations, please."

I laughed incredulously. "What? You're not serious! What are you doing here?"

Mabel staggered through a pirouette, then thrust the cap at me again. "Give us a pound and we'll tell you."

I scowled. "Don't be ridiculous!"

Mabel sniffed. "Suit yourself." And she turned away, whilst Glenda began a new song.

"All right, all right..." I grumbled, digging into my pocket and producing a gold pound coin which I dropped into the cap. "There. Now tell me what you're doing."

Mabel beckoned me closer and said, in a dramatic whisper, "We're undercover."

I gaped at her. "You're what?"

"Undercover. You know, like in disguise," said Florence helpfully, in between shakes of the tambourine.

I stared from her to Mabel to Ethel to Glenda and back to her. "But... why?"

Ethel leaned towards me. "To get information, dear. So we can help Seth... by finding the real murderer."

I didn't really see how caterwauling in the street while looking like bad imitations of old hippies would help Seth. "But... how?"

Mabel gave a sigh of impatience, as if I was being particularly stupid. "We needed a way to blend in with the street people, so we decided that busking was as good as any... It lets us spend time out here in the street, mingle with the homeless, ask questions about that tramp—you know, the one who was seen on the CCTV footage. Apparently, his name is Jim."

"How on earth did you know—?" I sighed. "Never mind. So, have you found out anything about him?"

"Not yet," said Mabel. She glowered around the square. "No one seems to want to come near us."

Yeah, I wonder why, I thought, wincing as Glenda's voice rose in a screech again.

"How did *you* find out about Jim?" Mabel looked at me suspiciously. "Did Inspector O'Connor tell you?"

"No," I said shortly. "I mean, yes, Devlin did mention him but I found out the rest myself from a *Big Issue* seller."

"Ooh, what did he tell you?"

I hadn't intended to say anything but they were looking at me like a group of eager puppies and I didn't have the heart to say no. I repeated what Owen had told me.

"The canal, eh?" said Mabel. "Right! We'll come with you—"

"No, no," I said irritably. "I'm going by myself and you—"

We were interrupted by a harassed-looking man in a cheap suit coming out of the travel agent on the other side of the street. He hurried up to us.

"Look," he said to Glenda, a desperate expression on his face. "If I give you some money, will you please *shut up*?"

"Don't worry, dear, we're packing up now," said

Mabel, hustling the others into action. "We're going to the canal."

"No, you're not—!" I protested but it was to deaf ears.

I thought I'd make a run for it but I hadn't realised how quickly the Old Biddies could move when they wanted to. In less than five minutes, they were trundling after me, fringed skirts, tambourines, and all. I sighed. Great. So much for trying to keep it low key so as not to scare Jim off—I couldn't have been more conspicuous if I tried.

We made our way across to Hythe Bridge— fittingly named as "hythe" was Old English for wharf or landing place, and this was where an ancient wharf had once marked the beginning of the Oxford Canal. A tow path ran alongside the canal and we started down this narrow dirt path, taking care to avoid the muddy patches. We hadn't had any snow in Oxford this winter, but plenty of sleet and rain, and the ground was wet and slippery in places. I wondered how on earth the big work horses had once managed to come this way when they used to tow canal boats and barges up and down the waterway. Weird to think that the canal had once been the fastest way to transfer coal, stones, and timber from the Midlands to London. Looking at the slow, peaceful surface of the water now, it was hard to imagine it as the fastest route to anything.

We hadn't been walking long when we came across a lock—an artificial "chamber" with gates at both ends, where the water level could be raised and lowered, so as to help boats navigate between two different stretches of water or across a land obstacle. This particular lock joined the Oxford Canal to a tributary of the River Thames and enabled canal boats to access the bigger waterway.

Locks were deep and could be treacherous—in fact, many drownings often happened in the locks, when a careless step on the side of a narrowboat could take you plunging into the swirling waters, to be crushed against the side of the boat or drown in the swell from the sluices.

But this one looked peaceful and idyllic in the winter sunshine as we approached it, spanned by a cast-iron bridge—Isis Bridge—and surrounded by the soft green of weeping willows. The tow path went over the bridge and continued on the other bank of the canal. Beyond the bridge, the water wound its slow, lazy way onwards into North Oxford, curtained on either side by hawthorn and crack willow, field maples, elder and ash trees.

There was a crowd milling around the bridge, which was obviously a popular photo spot, from the number of people taking family portraits and selfies. A young couple—the father wrangling a boisterous toddler and the mother pushing a stroller—came down the ramp towards us, followed by a woman walking a collie dog pulling eagerly on its leash.

"Morning!"

"Hello...!"

We nodded and exchanged smiles as we passed. Then we were climbing the ramp onto the bridge. A trio of young men—backpackers from the look of it, all wispy beards and shaggy long hair—gave me a cheerful smile and stood back respectfully for the Old Biddies as we passed them on the bridge. Then we were across and continuing along the tow path.

I was surprised at the number of people walking along the canal—perhaps the rare day of winter sunshine had prompted many of the locals to join the tourists along the waterway. It made the going much slower than I expected, having to dodge around families and dog walkers. Plus I found myself continually distracted by the pretty sights around the canal—the weeping willows forming graceful arches over the water, the brightly painted canal boats moored along the edge, and, as we approached Jericho, the tall Italianate tower of St Barnabas Church looming up on the opposite bank. I almost had to remind myself that I was here on a hunt for a murderer and not a scenic walk in the Oxfordshire countryside!

Finally, I paused and looked around, wondering if I should continue. We'd been walking for nearly half an hour now and had come a fair distance down the tow path. If we kept going, we were going to end up by Port Meadow, the huge area of ancient grazing land which had been left unploughed for four thousand years and was a free common ground on which local horses, ponies, and cattle grazed. At this time of winter, it was probably flooded and muddy and full of marsh birds, and I wasn't particularly looking forward to wading through that.

I peered down the tow path. We'd just passed a little humpbacked bridge and now, in the distance, I could see a large, modern, red-brick bridge, covered in parts with ugly graffiti. I wracked my memory. That was Frenchay Road Bridge, I remembered, and it was the last big bridge for a while until the canal reached Wolvercote. *I'll walk to there before I give up*, I decided.

I started forwards again, conscious of the Old Biddies who were still puffing along the tow path several hundred yards behind me. Then, just before I reached Frenchay Road, I saw him, hunched in the shadows underneath the bridge, smoking a cigarette. There was no mistaking that tall bulky figure and grizzled red hair, streaked with grey. He looked to be in his late forties or early fifties, with a long, mobile face and hard, suspicious eyes.

"Jim?" I said, approaching him with a smile.

He glanced up, his expression unwelcoming. "Yeah, whaddaya want?"

"I... um..." For a moment, I debated coming up with some story, then decided that for once, I was better being blunt and honest.

"You probably heard that Professor Barrow has been murdered."

He grunted but didn't say anything.

"I understand that you were outside Wadsworth

College around that time?"

He gave me a contemptuous look. "Yeah... so? It's a free country."

"Was there any particular reason why you were hanging around there?" I persisted.

"None of your sodding business."

I tried a different tack. "I also heard that Professor Barrow was opposed to the Domus Trust housing project? That he was trying to block it?"

Jim's face twisted into an ugly expression. "He was a bloody son-of-a—"

"You didn't like him," I said. It wasn't a question.

"Yeah, I didn't like him... So what?" he snarled. "Doesn't mean that I killed him!"

"I'm not saying you had anything to do with the crime at all," I said soothingly. "I just wondered... since you were around the college at the time of the murder... whether you saw anything suspicious?"

"No."

I bit my lip. Bloody hell, this man was hard work. I had run out of ideas for conversation. Behind me, I heard heavy breathing as the Old Biddies caught up with me at last. They peered around my back at Jim, who glared at them.

"Whaddaya staring at?" he snapped at Glenda, who gave a squeak and took a step backwards. But Mabel wasn't intimidated. She pushed her way in front of the others and looked Jim up and down disapprovingly.

"Young man, you need a good wash. And did you

know that smoking is bad for you?"

I groaned inwardly. Antagonising Jim was not going to persuade him to talk!

The tramp stood up and pushed past us roughly. "I don't need to listen to this sh—"

"Wait! Please!" I said, grabbing his arm. "Look, my friend, Seth Browning, has been arrested for the murder. I'm just trying to help him."

The homeless man's face softened slightly. "Yeah, I know Seth. He's a good bloke. Does a lot for the homeless." He swung around to face me. "But I can't help you. To be honest with you, I'd like to shake the hand of the person who killed that bloody drunk!"

"But do you have any idea who that might be?" I persisted. "Anyone who hated Barrow enough to kill him?"

"If I did, I wouldn't tell you! Why should I help the police catch the bloke who did us all a public service, getting rid of that bastard?"

He made a sound like a horse snorting, then turned and stalked away, heading down the tow path towards Wolvercote. He walked with a limp, I noticed, and it would have been fairly easy for me to catch up with him again, but I decided to let him go. I didn't think I'd get anything else out of him anyway.

"What an unpleasant piece of work!" Mabel stood staring after him, her arms akimbo. "I wouldn't be surprised if he was the murderer. Look at him! All unshaven and unkempt and skulking under bridges... "

I was almost inclined to agree except that I was uncomfortably reminded of Seth's accusation the night before: about how prejudiced people could be against the homeless. Jim might have been surly and hostile—and he could sure have done with a shave and a wash—but that didn't necessarily make him a criminal.

Just as a posh Oxford background didn't necessarily make you innocent either, I thought. Barrow had been an Oxford professor. The murder had taken place in an Oxford college. Somehow, I had a feeling that the key to this mystery was not out here in the homeless community but much closer to home.

CHAPTER THIRTEEN

Church bells were tolling the evening service across Oxford as Lincoln escorted me through the front gate of Wadsworth College and across the main quadrangle to the hall where the Oxford Society of Medicine dinner was to take place. We were slightly late as Lincoln had been delayed by an emergency case at the hospital, and when we stepped into the antechamber, it was already crowded with people and buzzing with the hum of conversation.

It was a typical Oxford event with all the men in "black tie", looking suave and elegant in their dinner jackets, snowy white shirts, and black bowties, and the women in glittering cocktail dresses and sumptuous evening gowns. As soon as I stepped in, I did the usual female ritual: an anxious inspection of the women around me to make sure that I wasn't overdressed or underdressed. *Whew.* It looked like I was okay. I had worn my trusty "little black dress" with long sheer sleeves and a flared hem, and I noted that several ladies had opted for their LBDs too. A flash of colour on the other side of the room caught my eye—a glimpse of turquoise chiffon and the sparkle of gold embroidery—I couldn't see her properly but I silently applauded the woman who had dared to stand out from the pack.

A waiter approached bearing a tray of drinks. Lincoln chose a dry sherry and I took a glass of champagne, then we mingled. Or rather, I should say, *he* mingled and I tagged along, trying to join in the polite conversation. Many of the guests were obviously old colleagues or friends of Lincoln's and I saw several of them eye me speculatively. I groaned inwardly. *Great.* I hoped that my coming as his date tonight wouldn't fuel any rumours. I didn't need anything else to help my mother's machinations.

Somehow, I got separated from Lincoln and found myself at the edge of a group who were having a good old argument about the best college at Oxford. I laughed to myself. This was almost like my student days again. What was it about humans—no matter which walk of life—they just loved belonging to a "tribe" and competing against each other! Inter-college rivalry was rife at Oxford and several of the colleges had long-standing feuds that spanned generations. And of course, there was the usual resentment towards the bigger, wealthier colleges—

like Magdalen, St John, and Christ Church—which tended to monopolise the limelight.

"Anyone would think that all there was to Oxford was Christ Church!" one of the men was saying in disgust as I joined the group. "Every blasted movie is filmed there and everyone I meet who has visited Oxford seems to only talk about Christ Church. I overheard a conversation at Heathrow Airport the other day on my way back from a conference—two tourists...and one of them had obviously just visited Oxford and was telling the other about it. She was making all these sweeping statements about 'Oxford colleges' and I felt like leaning over and saying, 'What you're saying only applies to Christ Church!' Not every college has a cathedral or those custodians with bowler hats!" He shook his head.

The woman next to him bristled. "As it so happens, Christ Church deserves its fame. It *is* one of the grandest Oxford colleges and has some of the most famous figures in literature and history amongst its alumni. Visitors love the stories. That concealed staircase, for example, through which dons come up into the dining hall to sit at High Table—that was supposed to be Lewis Carroll's inspiration for the rabbit hole in *Alice in Wonderland*—"

"Oh, not that old story again!" groaned the man. "Anyone would think that none of the other Oxford colleges have secret passages or fascinating stories and legends. What about Exeter College, where

Tolkien studied? In the library there is a book on Finnish grammar which is what first inspired him to start inventing languages—including Elvish for *The Lord of the Rings*. No one ever talks about that!"

"Well, I still think—"

A roar of laughter from the other side of the room distracted me and I glanced over. The crowd parted momentarily to reveal a woman surrounded by several men. She was clad in a floor-length turquoise gown, with long, wide sleeves and exquisite Middle-Eastern-style embroidery around her neck and cuffs. This was the woman I had glimpsed earlier, I realised, and even without her stunning gown, she would have eclipsed every other woman in the room. Not that she was conventionally beautiful—no, she was probably what one would have called "handsome" in the old days. She had strong features, a large, slightly hooked nose, dark brows, and big eyes with ridiculously thick eyelashes. Her mouth was wide and generous, outlined with vivid red lipstick, and she had big hair. I don't just mean a bit of volume—I mean seriously *big:* massive waves springing from her forehead and curling around her shoulders, like a lion's mane. I wondered how many gallons of hairspray had gone into that creation.

She was saying something and making everyone around her laugh uproariously. Suddenly, I knew that this was Leila Gaber. Her charm was palpable, even from across the room. I had to find a way to talk to her.

Casually, I drifted across and inserted myself into the edge of Leila Gaber's group. They were still laughing and it was easy to pretend to laugh along with them. It was a trick I had picked up during numerous networking parties in Sydney—by the time they stopped laughing, they'd already accepted you into the group and thought you were part of the conversation. I sidled up to Leila and at the first pause, I turned to her and used the line that usually worked with academics:

"Dr Gaber, I'm so pleased to meet you at last. I've heard so much about your work!"

The beautiful dark eyes regarded me shrewdly and I realised belatedly that Leila Gaber was no bumbling academic to be easily taken in by empty flattery.

"You are interested in Ethnoarchaeology? Which areas of my work on relational analogies do you find most interesting?" she said, a smile curling the corners of her mouth.

Yikes. "I... um... I didn't have a specific focus... Your... uh... your research is all so... interesting." Quickly, I changed the subject. "I love your dress," I said, this time with sincere admiration. "The embroidery is absolutely gorgeous. Is it a traditional Egyptian outfit?"

Leila Gaber smiled. "Well, not an ancient Egyptian one. This is a *thobe*, a traditional Arabic dress for ladies. Most of us modern Egyptians are descended from Arabs, you know, rather than from Cleopatra, and have assimilated Arabian culture into Egypt."

Her English was fluent but overlaid with a heavy Middle Eastern accent and the overall effect was charming.

"That's fascinating," I said. "Have you been at Oxford long?"

"Long enough," she said with another of those Mona Lisa smiles. "And yourself?"

"I was a student here," I said. "But I've been away—I was working in Australia—and I only returned a few months ago."

"To work for the University?"

I laughed and shook my head. "No, I run a tearoom in Meadowford-on-Smythe. It's a little Cotswolds village on the outskirts of Oxford."

"So did you study medicine at Oxford then?" she said, gesturing around the room. I realised she was wondering why I was a guest at this dinner.

"I'm here with a friend, who is a doctor," I explained. "He's the keynote speaker tonight, actually."

"Ah. Yes. Dr Lincoln Green." She glanced across the room at Lincoln, then back at me with a smile. "There are many who would think you very lucky."

I blushed slightly. "Lincoln and I are just friends," I said quickly. "And yourself? Do you have an interest in medicine?"

"I am here as a guest as well," she said. "The Tutor for Medicine at Wadsworth—Dr Al-Aker—is Egyptian and also an old friend. And he knows I am currently conducting research into the relationship between mortuary practices, society, and ideology. I am particularly interested in the increased use of hygiene, science, and medicine as agencies of social control."

"Do you have to do a lot of hands-on research?"

"Yes, although there is a large amount of literature to study as well. I am lucky, of course, to be working in one of the top universities in the world, with access to some of the rarest books and manuscripts available."

"I suppose you must spend a lot of time in the library," I said casually.

"Oh, many nights I am there until very late, yes."

I opened my eyes very wide, as if I suddenly realised something. "Oh! Were you at the library last Friday night? I heard that a professor was murdered here in Wadsworth!"

She gave me a sharp glance but I kept my expression innocently curious. Finally, she said, "Yes, I was here. In fact, I think I was in the library during the time the murder was taking place, just outside, in the Cloisters."

I gave a mock shudder. "Oh, that's horrible! When you found out, it must have been really creepy!"

"It was not pleasant," agreed Leila Gaber.

"Did you know him?"

She gave me a wry look. "Quentin Barrow? Only too well."

I said nothing, hoping that she would elaborate

but Leila Gaber wasn't Joan Barrow and the silence trick wasn't going to work on her. She simply gave me that mysterious smile again. After a moment, I said:

"Do they have any idea how he was killed?"

"He was stabbed through the neck. With a dagger that belonged to me," Leila Gaber added coolly.

I was thrown by her bluntness. "Oh... er... my God, really? But... how did the murderer get hold of your dagger?"

"It was a souvenir which I brought with me from Egypt. I was using it on my desk—to open letters and such. But it was not in my possession at the time of the murder. I had lent it—to the young Chemistry tutor at Gloucester College. In fact, it was he who discovered the body."

I gave another exaggerated shudder and said, "Aren't you scared at the thought of a murderer running loose around the college?"

"No." Leila Gaber looked amused. "I do not believe that this was a random killing. I believe it was—as the ancient Babylonians use to say—an eye for an eye, a tooth for a tooth."

"Revenge? You mean, he had enemies?"

"We all have enemies," she said with that sly smile again. "But yes, in this case, I think there were many times when Professor Barrow was careless in the way he treated others. You can only kick a dog so many times before it will turn around and bite you."

She looked away, then back at me. "It is wrong, I

know, to say such things, but in many ways, it is good that Quentin Barrow is dead."

I stared at her, disturbed at the casual way she had voiced such a ruthless sentiment in the middle of such an elegant, refined setting. She gave me that Mona Lisa smile again, knowing that she had shocked me, then turned and addressed a comment to the gentlemen around us, who had been hovering respectfully nearby. Instantly, they gave her their full attention, and soon everyone was laughing once more at some joke she had made.

I let myself be edged to the back of the group and stood watching the way they clustered around her. Oh yes, Leila Gaber was skilled at manipulating others and so charming that they wouldn't even realise they were being manipulated. She was ruthless and ambitious and capable of anything. The question was, did that include murder?

CHAPTER FOURTEEN

The tinkling of a fork being struck against glass announced that it was time to take our places at the tables. The rest of the evening passed pleasantly enough. I was seated with Lincoln and several other clinicians and I wondered if I had let myself in for a night of gory details about gross medical procedures and terrifying diseases. Doctors and medical types just can't seem to stop talking shop whenever they get together. But tonight, they seemed to be making an effort to behave themselves and I was treated to nothing more graphic than a description of a son's broken elbow while playing school rugby.

Dinner was a four-course meal, starting with broccoli and Stilton soup, then stuffed quail with roasted garlic, followed by rack of lamb on crushed minted peas and creamy mash potato, and then finally dessert: triple layered chocolate tart with orange compote. All washed down with glasses of red and white wine which were continually refilled by the college waiters.

It had been a while since I had sat down to such a formal meal and the array of knives and forks and spoons laid out around my plate was slightly intimidating. I remembered the basic rule, of course—start from the outside and work your way in, and always, always scoop *away* from your body when using the soup spoon—but it still felt slightly strange to be eating in such a formal setting. Life in Australia was so much more laid-back, with none of the fussy British etiquette, and I'd got used to a more casual way of doing things. Of course, most places in the U.K. weren't like this—Oxford was the epitome of British pomp and ceremony. Only Cambridge and Buckingham Palace could probably match it.

After the plates had been cleared, there was tea and coffee, cheese and crackers, and vintage port for those who hadn't had enough alcohol yet. I wasn't much of a drinker but I did love anything sweet and port was right up my alley. Wadsworth College had its own cellar and these were specially decanted bottles. I sipped the rich, sweet, plummy wine as I listened to Lincoln give his talk.

I had to admit, most of it went over my head and my thoughts wandered. I couldn't stop thinking about the murder—something I had heard earlier during the drinks was nagging at me. I had a feeling it was important but I couldn't put my finger on what the comment had been. It was frustrating. I also found that I was preoccupied watching Leila Gaber at the other end of the table. Every so often, she would glance over and our eyes would meet, and she would give me that secretive smile again. To be honest, I found it a bit creepy.

I was glad when the dinner was officially over at last and we all drifted out into the main quad. As we began strolling towards the front gate, I turned impulsively to Lincoln and said:

"Lincoln, can you help me with something?"

"Sure," he said, looking at me enquiringly.

"I want to try and recreate the night of the murder," I said, keeping my voice lowered so the other guests passing us couldn't overhear. "I want to see just how long it takes to run from the Cloisters, through the tunnel and the Walled Garden and the two quads, to get to the front gate. Professor Barrow was last seen alive around 12:10 a.m. and his body was discovered by Seth at around 12:30 a.m., so there's a twenty-minute gap when the murderer could have killed him and made his or her escape."

"Okay..." said Lincoln, looking slightly bemused. "How can I help?"

I looked at his evening clothes doubtfully. "Well, if you don't mind running in black tie... could you do a trial run for me? It's just that... you see, I've got this suspect in mind: a tramp who was seen on CCTV on the street just outside the college around the time of

147

the murder. He *could* have just been loitering there and it's all a coincidence, but I wondered... And he's a big fellow, you see—even taller than you—so it would be more realistic if you did the run. You'd have similar strides. Otherwise, I would have done it myself."

Lincoln still looked slightly bemused but he gave me a good-humoured smile and said, "Sure. Wouldn't hurt to work off that dinner anyway."

We walked together through the darkened college. It was quieter tonight, being a Monday night—no parties and most students would either be in their rooms studying or out at various University society meetings. The dining hall was on the opposite side to the Cloisters and we had to cross the main quad, the smaller Yardley Quad, walk around the Walled Garden, and finally through the tunnel behind the library building to reach the Cloisters.

I turned right as soon as we entered the Cloisters and walked a few steps along the covered arcade, then paused, getting my bearings. Based on what Seth had said—and on the vestiges of police activity in this area—I guessed that this was where the body had been found.

"Here," I said to Lincoln. "I think the murderer must have started running from around here."

"Okay," said Lincoln, shrugging out of his dinner jacket and handing it to me. "I'll stop when I get outside the front gate and check how long it took me—and then I'll come back."

"Thanks, Lincoln," I said gratefully. Then I caught his arm as he started to turn away. "Oh, wait! I just thought of something... the tramp... Jim... he had a limp."

"You want me to fake a limp too?" said Lincoln with a grin.

I laughed. "No, no... but maybe don't run at your top speed. Slow down a bit on purpose, to take the limp into account."

He nodded and took off. I watched him disappear around the corner, into the passageway, then settled down to wait. It was a clear, cloudless night and very cold, especially here in the darkness of the Cloisters. My breath drifted out in front of me like pale ghostly forms. I should have had a proper coat but vanity had made me only bring a pretty pashmina over my thin black dress and my feet, in the three-inch stilettos, were cramped and freezing. I shivered, then remembered that I was holding Lincoln's dinner jacket and draped it gratefully around my shoulders.

I walked over to the side of the arcade that faced the cloister garth—the open central courtyard—and huddled against one of the carved stone columns, pulling the jacket tighter around me for warmth. I looked around, up at the vaulted stone ceiling above my head, etched with intricate carvings, and the rows of repeating arches and pillars, stretching away from me in both directions.

I shivered again, though this time not so much from the cold. Okay, so I didn't believe in ghosts, but when you're alone in the darkened recesses of a medieval monastic structure... Not that I was unfamiliar with cloisters; several Oxford colleges had cloisters, including my own. I'd always found them a bit spooky, though. There was something about the Gothic architecture, the sinister gargoyles and the way light filtered in through the columns and was swallowed by the shadows of the arcade, that brought to mind medieval churches and secretive monks, and maybe even vampires and demons. And a murder had been committed here...

I laughed at myself and shook off my thoughts. I was letting my imagination run away with me. Pushing away from the stone column, I began to pace in a circle, partly to keep warm and partly to soothe my restless mind. I thought once more of the murder and the mystery of how the killer had escaped notice. There were not many rooms leading off from the Cloister: aside from entry to the college chapel, there were a few other doors which I assumed led to college administration offices, and on the opposite side was the back of the college library.

The murderer was unlikely to have hidden in any of the rooms—for one thing, he or she wouldn't have had the keys to the doors—and anyway, even if the killer *had* somehow managed to hide in one of the rooms, the police had checked them all and found no one. The chapel was also out... so that left only the library.

The library. Yes, Seth had mentioned that there

was a back door from the library storage room leading into the Cloisters. This would normally have been locked—but Leila Gaber had been in the library that night and Leila Gaber had the keys... It would have been easy for her to slip out, commit the murder, and then return to the library. We only had her word that she had been in the library the whole time and never knew about the murder taking place just outside.

But *would* she have done it? Knowing full well that she could be traced near the scene of the crime and that she had no real alibi, no one to vouch for her... Somehow, it seemed too bold, even for her.

Still, there *was* such a thing as a "double bluff". Perhaps Leila knew that no one would believe that she could be that reckless—and so in a way, this made it safer for her because people wouldn't consider that possibility seriously?

Argh. My head was spinning.

If it wasn't Leila Gaber—then who? Who else had reason to want Barrow dead? Jim? The tramp could have wanted Barrow out of the way. Without the professor's objections, the Domus Trust housing project was likely to go ahead and Jim would finally have a chance to get off the streets. But would someone really have killed for that? And how could he know that Barrow would be in the Cloisters at that time? I sighed. I couldn't shake off the guilty feeling that fixating on Jim was the "easy" answer—that Seth was right: it was easier to imagine a homeless man being a criminal than a respectable Oxford academic...

... Or even a mousy suburban housewife.

My thoughts returned to Joan Barrow. Now, she was someone who *did* have good reason to want Barrow dead. I realised suddenly that Lincoln's trial run would not only prove that Jim could have escaped in time before the police arrived but also that *anyone else* from outside the college could have too. Joan Barrow lived in Reading, but there was a regular train service from Oxford to Reading and vice versa. It was only a thirty-minute journey. And I knew that the trains ran late, with the last train from Oxford to Reading long after midnight.

I wondered if Joan Barrow had an alibi for last Friday night. Her invalid partner was hardly a reliable witness. In any case, he could have gone to bed early and she could have left the house quietly, come to Oxford, killed Barrow, and then taken the last train back—and no one would have been wiser. I had to admit, I had trouble imagining that pale, colourless woman I'd met in my tearoom as a violent murderer—but who knew what anyone was capable of? And it was obvious that she was passionately devoted to her partner and bitterly resentful of her brother's refusal to help them. She had said that she was familiar with Oxford. And she could have been familiar with her brother's habits... She wasn't a big woman, but Barrow would have been drunk, his senses dulled, his feet unsteady. Hadn't Seth said that they had both had too much to drink that night? It would have been only too easy to lay in wait for Barrow in the shadows of the Cloisters and jump out to stab him before he could react...

The sound of footsteps echoing on the flagstones interrupted my thoughts. It was Lincoln returning. A minute later, his tall figure stepped out of the tunnel and into the Cloisters. He was puffing slightly, his eyes bright with exertion.

"I'd forgotten how exhilarating it can be to have a good run, especially in the cold," he said with a grin. "Maybe I should take up jogging again."

"What was the time?" I asked eagerly.

"Twelve minutes, give or take. Of course, I don't know exactly how bad the tramp's limp is and how much it might hamper his running—but even so, I think he could have done it at a stretch."

I felt a surge of excitement. "Yes, and not just him but maybe a woman with shorter legs! I've been thinking, Lincoln: Barrow had a sister who—*ahh*!"

My words were cut off by a cry of pain. In my excitement, I hadn't been looking where I was going and one of my high heels had sunk into a gap in between the flagstones. I tripped and stumbled, feeling my legs twist under me and then a sharp pain stab my left foot. Lincoln caught me before I fell and I gripped his arms gratefully, regaining my balance.

"Gemma? Are you all right?"

"Yeah." I winced from the pain and looked down sheepishly. "I think I stabbed myself with my heel..."

We both looked down. I was right: somehow when I had tripped, my right foot had twisted over the left one and the sharp stiletto heel of the right shoe had sliced into the exposed fleshy part at the top of my left foot. I could see a deep gash and blood oozing freely.

Lincoln crouched down and removed the shoe, then turned my foot over, trying to see the damage. I hobbled on my right foot next to him, feeling stupid and embarrassed. Lincoln touched my foot with a gentle hand and I gasped with pain, tears coming to my eyes.

"You've got a nasty cut," said Lincoln grimly. "I can't see properly in this light but if it's deep, you might need stitches. Anyway, the first step is to get it cleaned and then we can have another look. I need to examine it properly."

Lincoln's voice had changed, become calm and authoritative—the doctor taking over—and I found myself meekly following his lead as he put pressure on the wound to stem the bleeding, then used his handkerchief to make a rough bandage. Then he directed me to put an arm around his shoulders as he supported me back through the tunnel. I hopped feebly alongside him and was glad that there weren't many people out and about in the college to see us. I was feeling like a clumsy fool.

We finally staggered into the Porter's Lodge and I saw a middle-aged man in a sombre brown suit, with a receding hairline, hurry out from behind the counter.

"Dear me..." He tutted. "What have we got here, sir?"

"Miss Rose has had an accident," said Lincoln crisply. "I'm a doctor. Have you got a first aid kit?"

"Certainly, certainly..." The porter hurried back behind the counter and returned a few moments later with a large plastic box bearing the symbol of a red cross. I gritted my teeth as Lincoln carefully swabbed and cleaned the wound, then applied antiseptic cream and a clean bandage.

"It looks okay," he announced, looking back up at me with a smile. "No need to go to A&E."

"Where did this happen?" said the porter, hovering around us.

"In the Cloisters."

"In the Cloister...?" He looked closely at Lincoln. "Erm... pardon me, sir, but didn't I just see you run through here a few moments ago? You went out of the gate and then came back in..."

"Yes, that's right," said Lincoln blandly. "I wanted to catch one of the other guests, who had left first, and ask him something. But when I got outside, I saw that he was already gone so I came back."

The porter looked from Lincoln to me. "May I ask what you were doing in the Cloisters, sir? I understand you're with the Oxford Society of Medicine party—that dinner was taking place on the other side of college."

"We fancied some fresh air after the meal and

thought we'd take a stroll around college."

"Ah, right..." He still looked doubtful. "Can I get you folks a taxi?"

"Can a taxi come down the lane here?"

"Certainly, sir. In fact, we have one particular taxi driver who is sort of 'on standby' for the college—we always give him a call first when we need a car and he is normally here within a few minutes, if he's not on a job."

I looked at the porter in mild surprise. "Really? Things must have changed since I was at Oxford—I don't remember ever using a taxi much. Most people just got around on bicycles or public transport, if they didn't drive." I laughed. "Gosh, you must have very pampered dons here at Wadsworth if they order taxis often enough to have a man on standby."

"Oh, well, it was one don really who often used taxis—Professor Barrow—he wouldn't drive after a bad accident years ago and, of course, he was a real stickler for punctuality, so he didn't like waiting on the off-chance for any taxi off the street... He was a gentleman of the old school, was the professor—always set great store by proper etiquette and appropriate dress... and students being late to tutorials was one of his great bugbears... blimey, I can remember once having to go all over college looking for a first-year who..."

He rambled on, whilst Lincoln and I exchanged a smile. My goodness, I had never heard a man talk so much. He was almost like a gossipy old woman!

Then I paused. Was this Clyde Peters? I remembered Seth's description of the garrulous head porter. I was sure it was him. Perhaps I could turn things to my advantage. I took a gamble.

"Actually, it was me who wanted to go to the Cloisters," I said, giving him a shy smile. "I heard about the murder on Friday night and I guess I was being nosy. Were you here when it happened?"

The man drew himself up and puffed his chest out in self-importance. "I was, Miss. I was the one who found the killer with the body."

I gave a mock gasp. "Oh my God! Really? Did you have to restrain him?"

"No," said Clyde Peters, sounding almost regretful. "'Twas that young Chemistry don over at Gloucester. I think he was in shock. Just stood there, holding the knife and looking down at the body. But he looked guilty, all right."

I gave the head porter a look of exaggerated admiration. "If it hadn't been for you, he might have got away! How did you happen to be there?"

"Ah, well..." Clyde Peters's gaze slid away from mine. "I guess it was just luck, Miss. I was doing a round of the college, you know, and happened to pass by the Cloisters. Anyway—" He clapped his hands together briskly. "I'll go and ring for your taxi now."

Lincoln thanked him, and ten minutes later, we were riding in the back of a cab, on the way to my parents' house in North Oxford. My foot was still throbbing, but I barely noticed. My mind was still back in the Wadsworth College Porter's Lodge.

Why had the head porter *really* been in the Cloister? I knew he said he had been doing a round of the college, but that struck me as odd. Porters didn't routinely do "rounds" of the colleges at night—not unless there had been reports of a really rowdy party which had gone on beyond curfew and needed to be shut down. There *had* been some parties in the college last Friday night—I'd seen some of the student party-goers myself—so the porter could have been checking up on them. But in that case, why had he been in the Cloister? All the student rooms were on the other side of the college; there would have been no reason for him to "happen to pass by" the Cloisters, as he had put it.

So the man had been lying. I thought of the way he wouldn't meet my eyes. Clyde Peters was hiding something. The question was—what?

CHAPTER FIFTEEN

It was hard to keep my mind on work the next morning; my thoughts kept drifting back to the night before and mulling over the different angles of the mystery.

"Gemma, wasn't this supposed to have been sent last week?" said Cassie, rising from where she had been rummaging below the counter and holding up a large sealed envelope. She frowned. "The bill's due this weekend."

I gasped and smacked myself on the head. "I completely forgot! Sorry." I glanced around the tearoom, which was still fairly empty, and said, "Listen, do you mind holding the fort yourself while I dash to the post shop now?"

"Yeah, sure," said Cassie. "In fact, do me a favour, will you, and pick up a couple of packets of gum for me while you're there. Ta."

I grabbed the envelope, slung on my duffel coat, and hastily wrapped my scarf around my neck, then stepped out into the cold. I shoved my hands into my pockets and walked briskly up the high street. Like many Cotswold villages, Meadowford-on-Smythe was centred around one main street running down its length, lined on either side by rickety old Tudor buildings with their distinctive black-on-white half timbering or stone cottages with heavy thatched roofs and tiny mullioned windows. I walked past Meadowford Antiques, the Starling Gallery, Cotswolds Olde Crafts, and the Meadowford Cobbler, and finally saw the village post shop, with its distinctive Royal Mail sign and the bright red pillar post box standing outside the door.

A relic from the times when glitzy shopping malls and gigantic chain stores hadn't yet dominated the nearby Oxford city centre, the village post shop was still the place to meet and mingle and get the latest gossip. As I approached, I could see why it was one of the most photographed buildings in the village and always had a few tourists posing in front of it. Even on this cold, wintry day, it looked gorgeous, with the gleaming ebony window frames accented against the soft honey colour of the stone walls and an old-fashioned climbing rose stretched over the doorway.

From the exterior, you expected to find a scene inside where the old bespectacled proprietor still weighed out flour on a brass scale. Instead, I stepped into a tiny space crammed with modern products and conveniences. Like many village stores before its time, the post office shop was great at multi-tasking. Aside from handling the mail, selling pretty postcards of the Cotswolds region and providing the senior citizens with their weekly pensions, it also sold the national lottery, provided a dry cleaning service, offered a rack of the latest newspapers and glossy magazines, as well as a table of fresh local produce: eggs, bread, milk, pies, cheeses, vegetables, and fruits from local farms. A row of shelves on the adjoining wall provided all the necessities of modern life—from toothpaste to USB adaptors, nappies to cigarettes. A sign above the counter informed customers that the post shop could order foreign currency on demand. I wouldn't have been surprised if they provided dog training and website design too!

I joined the queue in front of the counter to await my turn. At this time of the morning, the shop was crammed with villagers and a group of them were gathered by the counter, their heads together. For a moment, the sight of the woolly white hair, sensible loafers, lavender clasp handbags, and Marks & Spencer cardigans made me think it might be the Old Biddies—then I realised that these were some of the other pensioners in the village. As the line moved forwards and I shuffled alongside, I couldn't help overhearing their conversation.

"... and I heard that the murdered professor was a spy. That was probably why he was killed! You know the Secret Service recruits from Oxford academics—"

"That's not what I heard! I have it on good authority that he was part of some illicit University drinking club. It was another Oxford don who was arrested for the murder, wasn't it? They were probably involved in an initiation ritual or—"

"What nonsense! You're both wrong!" a third woman piped up. "My grandson works in Oxford city centre and he says there's been talk of a tramp seen lurking outside the college on the night of the murder. You mark my words, it will have been him. Nasty, dirty drunks and drug addicts—these homeless types are all the same!"

"NEXT PLEASE!"

I turned with a start as I realised that Mrs Sutton, the postmistress, had been calling to me several times. The space in front of the counter was empty and I was holding up the queue. I hurried up and handed my envelope over.

"Sorry about that."

She smiled. "That's okay, dearie. Everyone's been doing it this morning. It seems like the whole village can talk about nothing else! Everyone's got their theories and speculations..." She leaned forwards and peered at me curiously. "You were at the University, Gemma. Do you know anything about Wadsworth College and this professor?"

I shook my head, saying honestly, "Wadsworth wasn't my college and I don't really know it that well."

The postmistress gave an exaggerated shudder. "It's horrible to think about... That poor man stabbed in the neck like that and left for dead in the Cloisters!"

"I'd say it was good riddance," came a mutter from the other end of the counter. It was from a woman who had been examining a basket of soaps there. She turned slightly and I realised that it was Dora Kempton. She was wearing the same shabby tweed coat she had worn the day she came to my tearoom and her face looked even gaunter. She looked like she could do with a good meal. Her thin shoulders sagged under the weight of her coat.

"What was that, Mrs Kempton?" said the postmistress pleasantly. "Did you know the murdered professor?"

"As well as I ever want to," said Dora Kempton, her mouth pressed into a thin line.

"How did you know him?" I blurted out.

She hesitated, then said, "I was a scout at Wadsworth College for over thirty years. I retired recently."

Scouts were another of those unique quirks of Oxford University, shared only by Cambridge (where they were known as "bedders"). Every student had a scout assigned to him or her—a sort of housekeeper who cleaned their rooms once a week and kept a motherly eye on them. It was probably a relic from the days when only men were accepted at Oxford and they required a gentleman's valet to attend to their needs. In the early 20th century, scouts became more like domestic help, doing things like cleaning out the coal fires and carrying in water for washing. Nowadays, they mostly just vacuum the rooms, empty the bins, and clean the student bathrooms, although if you're super lucky, you might get an extra-motherly type who would even tidy your room, fold your clothes, and do your washing up and laundry!

Many of us got very close to our scouts. I still remembered mine fondly: a lovely lady named Jean who used to come in and quietly clean my room, and who was the first to find me that morning I woke up shivering in bed with the flu and called the college doctor for me. I was lucky that my own family lived nearby, but for a lot of students whose families might have been miles away or even overseas, having a nurturing presence in college helped to ease the feeling of being lost and alone in a strange new city. I glanced at Dora again and wondered what kind of scout she had been. Somehow, I didn't think she was the gentle, motherly type, though perhaps I was wrong. Perhaps there was a soft heart under that prickly exterior.

"Would you like one of those soaps?" said the postmistress, indicating the bar that Dora was holding.

Dora Kempton hesitated, then said gruffly, "I'm not sure I've got enough change on me..."

"Oh... I've got so many at the moment, there's a

bit of an oversupply," said Mrs Sutton quickly. "Why don't you take one to try for free and, if you like it, you can come back to get more."

Dora stiffened, putting the bar of soap back in the basket. "I will pay for my purchases like everyone else." She gave a curt nod. "I'll see if there are still any available when I pick up my benefit payment later this week."

There was an embarrassed silence as Dora turned and left the store.

"Well, for goodness sake...!" exclaimed one of the pensioners by the counter as soon as Dora was gone.

Another rolled her eyes. "That woman is too proud for her own good."

Her friend nodded. "I tried to offer her some spinach from my vegetable patch the other day, but she nearly bit my head off."

"What's a little bit of sharing between neighbours now and then?" said another of the pensioners and the others all nodded vigorously.

"Too proud," said the postmistress, shaking her head. "I've met types like that before. They'd rather starve and freeze to death than admit that they need help or accept a favour from anyone." She made a clucking sound with her tongue. "And it's not like the state benefits give you much, poor thing..."

"Has she just arrived in the village?" I asked.

Mrs Sutton shook her head. "About a year now, actually, although she hasn't made much effort to get to know anyone. She's never invited any of us to her house. Too embarrassed to show us how bare it is, probably."

"I heard she had to take early retirement," said one of the pensioners. "Not that scouts are paid that much anyway."

"Yes, she had to have a hip replacement, which meant she was off work for six months and then they didn't want her back."

"Isn't there anything she could do here in the village?" I asked.

"There probably is, dearie," said the postmistress. "But she needs to be willing to ask. Many of us would be more than happy to find something for her to do and pay her for her time—but the few times I've tried to offer, Dora took great umbrage." She shrugged. "You can't force charity on people who refuse to accept help."

I glanced at the clock on the wall behind her and suddenly realised the time. I had been standing here gossiping too long. "Oh heavens, I must be getting back to the tearoom."

"How is that going, dear?" said Mrs Sutton, giving me a warm smile. "I must say, Gemma, we were all so pleased when you came back to the village and resurrected the tearoom. I remember when you were a wee girl and could barely see over this counter." She chuckled. "You used to come in here with your mother and point to one of the sweet jars on the shelf and ask if you could have one. You were especially fond of the—"

"Fizzy cola bottles!" I said, remembering with a rush. I laughed. "Yes, you're absolutely right! I hadn't even thought about them till now." I peered behind her back. "I don't suppose you still stock any of those old sweets?"

"As a matter of fact, we do," she said with a smile. "You'd be surprised how many people still like them, and the tourists, of course, love them. They make great souvenirs—small, cheap, and light, and fit the image of 'vintage England'. More than one tourist has come in here to buy a postcard and left with a paper bag full of boiled sweets or sherbet fountains."

Five minutes later, I left the post shop laden with my own paper bag. Aside from the chewing gum Cassie had asked for, I had also bought large handfuls of sherbet lemons, Fizz Whizz popping candy, chocolate gold coins, chewy fruit jellies, mini love hearts, and, of course, the fizzy cola bottles— giant cola-flavoured jellies, covered with sugar.

I smiled to myself as I walked back to the tearoom. I had a feeling I was going to be sick eating these— but I was going to enjoy every moment of it.

CHAPTER SIXTEEN

I arrived back at the Little Stables Tearoom to find that the Old Biddies had come in and were helping out in the dining room. Cassie was nowhere to be seen. She must have been in the kitchen. We'd run out of many of the things my mother had pre-baked and so had started having to bake new batches ourselves. There was the faint smell of fresh baking drifting out from the kitchen and I looked forward to seeing Cassie's creations.

I shoved the paper bag of sweets under the counter, tied on my apron, and hurried over to join Mabel and her friends in serving the customers. I was just explaining the difference between a Bakewell tart and a Bakewell pudding to a group of German tourists when a loud bang in the kitchen made us all jerk our heads around. Then I heard Cassie's voice rising in a wail.

Uh-oh. I had a bad feeling about this.

I hurried into the kitchen. A scene of carnage met my eyes. Cassie was standing in the middle of the room, covered from head to toe in white flour. I had to fight to keep a straight face.

"Don't laugh at me!" Cassie snapped. "It's not funny!"

"What happened?" I asked, as I hurried forwards to help her clean up the mess.

"I was trying to make some Chelsea buns," Cassie said. "I followed the instructions your mother left, except that I thought I'd use a blender as it's such a bore mixing by hand in a bowl. So I put the flour and sugar and lemon zest and cinnamon and spices into the blender and then suddenly, the whole thing just exploded! I don't know what I did wrong. Honestly, Gemma, I never realised baking was so complicated."

It took us another twenty minutes to clean up the mess—flour and sugar had gone *everywhere* in the kitchen—and while we were doing that, the smell of burning suddenly made Cassie shriek and run to the oven. As I watched in dismay, she pulled out a tray of scones, each with a charred, black crust on top.

"Oh God, I'd forgotten I put these in to bake!" cried Cassie. She peered at them hopefully. "Well, they're only burned on top. Maybe if we slice off the top section, we can serve them anyway?"

"I can't serve those to customers!" I said, horrified. "We'll just have to bake some more and throw this batch away."

"It's such a dreadful waste of food," said Cassie, wincing. "Really, there's nothing wrong with them other than the top being a bit burnt..."

I agreed silently. I hated the thought of wasting all this food. I thought suddenly of Owen's cheerful face and Ruby wagging her tail as the two of them stood on that cold street corner, and grimaced.

"Maybe we can donate these," I said suddenly. "I'll ask Seth if he knows of any homeless shelters that might want them. I'm sure the homeless won't mind if they get scones that have the tops cut off and are a bit shorter than usual. They still taste just as good."

"Yeah, good idea. I'll get rid of the burnt bits and store them in the fridge, in the meantime," said Cassie. She sighed. "I hate to ask this, Gemma, but have you made a decision yet about those women you interviewed on Saturday?"

I gave her a despairing look. "Cassie, you saw what they were like! I can't hire any of them!"

"We need a proper baking chef," said Cassie. "I mean, I'm sure I'll get better with practice but..." She trailed off.

I sighed. She was right. People might think baking is just mixing things together in a bowl and sticking it in the oven, but I was convinced that there was more to it than that. Otherwise, it would be like saying Art was just dunking your brush in a pot of paint and dabbing it on a canvas. A great baker was just as much a talent as a great artist. There was something—some magic—that happened beyond just combining the ingredients together. And neither Cassie nor I had it. Oh, we could have probably produced some passable baking with a lot of practice, but to succeed, my little tearoom had to produce *incredible* baking.

And we weren't going to do it with Cassie in the kitchen. In fact, based on her progress so far, we'd be lucky to have something *edible* with Cassie in the kitchen.

"I've still got the advert running, so hopefully we'll get some more applicants soon... And my mother's back next Sunday, remember?" I said brightly. "So you've only got to manage until then."

"That's still another five whole days," Cassie groaned. "You'll be lucky if I don't blow up the kitchen by then!"

***

The rest of the day passed fairly uneventfully, if slightly meagrely. We were already behind with the baking and Cassie kept having to throw out botched batches and start again, so supplies kept getting lower and lower. For the first time since the tearoom opened, I found myself having to tell customers that certain items on the menu were unavailable. I winced each time I saw their disappointment and annoyance, and hoped that it wouldn't stop them coming back or recommending me to their friends.

Something else was bothering me too. I kept glancing at the clock on the wall and calculating the time difference... Shouldn't my mother have arrived in Jakarta by now? I checked my phone for the tenth time but there was no text message or email from her. A glance at the airline website told me that her flight had definitely arrived. So why hadn't I heard from her?

When my phone rang at last, I snatched it up, imagining all sorts of horrors, from the hospital calling to say that my mother had succumbed to some rare form of Ebola to the British Embassy calling to tell me that my mother had been captured by terrorists (okay, so I might have a slightly over-active imagination). I was so convinced it would be an overseas call that, for a moment, I was puzzled by the deep male voice in my ear and couldn't quite place it.

"Gemma? Are you there?"

"Devlin!" I said. "Sorry, I thought you were... I got a bit confused—"

"Can you talk?"

I was surprised by his uncharacteristically brusque tone. Then I heard the suppressed anger in his voice and realised that Devlin was furious. Casting a quick look around the tearoom, I went into the little shop area and shut the glass door behind me.

"Yes," I said cautiously. "Is something wrong?"

"Maybe you'd like to tell me why Seth rang you last Friday night."

Oh hell. My heart slammed in my chest. *How did he find out?*

"It was nothing," I mumbled. "He just needed support from a friend. I mean, he'd just found a colleague dead and then he was arrested for a murder he didn't commit... Anyway, how did you know he rang me?" I said, getting on the defensive. "I thought you were entitled to some privacy when you made your phone calls from the police station."

"You are—but you are also expected to be honest. Seth told the custody sergeant that he was ringing his solicitor for legal advice. He didn't say he was calling his friend to tamper with evidence."

I said nothing, my heart pounding uncomfortably.

"What did he ask you to do, Gemma?"

"Nothing! I told you, he just needed a friendly ear."

"Don't lie to me," said Devlin harshly. "I know he asked you to go to Wadsworth to get something."

I swallowed. "Ho-how did you know?"

"Cassie told me. Oh, she didn't mean to, but it slipped out. She came to see me last night, to beg me to help Seth, and unintentionally mentioned that he'd rung you. When I asked her about it, she fobbed me off with some lame explanation about a joke or something. But I'm not stupid, Gemma. Seth wouldn't ring you at that time of the night—and from the police station no less—unless it was something urgent and to do with the murder." Devlin's voice was cold and hard. "So are you going to tell me or do I have to bring Seth in again for questioning? And this time he will not be released on bail. In fact, I may even add 'attempting to obstruct a police investigation' to the list of charges against him."

I gritted my teeth, feeling a mixture of fury and betrayal. Devlin was supposed to be on *my* side! He was supposed to help, not be the enemy! Now, it felt like *he* was the one after Seth.

"It really wasn't a big deal," I said tightly. "Seth was still fuming when he got back to Gloucester, so he wrote a note to Quentin Barrow to sort of... well, have the last word on their argument, I guess. You know what it's like! And he put it in the old don's pigeonhole when he went back to Wadsworth—he popped into the Porter's Lodge first, before going to the Cloisters to look for his phone."

"If it wasn't a big deal, why did he need to wake you up in the middle of the night to go and fetch it?"

I shifted uncomfortably. "Well, it wasn't a very polite note..."

"You mean he made threats to Barrow."

"He'd had a bit too much to drink," I said quickly. "You say all sorts of things you don't mean in the heat of the moment. Don't tell me you haven't done it yourself."

"Yes, but I didn't murder anyone afterwards."

"Neither did Seth!" I snapped. "This is exactly why he wanted me to get rid of it—because he knew the police would think like that. He was already in such a bad position, he knew that even a harmless note could be incriminating."

"If he was innocent, then there was nothing to incriminate," said Devlin evenly. "Have you still got the note?"

"No, I destroyed it."

There was silence at the other end, but I could feel Devlin's anger and frustration coming down the line. I cast around for something to lighten his mood and thought suddenly of my encounter along the canal and the recreation in Wadsworth last night.

"Devlin, there's something else I've got to tell you."

"What is it?" His tone was curt.

"That tramp who was outside Wadsworth College on the night of the murder—I've been asking around town about him... His name is Jim... and... and he's got a pretty foul temper. I wouldn't be surprised if he's the kind of man who would bear a grudge."

"How would you know?"

"Well, I met him," I admitted. "I talked to one of the *Big Issue* sellers in town and got some information... And then I tracked him down by the canal."

"Gemma, are you playing at being amateur detective again?" said Devlin irritably.

"I'm not playing at anything!" I snapped. "I'm trying to help find the real murderer."

"You can help by staying out of the investigation."

"Well, it's too late for that," I said. "And you should listen to me! Last night, I did a recreation of the murder with Lincoln. I got him to run from the Cloisters to the main gate of Wadsworth and time how long it took. Even accounting for his limp, I think there was more than enough time for Jim to—"

"You were at Wadsworth with Lincoln?" Devlin cut in.

Was I imagining it or was there a note of jealousy in his voice?

"Yes, Lincoln invited me to go to the Oxford Society of Medicine dinner, which happened to be at Wadsworth this term," I said impatiently. "So anyway, I think Jim could be a strong suspect. He had no good reason to be loitering outside the college at that time of the night; he hated Barrow and had a motive for wanting him out of the way; he—"

"Gemma," Devlin cut me off. "It's unlikely that Jim was the murderer."

"Why?"

"Because we've had new information about the timeframe of the murder. Barrow's phone was damaged during the struggle, but the IT department have finally managed to retrieve some data. Barrow sent a text message at 12:17 a.m., so he was still alive then."

"How do you know it was him?" I said quickly. "I mean, anyone could have used his phone to send a message, to give a false impression of the time of murder."

"True," Devlin conceded. "But this was part of an

ongoing conversation. It looks like Barrow had some kind of text message interchange with a colleague at Harvard just after midnight. They were discussing a research project they're collaborating on and there were several messages back and forth, with the last one being from Barrow. The message contained too many details of the project—I doubt it could have been the murderer just sending a fake message."

"So what does this mean?"

"It means that Barrow had to have been killed between 12:17 a.m. and 12:30 a.m. when Seth found the body. But Jim was seen on CCTV outside the college at 12:23 a.m.—which only leaves a gap of six minutes when he could have committed the murder and made his escape. He would have had to kill Barrow and then run through the tunnel, around the Walled Garden, through the two quads before finally getting out the front gate. It's a long roundabout route. He couldn't have done that in six minutes."

Devlin was right. Even when the gap had been twelve minutes, Lincoln had said that it would have been a stretch for a man with a limp. Now, with it reduced to half that time, there was no way Jim could have killed Barrow and made it out of the college in time to be seen on camera on the other side of the street.

"Look, just stay out of it, okay, Gemma? Leave the investigation to the police," said Devlin. "You're playing around when you have no idea what you're doing."

I smarted at his condescending tone. "Well, I wouldn't have to get involved myself if you'd agreed to help prove Seth's innocence!" I snapped.

There was a stony silence from the other end and I realised suddenly I had gone too far. I heard Devlin take a deep breath and let it out slowly, then he said, his voice sounding colder and more furious than I had ever heard him, "I can't believe you have the gall to ask me to compromise my professional ethics when you've been lying to me and withholding evidence from the police!"

I winced. When he put it like that, it did sound pretty bad. But what did he expect me to do? I felt my own temper flare. At the end of the day, Devlin was an officer of the law and, in this case, we were on opposite sides of the fence, with Seth's freedom hanging between us.

"Devlin, I—"

"No. I don't want to listen to your excuses." He cut me off, his voice like ice. "I'm going to hang up now before I say something *I* will regret. Goodbye, Gemma."

I stared in disbelief at the dead phone in my hands. He had hung up on me! *How dare he!* Of all the arrogant, high-handed, self-righteous, odious... *Oooooh!*

I ignored the little voice at the back of my head which whispered that Devlin had justifiable reason to be angry and, in fact, had been pretty restrained and forgiving with me. Instead, I focused on my own anger and indignation. I was not speaking to Devlin again, I decided, until he crawled back grovelling to apologise!

CHAPTER SEVENTEEN

Devlin's final words left me fuming for the rest of the afternoon and I was glad when I could finally flip the "OPEN" sign to "CLOSED" on the tearoom door. It had been a strain trying to maintain a cheery façade in front of the customers. Cassie had left already so I went around by myself, drawing the curtains, pushing the last chairs back into place around the tables, switching off the lights. As I got onto my bike to begin the cycle back into Oxford centre, I decided to drop in to see Seth before returning home. I hadn't seen him since Sunday when we'd picked him up from the station, although I knew Cassie had popped in to check on him yesterday evening. I hoped he was keeping his spirits up.

I found Seth in his college rooms. From the papers

strewn across his desk, it looked like he had been trying to get some work done, but from the expression on his face, I didn't think molecular chemical reactions were what had been occupying his thoughts.

"Hi, Gemma," he said in a listless voice as he let me in.

"I thought I'd pop in to see how you are..." I said.

He shrugged. "I'm okay, I guess. Trying to focus on other things—but it's a bit difficult when all you can think about is the fact that you could be tried for a brutal murder you didn't commit!"

I reached out and gave his arm a reassuring squeeze. "Don't worry, Seth. You won't go to court. I'm sure we'll find the real killer before that and the police will drop all charges against you," I said with more confidence than I felt.

"Have you had news on the case?" he asked desperately. "My parents are arriving home next week. I don't want this to be the first thing my father hears when he gets off the ship."

I didn't know what to say. "The police are working on it," I said. "I... I just spoke to Devlin this afternoon and he's following up some leads." I didn't add that one of my top suspects had turned into a dead end. Then I remembered the original reason for Devlin's call and said, "By the way, Devlin found out about the note in Barrow's pigeonhole."

"What?" Seth looked at me in horror. "You didn't—"

"Cassie told him. By mistake," I added hastily. "She went to speak to him and you know what Devlin's like. He's incredibly sharp and he's a shrewd interrogator. And then he called me this afternoon and asked me outright—"

"What did you tell him?"

I gave him a rueful look. "I had to tell him the truth, Seth. But nothing in detail. Just that you'd written some things in the heat of the moment, after your argument with Barrow, and then regretted it afterwards. But given the circumstances... you didn't really want the police to see the note."

"Now Devlin will definitely think I'm guilty," groaned Seth. "Because why would I be worried about the note being found unless it was incriminating?"

That was pretty much what Devlin had said but I didn't want to make my friend feel worse. We sat in a morose silence for a moment, then I said brightly, "You should have seen the disaster we had in the tearoom kitchen this afternoon."

Seth made a valiant effort to follow my lead. "What happened?"

"Cassie tried to bake—"

I got no further because Seth burst into laughter. I looked at him severely. "I don't think she'd appreciate that."

"Sorry..." he gasped. "But I've seen her try to bake before. She's a public liability!"

My lips twitched. "Yeah, well, you wouldn't have

wanted to be anywhere near her today. Somehow, her blender exploded. There was flour and sugar everywhere. Took us ages to clean up the kitchen—and I don't think she'll ever get it out of her hair."

This sent Seth into fresh gales of laughter and I joined in. It was nice to see him lighten up a bit at last.

"Thanks, Gemma," he said with a grateful smile as he finally calmed down. He took off his glasses and wiped them. "God, I needed that."

"Just don't tell Cassie you found it funny," I said with a grin. "And in the meantime, we have a batch of burnt scones that we don't know what to do with... Hey, actually, I meant to ask you about that—do you know any shelters that might be interested in the food? The scones are perfectly good still; we've cut the burnt bits off—they just look a bit odd, but they taste fine."

"The Domus Trust would take them," said Seth. "Here, I'll give you their card and you can speak to the Food Donations Coordinator..." He got up and rummaged around in his desk. "They run regular soup kitchens for the homeless community in Oxford and also collect food donations from various businesses in the city. A lot of the cafés and restaurants have surplus food items, which is always appreciated."

"That's a brilliant idea!" I said. "I could do that too! Because the tearoom's reputation is built on fresh baking, I can't serve stuff that's over a day old—even though it's still perfectly good. Cassie and I try to eat as much as we can—" I looked down ruefully at my waistline, "—but we still often have to throw things away. It always makes me feel terrible. Maybe I can set up an arrangement with the Domus Trust to send all 'leftovers' to them."

"I'm sure they'd love it."

"Okay, I'd better go," I said. "Muesli is probably going to kill me when I get home. She'll be starving for her dinner."

"Give her a back scratch for me," said Seth with a smile as he accompanied me to the door. I was glad to see that he was looking much more cheerful. With a final wave, I left his room and started down the spiralling college staircase.

***

It was late when I got home and Muesli wasn't the only one who was starving. I fed her and then was pleased to discover some leftover split-pea soup in the fridge. As I took it out and transferred it to a pot to heat up, I mulled over the mystery again. If Jim was out of the picture, who did that leave as possible suspects for the murderer? Leila Gaber? Joan Barrow? And what about Clyde Peters himself? I couldn't shake off the nagging feeling that the head porter knew more than he was letting on.

While waiting for the soup to heat up, I checked my phone again for any message from my mother.

Nothing. I frowned. I'd tried calling her a couple of times earlier but it had gone straight to her answerphone. *She's probably just forgotten to switch her phone back on after getting off the plane,* I told myself. *Or forgotten to take it off flight mode.* I wondered briefly if I should call my father in South Africa, then decided against it. I didn't want to worry him. I'd wait until tomorrow, at least. If I hadn't heard from my mother by tomorrow, then I'd start worrying...

I was pouring the hot soup from the saucepan into a bowl when I became aware of a strange clattering sound. It came sporadically, sometimes softer, sometimes louder, and sounded like metal scraping against something...

I left the kitchen to try and find the source of the sound. Down the hallway... into the living room... I stopped short.

Muesli was hunched over in the corner by the curtains, pawing at something on the floor. As I got closer, I realised it was that vent—the one she had been fixated on before. I remembered my mother complaining about it just before she left. The little tabby had her face pressed against the bars of the ornamental grille, sniffing earnestly. I wondered what was in the crawlspace underneath the house to cause so much interest, then decided with a shudder that I didn't really want to know. I'd never been down in the cavity beneath the house—it was a typical architectural feature found in many old Victorian houses to help with ventilation—and I imagined that it was full of dead bugs and rats and Heaven knows what else.

Muesli, however, obviously didn't share my revulsion. She was shoving her nose against the grille and batting it every so often with an impatient paw, making the metal cover rattle in its frame.

"Muesli, stop that—" I started to say, when she gave the grille an extra hard shove and it bounced and shifted sideways out of its frame. Instantly, Muesli stuck her nose into the gap revealed in the corner and pushed the grille cover farther aside. Then, before I realised what she was doing, she had shoved her head and shoulders into the widening gap and started trying to wriggle through.

"Hey!" I cried, running across the room. "Muesli!"

I managed to grab her just before she slipped through the gap. Gosh, I hadn't realised how small she really was.

"*Meorrw!*" she cried sulkily as I picked her up and dumped her on a nearby armchair.

She gave me a reproachful look but I ignored her. Instead, I pushed the ornamental grille cover back over the vent, so that it fit securely into its frame. I gave it a prod experimentally. It rattled and shifted slightly. Years of use and general aging must have caused some shifting or deformation of the wooden floor, so that the frame of the vent no longer housed the grille cover perfectly.

I looked around, then saw my mother's knitting

basket nearby. I picked it up and brought it over, plonking it down over the ornamental grille, so that it covered the vent. *There, that should do it.* When my parents got back, I would ask them what they wanted to do to fix things more permanently.

I straightened and dusted off my hands, shooting Muesli a look of triumph. She turned disdainfully away from me and began washing her face, as if she had never been interested in the vent anyway.

I rolled my eyes. *Cats.* Leaving her to continue her ablutions in the living room, I headed back to the kitchen where my rapidly cooling soup was still waiting for me.

CHAPTER EIGHTEEN

"We're leaving a bit early today, Gemma," said Mabel, buttoning her coat and wrapping a scarf around her neck.

"Oh, are you going to catch a film?" I said, smiling at the Old Biddies. I knew that they often liked to go to the discounted senior sessions at the cinema in Oxford.

They glanced at each other and I got the sudden impression of naughty children planning something.

"No... We've got another engagement," said Florence formally. "We have to go get ready."

And with an air of great mystery, the four of them left. I watched their figures tottering away down the village high street. *What are they up to?* There wasn't time to ponder it, though. It was the tail end of "afternoon tea" and the tearoom was still full of customers. I flew around, delivering trays of tea and cakes, clearing away cups and plates, taking new orders... Finally, the last customer left with a satisfied smile on their face and I shut the tearoom door and changed the sign over to "CLOSED" with a weary sigh. I leaned against the door and closed my eyes for a moment. It was great that business was so good but oh my goodness, some days were exhausting. My feet were killing me. Maybe I could have a nice soak in a hot bath when I got home...

Then I remembered. Tonight was our first catering job. I would have to deliver all the food for the event before I could go home. It was only a small order but I was excited. It was the next step to growing my business. I knew that word of my Little Stables Tearoom was starting to get out and people were beginning to recommend our wonderful baking. If we could cater a few events—especially Oxford University ones—our reputation would be made. So this first job was a foot in the door.

This one was for a small gallery which had just opened in the village and was having an opening night party. They wanted to support local businesses so they had asked me to provide some food for the event. Nothing too fancy—just some good old British favourites: cakes and buns and such. Cassie had been busy in the kitchen all afternoon and from the smell of baking that was wafting out (and the lack of explosions or screaming) I was hopeful that we would have all the things ready to carry over soon.

Hmm... I tried to remember the layout of the gallery and whether they would have a big enough table for the food to be displayed. If not, we could take our own trestle table. I wondered for a moment if I should call to check, then decided I'd just walk over to see the place for myself. I needed a bit of fresh air, anyway, after being cooped up in the tearoom all day.

I bundled up quickly and started walking briskly down the village high street, my mind still busy with thoughts of catering. I knew that Eleanor Shaw, the owner of the gallery, was very active in the local church and community groups. A good recommendation from her could bring business from all over Oxfordshire. I smiled to myself, my thoughts turning into a pleasurable daydream. We could become a local institution, with the "Little Stables" name a coveted label on any baking. Maybe I'd start my own line of cakes and buns, packaged with the "Little Stables Tearoom Treats" logo. And we could even get matching napkins and maybe even—

My thoughts were interrupted as I nearly collided into a woman who was leaning against the school fence.

"Oh! Sorry, I didn't see—"

I broke off as I realised that it was Dora Kempton. Her face was ashen and she seemed to be clinging to the railings with all her strength.

"Dora! What's the matter? Are you all right?" I reached out to support her.

"I'm fine... fine..." she mumbled, attempting to stand up straight. "Just had... a bit of a turn, that's all..."

I looked at her sharply. Her face was haggard in the twilight, her eyes dull and strained. The hand that was clutching the fence was shaking slightly. Beneath the worn fabric of her coat, her body felt thin and frail. She was shivering in the cold, and suddenly I realised that she must be starving. I didn't know for sure but I was willing to bet that she had been fainting from hunger.

"Come on, come back to the tearoom with me," I said, putting a hand under her elbow.

"No..." Dora protested weakly. "I... I haven't got my purse with me. I've left it at home by mistake..."

"Never mind," I said briskly, and began hustling her across the road. She was too weak to resist, and within a few moments I had herded her back to the tearoom, through the dining room, and into the kitchen. Cassie looked up in surprise as we entered. She was standing at the big wooden table in the centre of the room, elbow-deep in flour, with white smudges on her nose and forehead. Her hair was sticking out wildly from her head and she looked completely frazzled.

"When was the last time you ate anything, Dora?" I said as I helped her to a chair by the table.

She flushed and looked away. "I... I didn't have time for breakfast this morning." She dropped gratefully into the chair, mumbling, "Thank you. I'll be fine in a moment... I just needed to rest a bit, that's all."

I ignored her and went over to the sideboard, where I cut a thick wedge from the remainder of a lemon meringue cheesecake on a platter there. I transferred this to a plate while I set the kettle to boil and it was soon whistling merrily. I filled a warmed teapot with fresh tea leaves and added hot water, then let it brew for a few minutes before pouring out a cup of the rich red brew. I took this and the plate of cake over to Dora, setting it down in front of her.

"Would you like milk with your tea?"

"I..." she trailed off, her eyes going hungrily to the plate. Then she straightened her shoulders and sat back resolutely, her mouth compressed in a thin line. "I don't need your charity."

"It's not charity!" I said impatiently. "It's being environmental. The tearoom is closed now and I would have to throw this out if it's not eaten. I can't serve it tomorrow." I pushed the cake closer to her and softened my voice. "Go on, have some."

She hesitated, then finally, as if she couldn't help herself, she picked up the fork and cut a piece off the edge of the cake. I watched her raise the fork to her mouth and swallow the piece hungrily. Then she picked up the teacup and took a gulp of the hot tea, inhaling the fragrant steam with a sigh of pleasure. Without a word, I loaded another plate with some of our leftover finger sandwiches and a (very slightly burnt) Chelsea bun, and set it in front of her.

Dora hesitated again, then said quietly, "Thank you," and began to eat.

I averted my eyes politely and went over to Cassie, who seemed to be having some kind of meltdown.

"I don't know what happened!" she said. "I'm sure I followed the recipe exactly!" She stared in dismay at the Victoria sponge cake in front of her—or what should have been a fluffy, moist sponge cake, except that the middle of the cake had somehow caved in. It looked like a crusty brown volcanic crater.

"We can't serve that," I said in dismay.

"Maybe if we add some frosting on top, no one will notice?" Cassie said hopefully.

I looked at her in exasperation. "Cassie! A blind person would notice that crater in the middle of the cake!"

"What are we going to do?" Cassie wailed, clasping her hands to her face. "This is for the gallery party that we're catering this evening."

I gasped. "*What?* I thought you made the cake for that already!"

Cassie looked a bit shamefaced. "I did... But when I tasted it, I realised I must have used salt instead of sugar," she said sheepishly. "So I thought I'd just make up another one really quickly. After all, it doesn't take that long to bake and I whacked up the oven temperature higher than normal—I thought it would bake faster—and I kept checking it—but then this happened!"

I wanted to roll my eyes but I knew I was in no

position to complain. It was exactly the kind of thing I would do too.

"What are we going to do, though?" I said, starting to panic. "They're expecting the food any minute. We haven't got the time to bake another cake. And the Victoria sponge was supposed to be the centrepiece!"

"You could simply cut the middle of the cake out," came a calm voice from the other side of the table.

We both looked up in surprise to see Dora Kempton regarding us kindly. I had completely forgotten that she was there.

"You could turn it into a ring cake," she said.

"A what?" Cassie gaped at her, completely lost.

"Have you got a sharp knife?"

I picked one out from the knife block next to the sink. "Will this do?"

Dora nodded. "Just cut out a circle in the middle of the sponge and remove the crusty dry brown sections. Then frost the rest of the cake and serve. No one will be any wiser. In fact, you could even fill the hole in the middle with fresh fruit and some whipped cream on top. It will look very attractive and novel."

I smiled. "That sounds like a brilliant idea! Oh, and we've got some fresh Blenheim Orange apples from a local farm," I said. "We can slice some up, arrange them in a swirl in the centre, and drizzle some honey on top. It would go really nicely with the theme of the exhibition, which is celebrating local Cotswolds bounty."

Cassie was looking more hopeful. "Yeah! And we could also add some—" She stopped and sniffed the air. "Wait... is something burning?"

She gasped and ran to the oven, yanking the door open. Smoke billowed out.

"Noooo!" Cassie wailed, flapping her arms around. I ran over and grabbed an oven glove. A few minutes later, we stood looking in deep dismay at the crammed baking tray on the wooden table.

"Um... What were you trying to make, Cassie?" I said.

"A lemon drizzle cake," said Cassie forlornly. "It sounded so easy from the recipe. And also some chocolate fudge fairy cakes. These are for the gallery party and I was running late, so I thought I'd just put them all in to bake together—that would speed things up. But why have they all gone hard and crusty and cracked?"

Dora spoke up from the other end of the table. "That often happens if the oven is overcrowded and it gets too hot."

I wanted to berate my best friend but I could see that Cassie was upset enough already. She was blinking back tears and I had never seen her look so defeated.

"Oh God... look at that hideous bump!" she whispered, staring at the lemon drizzle cake, which had a bump like a huge pimple in the centre of it, covered with an ugly, cracked brown crust.

Dora stood up and came over to us. She prodded

the cake with an expert finger. "It feels all right aside from that. Just slice this bump off, then flip it over and ice the bottom. It should still taste fine and no one will notice."

"What about these?" I said, looking in horror at the lumps of ugly fairy cakes. "They're supposed to be soft and moist... These have gone completely dry and cracked, and the edges are burnt."

Dora Kempton pushed her sleeves back. "Get me a chopping board and a knife," she said. "And some whipped cream, ice cream, and several large glasses. And have you got any berries?"

"I haven't got fresh berries but I've got some lovely forest berry compote from one of the local farms," I said.

"That'll do nicely. Get those things for me."

Cassie and I hurried to comply. Then we watched in fascination as Dora expertly cut the fairy cakes up. She discarded the burned sections, then sliced the remaining chocolate fudge into bit-sized chunks. These she put into the large glasses, layered with the rich berry compote, whipped cream, and home-made ice cream until it turned into a delicious-looking trifle. Finally, she got some chocolate flakes and sprinkled them on top. The result was amazing.

"Wow..." I said. My own mouth was watering. "They look incredible, Dora. I want one for myself!"

"Here," said Dora, making up a last glass with the leftover bits of chocolate fudge fairy cake and a dollop of the other ingredients. She handed this to me and

Cassie and we took turns spooning from the concoction whilst she stored the other glasses in the chiller.

"Ooh, delicious!" Cassie smacked her lips.

It was. You would never believe that something which was such a baking disaster could turn into something that tasted so heavenly.

"Are you sure you used to be a scout?" I said jokingly. "These look like the work of a professional baker!"

Dora's stern face broke into a rare smile. "My mother used to love baking," she said. "I used to help her a lot as a little girl, and I just kept on doing it as I got older. I find it relaxing."

"Relaxing—!" Cassie choked on a bit of chocolate fudge and berry trifle.

Dora laughed softly; it was a pleasant sound. When she was smiling like this, her eyes warm and happy, she looked like a different person.

I said earnestly, "I don't know how to thank you enough, Dora. You saved us! These are going to go down a treat at the gallery party!"

"It's nothing," she said gruffly. She waved towards her empty plate and teacup at the other end of the table. "It's the least I can do..."

I hesitated, then said nervously, "Can I offer you some reimbursement for your time—?"

"Certainly not!" Dora snapped. "I'm happy to help."

"Okay," I said, quickly retreating. "But won't you

take some more of our leftovers from today? Just so it's not wasted," I added hastily. "And you can tell us how we might improve."

Dora accepted this and left, bearing a large paper bag of buns and muffins. As soon as she had gone out the door, Cassie gripped my shoulders and said:

"We've found our chef, Gemma! You've got to hire her! Tomorrow!"

I smiled. "Do you think I can get her to agree without thinking I'm offering her charity?"

"Bloody hell, at this stage, she'd be the one giving us charity!" said Cassie, flopping down onto a chair. "I'm absolutely knackered! Baking is the most stressful thing ever. I never want to go through another afternoon like this again."

I laughed, then gave her arm a sympathetic squeeze. "I'm sorry, Cass—it wasn't fair to put this all on you."

She waved me away. "Hey, I volunteered. I thought it looked a lot easier than it actually is. Your mother certainly made it look easy... oh, by the way, have you heard from her?"

I gave a smile of relief. "Yeah, *finally*! I got a text from her this morning. It seems that she *had* sent a text to me after they arrived in Jakarta but then she discovered that she had only typed it out but had forgotten to press 'Send'." I rolled my eyes.

"Well, at least she's safe and sound," said Cassie. She looked around the kitchen. "And maybe by the time she gets back, we'll have a new chef in the tearoom!" She grinned at me. "I think I'm safer sticking to my paintbrushes."

"Well, you make *that* look a lot easier than it actually is," I said with a smile. "You can produce a beautiful landscape in the time it takes someone to draw a stick figure."

"Guess we all have our talents," Cassie agreed. She grinned at me. "Yours is sticking your nose in people's business."

"It's not!" I said, horrified. "You're making me sound like the Old Biddies!"

"No, no, not like them," Cassie assured me. "I meant that in a good way. I mean... I think you've got a knack for solving mysteries, Gemma."

"It doesn't seem to be helping Seth much at the moment."

At the mention of Seth, Cassie's face fell and I wanted to kick myself for ruining the mood.

"Gemma, you don't really think he's going to end up being charged for the murder?" Cassie said, her face worried.

"I don't know," I said miserably. "At the moment, it doesn't look good."

"Why don't we get together with him tonight after we drop these things off at the gallery and go over the case again?" suggested Cassie. "Maybe we can come up with a new angle."

I blushed slightly. "I... Actually, I've got a date tonight."

Cassie raised her eyebrows. "I thought you hadn't

forgiven Devlin for what he said yesterday? You said you weren't talking to him again until he apologised."

"It's... it's not with Devlin, actually. I'm going out with Lincoln. He rang this morning and asked if I'd like to have dinner with him tonight."

Cassie said nothing but she gave me a look.

"Hey, I'm a free agent, still. I can go out to dinner if people invite me," I said defensively. "And Lincoln's great company."

My best friend leaned forwards. "Do you *like* Lincoln, Gemma? I mean, seriously?"

I hesitated. "I... I could, I think. I mean... he's not Devlin but... well, it's nice being with him. We're not always fighting and arguing all the time, and we don't have this painful history between us—it's just... pleasant. And Lincoln's so calm and solid and dependable... He doesn't make me furious all the time..." I sighed. "Oh, Cassie, I don't know. I'm so confused!"

Cassie's face softened. "Well, I suppose it wouldn't hurt to get to know him better—before you decide which one to choose."

"Cassie!" I gasped. "It's not like deciding what to order from a menu!"

"Why not?" she said with an impish grin.

I rolled my eyes, then I said forlornly, "I just... I don't want to hurt anyone..."

"Someone always gets hurt when people fall in love. You can't think about that. You have to listen to what your heart says and be true to yourself. Even if it scares you. Even if it isn't the easy way. It wouldn't be fair to either of them otherwise."

"Since when did you become Ms Love Guru?"

Cassie gave me a smug smile. "I'm an expert on relationships. I can see things."

Yeah, well, you can't see your own feelings about the boy who has always adored you and who is under your very nose, I thought. But I kept my thoughts to myself. Things were awkward enough with Seth without me making things worse by opening the subject up with Cassie. I started to carry some of the cakes out of the kitchen.

"You know I expect a full report tomorrow," Cassie called after me. "Especially on what kind of kisser Lincoln is."

"*Cassie!*"

Her teasing laughter followed me out of the room.

CHAPTER NINETEEN

Whenever I had gone out with Lincoln in the past, I had always taken great pains to stress the "non-date-ness" of our outings, that we were simply going out as friends. And I had dressed accordingly, going for a casual girl-next-door look, so that Lincoln wouldn't think I was making any special effort for him. Tonight, though, I hesitated in front of my wardrobe. If I was going to give Lincoln a fair chance, then I had to act like it was a date, instead of working overtime not to see him in a romantic light. Maybe Cassie was right: I needed to embrace this fully to really know my feelings.

It was so easy, now that I was back in Oxford, visiting the old haunts, reliving my student days, to just fall back into old patterns of behaviour. Devlin had been my whole world then and I had loved him with the single-minded, all-consuming passion of first love. But I didn't know if what I felt for him now was simply an echo of those feelings or something real that had stood the test of time. Maybe if I let myself fall for another man, with no doubts or reservations, I would know at last what my true feelings were.

Besides, just because Lincoln didn't make my heart race when I saw him... so what? Did it have to be felt so intensely for it to be considered "real love"? Could you love someone just as much if the feeling grew from respect and liking instead of an instant attraction and intense passion?

I wished I knew the answer.

When Lincoln arrived to pick me up, I saw his eyes light up in surprise and appreciation as he saw me. I had chosen a navy silk dress with an empire line waist and flowing skirts, and placed a jewelled barrette in my short pixie crop. I felt very grown up and elegant as I allowed him to help me into my coat and escort me out the front door.

Thank God my mother was away. It had been hard enough dealing with her heavy-handed matchmaking when I had maintained an offhand attitude. It would have been impossible if she saw that I was making any kind of effort with Lincoln.

"You look beautiful," said Lincoln, as he opened the door of his car for me.

"Thanks," I said lightly. "Where are we going?"

"I've booked a table at Gees."

"Oh! I haven't been back there since I left England," I said enthusiastically.

Gees was one of the top fine dining restaurants in Oxford, which was saying something. In a city with the kind of spectacular architecture that Oxford has, you were pretty spoilt for choice when it came to looking for a picturesque place to dine, from a former castle prison complex to a mediaeval Grade-II-listed building, from a quaint boathouse to a converted chapel church... Gees offered a posh option mixing the modern with the historic. It was housed in an enormous Victorian glass conservatory, with a spacious interior filled with potted trees and marble-top tables, spread out across the chequered floor. It was the place you went to for special occasions—the wedding anniversary dinner or graduation celebration with your parents.

We were shown to our table by an unobtrusive waiter and seated in a corner of the conservatory. I looked around with interest: the place had been refurbished since my student days at Oxford and some things had changed—the iconic chandeliers, for example, had been replaced by modern feature lighting—but overall, it had the same elegant ambience combined with a sort of restrained rustic charm.

As we perused the menu, ordered, and then waited for the food to arrive, Lincoln chatted lightly about his work and the new developments at the hospital. I found myself enjoying the evening much more than I had expected and liking Lincoln the more time I spent with him. I eyed him surreptitiously as we tucked into our main courses. His soft brown eyes were twinkling as he recounted some humorous story from the hospital and his long-fingered hands—doctor's hands—gestured as he illustrated his story. I thought of Cassie's teasing comment and wondered suddenly what it would be like to be kissed by him. Would he make my heart pound the same way Devlin did? Would I be swept away on a wave of feeling so intense, it made me forget everyone and everything? Didn't I owe it to myself to find out?

"Gemma?"

I started and realised that I had been staring. "Sorry, my mind wandered for a minute..." I blushed and looked down, hastily cutting up an artichoke.

"What do you think of the new menu?" asked Lincoln, as he forked up some of his fettuccine with venison ragout.

"Great so far... but I'm looking forward to their pudding menu."

"Yes, I would have thought that as a tearoom owner, it's their pudding menu that would interest you the most. See how their desserts compare with yours."

I laughed. "I could hardly hope to compare with an institution like Gees!"

"Oh, I don't know..." said Lincoln with a smile. "Your Little Stables Tearoom's reputation has been growing. I've heard quite a few people talk about you at the hospital."

"Really?" I said, delighted.

He nodded. "People telling others they must go or saying that they took friends and relatives and everyone loved it. You've done really well, Gemma, in such a short time too. How long have you been open?"

"Just over four months," I said, surprised now that I actually thought about it. In a way, it felt like a lifetime had passed since I had returned to England.

"Well, I think you're doing a fantastic job."

I felt a warm glow at the praise. "Thanks."

"By the way, how's Seth? How are things going with the murder investigation?"

I sobered. "Not so good. I think it's getting Seth down a bit."

"Don't the police have any other suspects? What about that tramp that you were interested in last time? Weren't we doing that recreation to check that the timing could have worked for him?"

"Yeah, but I've since learned that Professor Barrow sent a text message at 12:17 a.m.—which means that he was still alive then. And since Jim was seen outside the college at 12:23 a.m., that only leaves a gap of about six minutes which—"

"Which he couldn't have managed, especially with a limp," Lincoln finished for me.

"Yes." I fiddled with my fork. "The problem is, there *are* other suspects but none of them are as strong a suspect as Seth. There's Dr Leila Gaber, who's a colleague of Barrow's and hated him. There's Barrow's own sister who benefits by a lot of money from his death—and there wasn't much love lost between them either. And then there's that head porter we met—Clyde Peters—he seems to have been in the Cloisters a bit too conveniently the night of the murder and I'm sure he's hiding something, although on the face of it, he doesn't seem to have a motive or benefit from Barrow's death..."

Lincoln shook his head in sympathy. "What a crummy situation. I'm really sorry..." He paused, then mused, "Dr Leila Gaber... That name sounds familiar..."

"She was at that Oxford Society of Medicine dinner."

"No, that's not it... I think I heard some gossip about her at the hospital."

I sat forwards. "Really? What?"

He gave me a sheepish smile. "I have to confess, I don't pay much attention to hospital gossip. It was just that the name was unusual so it stuck in my memory." He furrowed his brow, thinking. "From what I can remember, I don't think it was very complimentary... but then, what gossip is?" He grinned. "It's never any fun unless you're talking about scandals and misdemeanours. People aren't interested in the nice stuff. They want to hear your deepest dirty secrets."

"Mmm..." I would have given a lot to hear Leila

Gaber's deepest dirty secrets. "I wonder who might know... "

"You could try her colleagues at the Department of Ethnoarchaeology," said Lincoln. "Those who work with her would have the best knowledge about her background, I should think. And Leila Gaber is the kind of woman who would get herself talked about," he added with a wry smile.

He was right. With her larger-than-life personality, Leila wasn't the type to be ignored: you either loved or hated her. And I was pretty sure most of the men loved her, and probably a lot of the women too. Even *I* found myself reluctantly liking her. There was something so charming about her blunt, vivacious personality.

The waiter came quietly to remove our empty plates and I excused myself to go to the Ladies. As I made my way across the conservatory, I scanned the tables absentmindedly... Then I did a double take as I passed a table where a little old lady in a bright floral dress and pink cardigan was sitting.

It was Glenda Bailey. And facing her was Clyde Peters, the head porter of Wadsworth College.

CHAPTER TWENTY

"Glenda!" I cried in surprise.

She started and looked up, whilst Clyde Peters stopped speaking abruptly. They had been leaning forwards across the table, heads together, talking earnestly, and from the furtive look they sent me, I wondered what they had been talking about.

"Oh, it's you, Gemma," said Glenda, looking none too pleased to see me.

I was surprised. The Old Biddies were usually so warm and friendly towards me—if slightly too friendly. They treated me like an honorary great-niece or grand-daughter and delighted in meddling with my life. So I had never seen one of them look at me with as much displeasure and annoyance as Glenda was looking at me now.

I stole a glance at the man opposite her. Clyde

Peters was sitting back with a bland smile on his face, his expression shuttered. From the way they were dressed and the romantic setting, it was obvious that they were on a date, but why would Glenda Bailey suddenly be going out with the head porter of Wadsworth? What was she up to?

I scanned the restaurant again and saw something I hadn't noticed before. In the far corner, behind one of the large potted trees, was a table with three little old ladies. They were huddled over their plates, pretending to be pre-occupied with their food and obviously hoping not to be noticed, but I recognised them instantly: Mabel Cooke, Florence Doyle, and Ethel Webb. The rest of the Old Biddies. What were they doing here? I glanced back at Glenda suspiciously. This was no ordinary date. This must have been what they had left the tearoom early today to prepare for.

"Fancy seeing you here," I said to her. I glanced at Clyde Peters, then looked back at her expectantly.

"Er, yes... Gemma, this is Clyde. He's the—"

"I'm just a friend," he interrupted quickly.

So, he didn't want to raise the subject of Wadsworth College. Did he think I wouldn't recognise him? There was an awkward silence. It was obvious Glenda wanted me to leave.

"Well, I'll leave you to get on with your meal," I said at last. "Nice to bump into you."

Glenda murmured something similar in reply although I could tell she didn't mean it. I continued on my way to the Ladies, pondering what was going on. What were the Old Biddies up to? Their attempts to "help" investigate a murder usually ended with me stuck in some embarrassing situation. I shuddered to think what they were involved in this time.

I didn't have much chance to find out any more about it. By the time I returned to the conservatory, Glenda and her companion had gone. I looked quickly across the room. The other table was empty as well. They must have all left in a hurry. I frowned. What on earth was going on?

The little interlude kept me preoccupied for the rest of the dinner, in spite of the delicious sticky toffee pudding with toffee sauce and pecan pie with caramel ice cream that we had for dessert.

"You're very quiet," Lincoln remarked, as he walked me to the front door of my parents' house.

"Sorry." I gave him an apologetic smile. "I've been really rude. It's just that this case with Seth... It's been worrying me and I can't seem to stop thinking about it..."

"Ah. As long as it wasn't because I was boring you to death."

"No, no, of course not! I really enjoyed tonight."

"Then... maybe we could do it again sometime?" said Lincoln.

I knew what he was asking. I looked up and read the intent in his eyes as he stepped closer to me. My heart pounded. I could still diffuse the situation— step away and make some light remark, pretend to fumble with the key in the lock—or I could let Lincoln kiss me.

My mind whirled. I didn't know what I wanted. He came even closer and leaned towards me. I held myself still, my breath in my throat... and then—

The air was suddenly pierced by a bloodcurdling yowl.

We both jumped.

"What on earth—?" Lincoln looked around.

I gasped. "*Muesli!*"

I fumbled with the lock for real and let myself into the house, dashing into the hallway and switching on the lights. "Muesli? Muesli? Where are you?"

Another yowl answered me. It seemed to be coming from the living room. I ran in, Lincoln at my heels. I looked frantically around. I couldn't see the little tabby cat anywhere.

"Muesli? Where are you?"

A soft meow this time. Forlorn. Scared.

"Sounds like it's coming from behind the wall, in that corner..." Lincoln pointed.

I ran to the corner and placed a hand on the wall. Then my eyes caught sight of the vent on the floor. My mother's knitting basket had been shoved aside and the ornamental grille cover had been pushed out of its frame again, to reveal a gaping hole. Large enough for a very small cat to have squeezed through.

"Oh, bloody hell... she's gone into the vent," I said. I knelt down, removed the cover completely, and peered down into the black hole. "Muesli?"

"*Meorrw!*" came a faint reply. But it didn't seem to be coming from below me—it seemed to be coming from the side.

"She sounds like she's behind the walls?" I said in puzzlement.

"These old Victorian houses have a crawl space underneath and that's probably connected to the wall cavities," said Lincoln. "She might have somehow got into the walls that way, especially if she's a very small cat..."

"How am I going to get her out?" I wailed.

"Maybe if you just leave the vent open, she'll come back of her own accord?"

I looked at the black hole in front of me dubiously. "But what if she's stuck somewhere? What if she's hurt? I can't just leave her..."

"Then you'll have to call the fire brigade," said Lincoln.

I sighed, thinking of all the times I'd made jokes about Britain's Fire Brigade spending more time rescuing cats than putting out fires. Well, I guess this was poetic justice. I made the call and was relieved when the operator sounded more amused than annoyed.

"Don't worry, we're used to dealing with naughty kitties," the woman laughed. "You're not the first owner to have made this call this week."

However, she told me that there were a few other incidents that had to take priority so the firemen might not be with me for several hours. I hung up and felt slightly sick at the thought of the delay. I imagined Muesli stuck somewhere, bleeding, in pain...

"You really love her, don't you," said Lincoln, observing my distress.

I gave a sheepish laugh. "It seems stupid, doesn't it, to be so attached to a little cat? Do you know, I never thought I was a cat person? I always thought I preferred dogs. I mean, I do still love dogs but Muesli is just... special. I can't imagine life without her now."

I was surprised to feel tears starting to my eyes and blinked rapidly, looking away. Lincoln shifted from foot to foot, looking intensely uncomfortable and unsure what to say—the typical Englishman when faced with excessive displays of emotion.

He cleared his throat. "I'm sure she'll be fine," he said, giving my shoulder an awkward pat.

I sniffed and dashed a hand across my eyes. "Look, you might as well go home," I said. "It's silly, us both hanging around here waiting. And you've got work tomorrow morning, haven't you?"

"Yes, I've got an early ward round," he said regretfully.

"Go. Don't worry, I'll be fine." I dredged up a smile. "And I'm sure the firemen will be here soon."

When he had left, I tried to sit in a chair and wait calmly but I just couldn't keep still. After a while, I sprang up and paced the room. Every so often, Muesli would let out a pathetic meow but it seemed to be coming from a different place each time. I followed the sound around, splaying my hands on the walls, calling to her, trying to place her location. It was incredibly frustrating.

Then at last, the firemen arrived. I was surprised at how matter-of-factly they took my story. I guess rescuing cats from weird places was a weekly habit for them.

"We have to work out where she is first," said the older firemen whose face was lined with experience and good humour. "Then we can decide whether we should drill through the walls or remove panelling to get access."

"Drill? Remove panels?" I paled. I thought of my parents returning home and me having to explain why there was a gaping hole in their living room wall. "Um... Isn't there any other way?"

"That's if she is in the wall cavity," said the fireman. "If she's underneath the house, we might be able to access the crawl space through a vent on the outside. But that can take longer because we would have to go down there and then search for her. It would be a lot quicker and easier to pinpoint the location from within the house and go straight through."

At that moment, Muesli let out an indignant yowl and we all rushed to the spot where the sound had come from.

"Looks like we might be in luck," said the old firemen. "If we could pull out this panel here and go through..."

I watched apprehensively as he and his colleague began taking apart the panelling, revealing a huge hole in the wall. Another *meorrw* drifted out but this time from the other side of the room.

The fireman frowned. "I could have sworn it was here—"

"*Meorrw!*" This time it was close again, but behind me, by the windows.

"She seems to be all over the place!" I groaned.

"Not to worry, luv, we'll find her," said the old fireman cheerfully. "We rescued a cat once that had been stuck in a wall for a week. Took us three days to get him out and we had to drill holes everywhere and dismantle half the living room, but we got there in the end!"

Okay, if that particular piece of information was supposed to cheer me up, it wasn't working. Still, I appreciated what he was trying to do.

"Have you tried enticing her with some food?" the younger fireman spoke up. "See if you can get something nice and smelly and put it near the first vent."

"Great idea!" I scrambled to my feet and ran into the kitchen.

A few moments later, I was thrusting a small plate of tinned tuna into the gap in the floor. The strong fishy odour wafted up and I wrinkled my nose. I hoped I wasn't attracting rats with this. Muesli had gone eerily quiet and I looked at the firemen uneasily.

"She hasn't made a sound for a while—do you think something's happened to her?"

"Maybe she's just busy coming this way," said the younger fireman hopefully.

We waited a few moments longer. Nothing.

"Try calling her," said the older fireman.

"Muesli? Muesli? *Muuuuuuesli!*"

Nothing.

And then suddenly—

"*Meorrw?*"

We whirled around. A little tabby head had popped out on the other side of the room. I sprang up and ran over to her. She was climbing out of another floor vent, wriggling through the triangular gap at the side of the cover, which had been knocked askew. She must have come up underneath, butted it with her head, and shoved it aside. I pounced on her and scooped her up.

"Muesli! You little devil!" Now that she was safe and sound, I was furious at her. "I can't believe you just popped back up like that—after you made us open up a huge hole in the wall!"

"Ah well, as long as the kitty's fine," said the older fireman with a grin as he came over to join us. "You can always patch up a wall but you can't always patch up a cat."

He was right but still, I wanted to throttle the little minx. She was lying in my arms, looking up at the fireman, her head tilted to one side, her green eyes enormous.

"Ah now... isn't she a pretty little thing," said the old fireman with a smile, reaching out a big hand to tickle her under the chin.

Muesli shut her eyes with pleasure and purred loudly, the picture of smug contentment. I scowled at her. I couldn't believe the trouble she had caused and here she was, acting like some celebrity receiving her adoring fans.

"We'll fix those grates for you," said the old fireman. "It's only temporary, mind—you'll have to get someone to come out and sort them out properly. But at least it'll stop this little one doing another escape act."

"Thank you."

I hugged my cat to me and watched as they checked every vent in the house, then with a last pat for Muesli and good-natured chuckle, they left. I stood on the doorstep watching the fire engine drive away, Muesli in my arms.

"*Meorrw?*" she said.

"What are you looking so smug about?" I said, giving her a sour look. "Do you realise how much trouble you've caused tonight?" I thought back to earlier in the evening and that almost-kiss. "And you ruined a romantic moment too," I grumbled.

"*Meorrw...*" said Muesli with a glint in her green eyes.

I almost wondered if that had been her intention all along. And I didn't want to admit it, but a part of me was almost glad that she had succeeded.

TWO DOWN, BUN TO GO

CHAPTER TWENTY-ONE

The next morning, I wasted no time as soon as the Old Biddies arrived in the tearoom. I marched over to them and demanded:

"What were you doing in Gees last night?"

They gave each other shifty looks, then Ethel leaned forwards and said excitedly:

"We were undercover again."

Oh God.

"What does that mean exactly?" I asked nervously.

Glenda giggled. "I was the honey pan."

I looked at her in puzzlement. "The what? Oh, you mean a honey pot!"

She gave me a coy smile. "Of course, he's not my usual type. I like them a bit younger. But I suppose one has to do one's duty for one's country."

"Uh... right," I said, trying to imagine Glenda in

the role of Mata Hari and not quite managing it.

"You probably weren't *his* type," grumbled Florence. "That's why he wasn't telling you much."

"Nonsense!" cried Glenda indignantly. "It wasn't easy, but I was working my charm on him and I would have found out more if Gemma hadn't appeared!" She looked at me reproachfully.

"Me?" I gaped at them.

"Yes, you. You ruined our operation, Gemma," said Mabel with a scowl. "Now we won't get a second chance at Peters again."

"What do you mean?"

"He was telling me all about the murder on Friday night," said Glenda. "He—"

"Oh!" I clutched her arm eagerly. "Did he tell you what happened before he found Seth? Did he see anyone in the tunnel? I was thinking about this last night as I was going off to sleep: the tunnel is the only way in and out of the Cloisters so the murderer had to have escaped that way. And if Clyde Peters had been coming from the opposite direction, surely he would have passed the murderer on the way?"

Glenda frowned. "But he didn't go through the tunnel until *after* he had found Seth with the body."

"What...?" I stared at her in confusion. "What do you mean he didn't go that way till *after* he found the body? Didn't he come that way in the first place? He told the police he had been doing a round of the college and had just gone into the Cloisters when he saw Seth with the body."

Glenda shook her head. "No, that can't be right. He told me that he was already in the Cloisters—in fact, he was just on his way back out when he found Seth."

I stared at her. "But... but that completely changes things! Are you saying that he hadn't come from the Porter's Lodge? That he was already in the Cloisters before Seth even arrived?"

"Yes, Clyde was in the college guest room. He told me he had just come out of the guest room, by the chapel, and was heading back to the Lodge when he found Seth and the body. Gave him such a fright, it did."

"What was he doing in the guest room? And why didn't he mention this to the police?"

"Ah... well, Clyde has been running this little scheme on the side, you see. The guest room is often empty and he's in charge of all the bookings anyway. So he started quietly renting it out, if someone wanted somewhere to stay in Oxford for a night or two, as long as they gave him a little something to put in his pocket. He would smuggle them in and no one would be any wiser. The Cloisters are in such a secluded corner of the college, anyway, hardly anyone goes there much. It was a nice little side earner and it's been going on for years. The college authorities don't know about it, of course, and Clyde certainly doesn't want them to find out, so that's why he didn't mention it to the police."

I rocked back on my heels. "So... are you telling

me that there was someone else in the Cloisters the night of the murder that nobody knew about? Not even the police? Who was this person staying in the guest room?"

"It was the murdered professor's brother, Richard Barrow," said Glenda. "It was actually Professor Barrow himself who asked Clyde to put his brother up. Apparently Richard appeared in Oxford on Friday morning, asking his brother for help. He didn't have money and would have had to sleep on the streets, so the professor stepped in. But he didn't want anyone to know about it, so it suited him to have Richard be one of Clyde's 'unofficial guests'."

"I can't believe Clyde Peters never mentioned this to the police!" I said savagely. "This changes everything! Richard Barrow stood to gain a great deal by his brother's death—and it sounds like he needed money desperately. And now we know that he was actually on the spot the night of the murder!" I frowned. "Wait... the police checked all the rooms after they arrived and they didn't find anyone in the college guest room."

"Clyde said he managed to get Richard away before the police arrived."

"How did he do that?"

"Well, he was just about to tell me and then you arrived," said Glenda, a bit tartly. "And afterwards, he shut up like a clam and wouldn't say another word. I think he had got a bit carried away while he was talking to me and hadn't realised what he was saying. You know how men do love to boast and if you look admiring and pretend that you're a silly little woman who can't understand how clever they are, they will completely forget themselves and tell you anything."

I looked at Glenda with new respect. Perhaps she had more in common with Mata Hari than I thought.

"So what do we do now?" said Mabel briskly.

"I've got to tell Devlin about this," I said. "The police have to know that there was someone else in the Cloisters that night who had good reason for wanting Barrow dead." I paused as another thought struck me. "Do you know, this means that Joan Barrow lied as well. She told the police that she had no idea where her youngest brother was…"

"Maybe she doesn't?" said Florence.

I shook my head firmly. "No, I had the feeling that she was hiding something. I'm willing to bet that she knew her brother was here in Oxford on Friday night and in fact…" I added excitedly, my thoughts racing now. "I wonder if that was why she was so adamant that the police shouldn't come to her place to interview her? Maybe it had nothing to do with her sick partner at all! Maybe it was because Richard was hiding at her house. After all, he had to go *somewhere* after he escaped from Wadsworth—if he didn't catch the last train from Oxford to Reading, he probably passed the rest of the night on a University Park bench somewhere and then caught the first train the next morning. I think the first train from

Oxford to Reading goes at 4 a.m. so that would only be a few hours after the murder."

"Do you think they might be involved in the murder together?" Ethel shivered. "It seems dreadfully ruthless to plan to murder their brother in cold blood."

"I don't know," I mused. "I haven't met Richard Barrow so I don't know what he's like. Reading between the lines of what his sister said, he sounds like a small-time crook, so maybe... But Joan... well, she seemed like one of those mousy, suburban housewives. I wouldn't have thought she would have the nerve for murder... but I guess you never know, do you?"

"I think it's *very* possible," said Mabel darkly. "Brothers and sisters have been murdering each other since the time of the Bible."

I looked at her askance. Somehow, I didn't remember Sunday school being so violent.

"There's something I don't understand, though..." I frowned. "How did Clyde Peters get Richard out without anyone seeing? I mean, I know Seth was in shock but I think he would have noticed if Clyde Peters was hustling a strange man past him—and he was standing right by the entrance to the tunnel, which is the only way out of the Cloister..."

Something nagged at me—something I had seen or heard—maybe that night of the Oxford Society of Medicine dinner? What was it? I felt instinctively that it was something important, but I couldn't put my finger on it. I furrowed my brow, thinking hard. It was hovering there, on the edge of my mind, but I just couldn't grasp it.

I sighed and gave up. Anyway, the important thing now was to call Devlin and let him know about this new information. He would be able to ask the head porter all the details of Richard Barrow's movements on Friday night. Devlin's phone was busy so I tried his office at Oxfordshire CID, thinking I'd leave a message there. I was surprised when he answered it himself.

"O'Connor speaking."

My heart gave its usual jolt at the sound of his deep baritone. The last time we had spoken was when we had that huge row about the note in Barrow's pigeonhole. A part of me was still angry at him, but I knew I had to put aside my personal feelings for now.

"Devlin? It's me, Gemma. I haven't caught you at a bad time, have I?"

"There's never really a good time," he said, but I relaxed slightly as I heard the sardonic humour in his voice.

Quickly, I recounted my conversation with the Old Biddies. Devlin whistled under his breath.

"That old weasel! So Peters lied to us and withheld important evidence in a murder investigation."

"Well, you can get the truth out of him now, can't you?"

"Just as soon as I get off the phone with you," said

Devlin. "Mr Peters and I are going to have a little talk."

I winced at his tone and almost felt sorry for the head porter. "And what about Richard Barrow?"

"I'll be speaking to him too," Devlin said grimly. "And that sister of his. I'll be on the first train to Reading tomorrow. And I'll be going over everyone's alibis again. This does change everything. The very fact that Richard Barrow concealed his presence in the Cloisters that night and then ran away from the scene of the crime makes him look guilty in my book. Thanks, Gemma, for passing this along—this is crucial information for the investigation."

"I'm glad I could help," I said shyly.

Devlin hesitated, then said, "Actually, Gemma, I've been meaning to ring you as well... I wanted to say I'm sorry—about the other night. I shouldn't have been so brusque with you."

His apology took me by surprise. "That's okay," I said slowly. "I... I want to apologise too. For what I was asking—what I was expecting you to do. I mean, I understand that you can't... that you wouldn't... You wouldn't be *you* if you had said yes," I finished lamely.

"It's difficult to be 'me' sometimes, especially when I know it will hurt those I care about." There was a pause, then he added, "It can be hard to let go... sometimes you have a case that just doesn't get resolved and then something comes up—months, maybe even years later—and suddenly you see a chance to close the case at last. And you feel morally obliged to do everything you can to go back and get that closure. You owe it to the victims, if not to yourself."

I realised suddenly that he wasn't talking about this case but about his recent recall back to Leeds. In his own way, Devlin was trying to apologise, to explain why he had left so suddenly before Christmas and been so preoccupied with his old case up north.

"It's okay," I said. "It's... your work. I understand. It's what makes you such a good detective."

Devlin would always be driven, I realised, consumed by his work and his desire to find justice. And he would probably always put his morals above his personal feelings. But in a way, if Devlin had caved in and indulged me, I would probably have admired him a lot less. It was his very integrity and nobility which was one of the most attractive things about him. This was Devlin O'Connor and this was the man I would be choosing if I decided to give my heart to him.

CHAPTER TWENTY-TWO

"Gemma—have you spoken to Dora yet?"

I looked up from the napkins I was folding. "No, not yet... I was going to do it on the way home."

Cassie came over and took the napkins off me. "Go. Leave early. I'll close up. We need Dora more than anything else."

A few minutes later, I was bundled up in my coat and scarf and hurrying down the village high street in the fading afternoon light. Dora Kempton lived on the other side of Meadowford-on-Smythe, down by the embankment along the river. There, sandwiched between a row of newly-furbished Cotswolds cottages and a development of mock Tudor housing, built for the wealthy London commuter brigade, were a couple of tiny workers' cottages.

They were slightly rundown and lacked many of

the modern amenities, but they were snug and solid. They were owned by a kindly local landowner who had decided to let these cottages out at a vastly reduced rate to pensioners in straitened circumstances. He could easily have made several times what he was getting if he had rented them out to the London set—or even sold them—but thank goodness, there were still people like him in the world.

Dora looked surprised to see me when she opened the door and I saw her hesitate, glancing involuntarily over her own shoulder. I could guess what was going through her mind. She was probably embarrassed to have me come in and see the bare poverty of her house, but it was too rude to keep me standing out here on the doorstep, especially in this weather. She invited me in reluctantly and showed me into the tiny living room.

I sat down on the faded sofa and tried not to shiver. There was no heating in the house and I wondered how Dora managed at night. I'd often heard news reports in the past of the elderly and the impoverished who died of hypothermia in the winter because they were afraid to use the heating and rack up bills they couldn't pay, but you know how things on the news never seem real to you until you meet it in your personal life?

"Would you like some tea and biscuits?" said Dora formally.

"Oh no, that's okay I don't—" I started to say, not

wanting to deprive her of her meagre supplies. Then I saw the look in her eye and the way she drew herself up. I realised that as a guest in her house, the best gift I could give her was the sense of pride in being a hostess.

I smiled at her. "That would be lovely, Dora. Just a cup of tea, thanks."

She went into the kitchen and I heard her clattering around, to return in due course with two mugs of tea and a small plate of biscuits—although these were so thick and chunky that calling them by the American term, "cookies", was probably more fitting. I helped myself to one, biting into it gingerly, then again with more enthusiasm. They were wonderfully buttery, crumbly, and crispy, tasting of oats and honey, and perfect for dunking in tea.

"My goodness, Dora, these are delicious! What are they?"

Her chest swelled with pride. "I made them myself. They're hobnobs, although I changed the recipe slightly. I used honey instead of golden syrup."

"They are wonderful," I said, taking a sip of tea and chewing slowly. "And they go so nicely with the tea."

"I can let you have the recipe if you like," said Dora, her eyes glowing with pleasure.

I could see that for a woman as proud as her, the ability to be in a position to *give* something for once meant a lot to her.

"Thanks, that would be great..." I paused, then

pounced on the opportunity she had given me. "Actually, that's sort of why I've come to see you today."

She looked at me enquiringly.

I leaned forwards. "Dora, would you consider coming to work for me as the chef at the tearoom?"

She looked surprised. "But surely... You must have people who are trained baking chefs—"

"I've interviewed a few people, but so far I haven't found anyone suitable. Besides, this would be a great arrangement because it would also give you something to—" Too late I realised my mistake. I cursed myself.

She stiffened. "If you're offering me this out of charity, I thank you for the offer but that isn't necessary."

"No, no, this isn't charity in the least!" I said. "To be honest, *you'd* be the one doing us a favour. We desperately need a chef and you're obviously a fantastic baker. I've been trying to find someone suitable but I've just been pulling my hair out! And poor Cassie is trying her best, but you saw how she's managing so far."

A smile twitched the corners of Dora's lips. "Yes, Cassie doesn't quite seem to have the knack."

Oh God. Understatement of the year.

"Neither do I," I said honestly. "We're both better using our time outside looking after the customers. And when you came in the other day and saved us for that gallery party, I suddenly thought—how wonderful it would be to have you helping us full time." I took a deep breath and put on my best corporate manner. "But I would want to pay you for your expertise. Exactly as if you were a professional chef. This is not me offering you a job out of pity— this is me offering you a working arrangement, based on my assessment of your skills."

There was a long pause.

I added in a pleading voice as I saw her waver. "Please, Dora. We really need you. As Cassie said, you'd be the one providing charity for us at this stage if you came to help!"

Dora was silent for a moment, then she said, "If I do come, I want it to be on a trial basis. One month with no pay. And if you're happy with my performance after that, then we can work out a permanent arrangement."

"It can't just be a free trial," I protested. "A probationary period is normally on full pay."

"I won't take money until I feel I'm suitable for the role."

"Half," I said firmly. "I will pay you at least half the normal hourly rate." *This is ridiculous,* I thought. *I must be the only person in the world who's negotiating with an employee to pay them more!* "And the trial period will be two weeks, no more," I added.

Dora gave me a wry look. "You drive a hard bargain, young lady."

And you're a stubborn old hen, I thought, with a mixture of exasperation and affection.

"Very well," said Dora at last. "I accept."

"Great!" I felt the smile spreading across my face. "When can you start? Tomorrow? Can you make more scones immediately? Because we've completely run out and we're really panicking. And muffins too. Oh, and Chelsea buns. We've got everything ready for you already. If you can come in first thing, I can show you where everything is and then maybe Cassie can help you bake the first batch so that we've got fresh buns and scones before the customers arrive..." My words were tumbling over each other in my eagerness.

Dora's stern face broke into a laugh. "Yes, I can start tomorrow. What time would you like me to be there?"

"We don't open until ten-thirty but usually get there by seven to start the baking..."

She nodded. "Seven it is."

I had to fight the urge to throw my arms around her and give her a hug. Instead, I contented myself with giving her a warm smile.

"Thank you so much, Dora; you don't realise how much your help means to us." I glanced at my watch. "Oh, I'd better dash. I need to stop off at the Domus Trust office before going home. I hope they won't have shut."

She accompanied me to her front door. As we walked past the small hall table, I noticed a few framed photos grouped on its surface. In amongst pictures of a much younger-looking Dora holding a baby, Dora standing with an elderly couple, Dora sitting at a grey, pebbly seaside...there was one of her in a pinafore apron, standing in what looked like an Oxford college quadrangle. She was next to another woman of similar age and dress, and they were both smiling cautiously into the camera.

I stopped and looked closer. "Was this from your scout days?"

Dora glanced at the faded photo. "Yes. One of my students took that and gave it to me. That's my friend, Agnes, who was another scout."

"That's the Great Quad at Wadsworth, isn't it?"

"Yes. I used to look after the staircases off the main quad and a few of the rooms in the Yardley Quad. In the earlier days, the new student dormitory building hadn't been built on the other side of the college, so many more of them used to stay in rooms on this side. That's all changed now, of course." She sighed, looking wistful for a moment as she stared down at the photograph in my hands. "I haven't been back to Wadsworth since I was made redundant last year. It seems strange to think that I spent most of my working life there—every day, for years and years—and now, I never see it at all. Wadsworth was almost like my home; I knew every nook and cranny, every spire and gargoyle." She laughed a bit sheepishly. "I think I probably knew it better and felt more part of it than many of the students there."

"I'm sure you did," I agreed. I put the frame carefully back amongst the others, then pulled the collar of my duffel coat up around my neck and gave her a parting smile. "Well, thanks again for the tea, Dora... and thank you for agreeing to come and help us at the tearoom."

"No, thank *you*," said Dora suddenly. "I know you said you're not doing it out of charity and I believe you. But I also know that you've taken an interest in me out of the kindness of your heart. You're a nice girl, Gemma Rose. And I... I'm glad I met you."

I stared at Dora in surprise, then gave in to that urge and threw my arms around her in an impromptu hug.

"Here! Now! Get away with you..." Dora said gruffly, disentangling herself.

But I could see from her flushed cheeks and bright eyes that she was touched and pleased, and her smile warmed my heart as I stepped out into the cold twilight.

CHAPTER TWENTY-THREE

It was almost completely dark by the time I cycled back to North Oxford, where the Domus Trust office was located. I pulled my bike off the road, propped it against the front railing of the elegant brick Georgian building and hurried up the front steps, hoping that it hadn't closed. I was in luck. A young woman looked up as I entered the warmth of the reception but my spirits fell a minute later when she told me that the Food Donations Coordinator had already left for the day.

"If you leave your name, I can give him a message and get him to ring you tomorrow," she offered.

"Thanks, that sounds like a good idea." I gave her my details, then as I turned to go, I noticed a large artist's sketch of a housing development. I went towards it for a closer look. "Is this the new project?

The one that might be built on college-donated land?"

"Yes, if we can only get the approval through," she said despondently. She sighed. "There was quite a lot of resistance and attempts to block the project, particularly from Wadsworth."

"Yes, I'd heard that," I said. "But surely now with Professor Barrow dead..." I paused, embarrassed, and cleared my throat. "I mean, I thought he was the main person objecting to the proposal?"

"He was—but it seems that he had great influence with other members of the college committee, particularly the Master of Wadsworth College, and he had somehow managed to persuade them to his way of thinking..." She trailed off.

"I'm sorry," I said, thinking suddenly of Owen and Ruby, and feeling a wrench in my heart. "I hope something can be done... I know the homeless community in Oxford are really depending on this."

"Oh, you can't imagine! Everyone is in really low spirits at the moment, especially the ones who've had a hands-on involvement with the project. Jim was furious—he's one of the homeless who has very involved."

"Yeah, I've met Jim," I said without much enthusiasm.

She gave me a wry look. "He's not exactly a barrel of laughs, is he? But I have to admit, he's been really helpful, especially in working with our planners to design the development." She waved a hand at the artist's sketch.

I glanced up at the poster again. "I suppose he was hoping to get his own place at last."

"Well, funnily enough, Jim didn't apply for one of the units," said the receptionist.

"He didn't?"

She shrugged. "We all expected him to be the first in line to request a unit—and he would have got first dibs too, given all the hard work he's done. But ironically, he won't be one of those who would benefit directly from the project." She shrugged. "People are weird. I think sometimes they care more about the 'cause' and the principles and everything, than the actual material benefits."

I thought of Seth, secure in his comfortable Oxford college life, getting all worked up for something he had no direct benefit from, and for people he didn't really know and would probably never spend much time with. "Yeah, you're right. People are weird sometimes," I agreed.

"Still, with the way things are going, it's not going to matter either way..." she said and gave another sigh.

Back outside the Domus Trust offices, I was about to get astride my bike again when I noticed the building on the street corner opposite. In large letters etched above the front entrance were the words: "DEPARTMENT OF ETHNOARCHAEOLOGY".

This must be Professor Barrow's department... and Leila Gaber's too, I thought.

On a sudden impulse, I went into the building. It

was full of students, post graduate research fellows, and academic dons, busily walking and talking in pairs, most of them leaving the building, on their way back to their homes or colleges. I wandered casually over to the department directory and glanced through the list of names. Then I turned towards the main staircase leading up from the lobby—but I had barely gone up a few steps when I paused.

What was I doing? Even if I could find out where Leila Gaber's office was, how was I going to get any information about her? I didn't know any of her colleagues and they weren't likely to just strike up conversation with me and tell me all the sordid details of the gossip about her. I didn't even have a legitimate reason for wandering around the department...

Then my eye caught sight of a few signs at the top of the stairs: "TOILETS", "LECTURE THEATRE", and then "CANTEEN" with a little arrow next to it.

I brightened. I might not be able to talk about the intricacies of ethnographic data in archaeological records, but there was one thing I could talk about with ease: tea and cakes.

I hurried up the rest of the steps and made my way to the canteen. It was almost closing and I was grateful that I'd got there just in time. A single woman was wiping one of the counters whilst humming to a song on a radio in the kitchen behind her. She was plump and motherly, with a pleasant, good-humoured face, and looked the epitome of the traditional British "tea lady", employed to make and serve tea in a workplace. I thought she also looked the type to enjoy a good gossip. Crossing my fingers behind my back and hoping that I was right, I approached her.

"Hello... Is the canteen closed?"

She looked up. "Ah, well... I can do one more," she said with a smile. "What can I get you, love?"

"Oh, that looks delicious," I said, pointing to a sad-looking plate of congealed apple crumble. I wouldn't have been seen dead serving that in my tearoom, but I said enthusiastically, "You can't beat a good old-fashioned British pudding, can you?"

"No, dearie, you certainly can't an' that's what I tell my Norman. He's always rabbitin' on, wantin' to move to places like Spain. Costa del Sol, he says! 'Coast of the Sun', it's called. We could get a villa by the beach an' everythin'." She made a face at me. "Coast of the Sun, my foot! They don't know how to serve proper tea in these foreigner places! And I'm not goin' anywhere I can't get a decent cuppa."

"You're so right," I said quickly. "I was in Sydney for eight years and I went to some of the best cafés in Paddington, but none of them could serve a decent cup of tea," I lied, hoping that some of my favourite cafés Down Under would forgive me.

She nodded. "Oh yes... those Australians. They've got some right awful tea, don't they? Billy tea, I heard it's called! Has the most disgustin' smell."

Actually, billy tea was a beloved Australian icon—

a bush tea that was a blend of tropical tea leaves from northern Queensland and eucalyptus leaves. It got its name from the "billy can"—the traditional tin can used to heat hot water over the campfire—and had a strong, smoky flavour which *was* a bit of an acquired taste for some people, but hardly the horror she was making it out to be. Still, I made a sound of agreement and said:

"I don't think anything compares to a proper cup of English tea."

She slapped the counter in agreement with me. "That's right, dearie. I'm sure now that you're back in England, you'll be glad to have some *real* tea."

And she proceeded to prove her point by pouring me a cup of thick brown brew that was practically a sludge of solid tannins. I kept the smile on my face with effort as I accepted the cup from her, praying that my gastrointestinal tract was coated with enough acid to cope with it.

"Go on," she urged me. "Take a sip. Tell me—isn't that how a cuppa tea ought to be?"

I took a cautious sip, stopping myself just in time before I grimaced and spat it back out. It was sharp and bitter and so astringent that my teeth almost shrank in my mouth.

I swallowed with some difficulty, then pasted a shaky smile on my face and said, "Yeah, this... this is just what I've missed."

"Oh, silly me—I forgot to add milk," she said. And without asking me, she reached over and poured a large glug of yellow milk into my tea, which promptly turned a sickly shade of brown.

"Er... thanks. That's great." Terrified that she would urge me to take another sip, I added quickly, "You must meet a lot of foreign students and academics working here. Do you find that they don't really know how to appreciate proper English tea?"

She gave me a dark look. "Oh, them foreigners. The whole department's run amok with them. Most of 'em are all right," she said generously. "The students especially—they seem to make a real effort to try new things... But some of them top lofty academics... professors an' such... Think they know everythin', they do."

"That must be really exasperating for you," I said, giving her a sympathetic look.

"Jolly right! Only yesterday I had to tell Professor Wang that there was nothin' wrong with the peas. They're *supposed* to be all mushy an' brown in colour. That's why they're called mushy peas, see?"

"Mm, yes..." I said, wondering how to bring the subject around to Leila Gaber in a natural way that wouldn't raise suspicions. Then I realised that I was worrying too much. Someone like this tea lady loved the chance to gossip so much, it would never enter her head to wonder why I was asking.

I took the plunge and said, "What about Dr Gaber? I met her at a party recently and she seemed quite... um... exotic. I don't suppose she would take very well to English customs?"

"Her!" The tea lady sniffed. "Thinks she's the Queen of Sheba, she does! Complainin' about this and complainin' about that. Last Tuesday, she had the cheek to tell me that my sponge cake was dry! As if I don't know how a sponge cake ought to taste like! Well, I told my Norman, I said, I've been makin' sponge cakes since the time when she was—"

"Uh... yes," I said hurriedly. "I... um... I'd been hearing stories about Dr Gaber—seems she's been involved in some sort of scandal?"

"Ooh, yes, I've heard those stories goin' round the department too..." She leaned towards me and lowered her voice conspiratorially. "They say she's in Oxford because she's runnin' away from somethin' back in Egypt."

"Running away from what?"

She wagged her finger at me. "Well, there's been talk... Katie in HR was talkin' to Sue May who mentioned it to Mel, who told me... They say she was arrested."

"*Arrested!*" I stared. "What was she arrested for?"

"Well, as to that, no one's quite sure..." She shrugged. "Something to do with a colleague, I think. She drowned in the Nile, you see—the colleague, I mean—an' they said it was an accident... but then there was some talk, maybe it wasn't an accident after all... an' the woman worked with Dr Gaber, you know. But in the end, they couldn't pin anythin' on her so they had to let her go. But there was more talk and people were scared to work with her after that..."

She leaned towards me. "Mind you, I think that woman is capable of anythin'. You've only got to look in her eyes to know. Don't think she'd think twice about doin' away with someone…" Then she leaned back, clasped her hands under her bosom, and said: "Now, what else can I get you, love?"—as if she hadn't just been accusing a woman of murder.

"Um… nothing, thanks," I said, desperate to keep her talking. "So did you hear anything else about Dr Gaber's background? Why do you think the Egyptian police suspected her of her colleague's murder? How—"

I broke off as I realised that the tea lady was no longer listening to me. Instead she was looking over my shoulder with an expression of horror and dismay on her face.

I whirled around and found myself facing Leila Gaber.

CHAPTER TWENTY-FOUR

"D...Dr. Gaber," I stammered. "I was just—"

"Yes, I heard," said Leila Gaber, taking a step towards me.

I stumbled backwards and felt the counter bump against my hip. It was stupid, but looking into the woman's dark eyes in front of me, I felt a flash of fear. I could see that she was furious, though she kept her temper under control and her voice was silky as she said:

"You seem to be very inquisitive about my past, Miss Rose. Perhaps I can help enlighten you. In Egypt, we believe it is only polite when someone has questions to ask that person directly first—I had thought that the rules would be the same in England but perhaps I was wrong?"

I flushed, feeling like a schoolgirl being chastised

by the headmistress.

"I... I'm sorry," I stammered. "I was just curious..."

She raised a well-groomed eyebrow. "Ah... well, you know what they say about curiosity and the cat..."

That Mona Lisa smile was in place again but there was no mistaking the sense of threat emanating from her. Although her lips offered explanations, her eyes dared me to ask further. I didn't like to admit it, but she intimidated me. I lowered my eyes from her gaze and fumbled with the handle of my teacup.

"Dr Gaber—are you after a nice cuppa tea?" the tea lady said behind me with false cheerfulness. "Else I'm closin' up."

"Yes, and I'd better get going too," I said hastily.

I fished in my pocket for some change and put it on the counter to pay for my tea, then gave Leila Gaber a slightly shame-faced smile and quickly left the canteen. I knew I was running away like a dog with its tail between its legs, but I also knew that it was useless to stay and fight. Leila Gaber was on her home ground here and would always have the advantage over me. Better to regroup and tackle her another day.

***

There was something ominously familiar about being dragged out of sleep by the shrill ringing of my phone. I rose on an elbow and groped on my bedside table, my heart pounding. It was like a repeat of a bad dream—I almost expected to hear Seth's voice on the other end of the line—so it took me a moment to realise who was speaking.

"Darling, you simply must help me talk to this man!"

"Mother?" I sat up groggily. I leaned over and glanced at the clock on my bedside table. The glowing numbers read 2:35 a.m.

"Mother, is everything all right? Are you still in Jakarta?"

"Yes, yes, we're at Carita Beach. You *must* help us speak to this fisherman."

"Fisherman?" I was struggling to gather my thoughts. "What fisherman? What are you talking about?"

"The fisherman who is taking us to Krakatoa, of course!" said my mother impatiently. "He is ever so stubborn and just will not budge. Helen and I have been trying for the last twenty minutes—and really, I must say, we've become *quite* the experienced hagglers—we have been following your instructions to the letter and I even told the hotel yesterday that I should get a discount on the room rate since I've brought my own toiletries and I'm not using theirs," she added proudly. "But we just can't seem to persuade this fisherman to agree to anything! I wonder if the problem is that he doesn't speak English? Anyway, I thought you could speak to him…"

I groaned. "Mother, you didn't just ring me up at

two in the morning to haggle with an Indonesian fisherman on the other side of the world?"

"Oh, is that the time? I was so sure that I got the time difference right. Isn't it four-thirty in the afternoon in Oxford?"

"No," I growled. "It's two-thirty in the morning."

"Oh dear. I suppose I must have read the time zones the wrong way around or something. I downloaded an App on my phone, you see," she said importantly. "Dorothy Clarke told me about them and you can get an App for all sorts of things—it really is marvellous—and I've got one to tell me the different times around the world. Let me see..." My mother's voice faded away slightly as she looked at her screen. "Is it this one? No... That's the Melon Meter App—it tells you when a watermelon is ripe, darling—isn't that wonderful? Hmm... and this is the Anti-Mosquito Sonic Repeller App—so clever, it gives off a special frequency which repels mosquitoes and other nasty bugs—although I must say, it doesn't really seem to work... Maybe this one? Helen, do you think the App for the time zones was called Rooster Time Clock?"

"Never mind, Mother," I said wearily. "Please just remember that we are seven hours behind you in the U.K.... Mother? Are you still there?"

"Sorry, darling... what was that? Oh, Helen's just waving to me. The fisherman seems to have agreed! Marvellous! Right, must dash—"

"Wait, Mother—"

But she was gone. I put the phone down and stared at the glowing screen, then flopped over backwards on my pillow with a sigh of exasperation. *Aaaargh! My mother!*

"*Meorrw...*" said Muesli sleepily from the foot of the bed, where she was curled up amongst the folds of the blanket. She yawned widely, showing me her sharp little white teeth, then lowered her head, tucked her tail under her chin and shut her eyes again, purring softly.

I pulled the covers over myself and tried to go back to sleep, hoping that the sound of my purring cat would lull me back into slumber.... but I was wide awake now, my head buzzing with Indonesian fishermen and ripe watermelons. I tossed and turned, trying all the tricks that I had been told: emptying the mind, focusing on my breathing, visualising my body relaxing, counting sheep, counting watermelons...

Finally, I turned onto my back again and stared up at the ceiling in the dark. It was no use trying to keep my mind blank so I let it wander where it wanted to... which was right back to the murder. Something was still nagging me... it had been bothering me for a while now... like a piece of food stuck between your teeth: you can't find it with your fingers when you try to pluck it out and yet you know it's there, you can feel it... probing it with your tongue...

It was something to do with Richard Barrow and

his escape from Wadsworth... Why hadn't anyone seen him?

And something else too—something I had heard at the Oxford Society of Medicine dinner... and...

... *and something about Muesli*, I thought suddenly. Something that had struck me last night after the firemen had left... of how she had managed to go down one vent and come up another one on the other side of the room, where we had least expected it...

That's it!

I sat bolt upright in bed, causing Muesli to give a disgruntled *meorrw!*

That's the answer! It has to be!

I realised now what had been nagging me from the Society of Medicine dinner. That conversation about Christ Church's concealed staircase leading from the dining hall down into the S.C.R. below, which was the inspiration for the rabbit hole in *Alice in Wonderland*... And Christ Church wasn't the only Oxford college with hidden staircases and passageways...

There must have been another way out of the Cloisters—a shortcut—that led directly from the Cloister arcades out of the main gate, without the need to go through that long roundabout detour, through the tunnel and Walled Garden and then across the two quads of the college.

Yes, I was certain of it. Wadsworth must have its own secret passage which connected the Cloisters with the outside world. And the murderer must have used it to escape.

CHAPTER TWENTY-FIVE

At last, I fell into an uneasy sleep and was deeply unconscious when my phone rang again. I opened my eyes blearily. *It must be my mother again. God knows what she wants me to do now.* Struggling out of the tangle of blankets, I scooped up my phone and snarled, "What is it *now?*"

"I see you're still not a morning person," came an amused male voice.

"Oh! Devlin..." I spluttered, sitting up slowly. "Sorry... I thought... I thought you were my mother."

"Your mother?" He sounded faintly puzzled.

I sighed. "My mother's gone off to Indonesia with her friend and she woke me up in the middle of the night to ask me how to bargain with a fisherman at the beach..." I heard something that sounded suspiciously like laughter and said grumpily, "It's not funny. It took me ages to get back to sleep afterwards and—*Oh!*" I remembered what I had been thinking as I'd drifted off to sleep again. "Devlin, I've got something to tell you! I think I've figured out how the murderer escaped from the Cloister! I think Richard Barrow—"

"That was why I was ringing you, actually," said Devlin. "This is confidential information, you understand, but I appreciated what you did yesterday, telling me immediately about what Glenda Bailey had learnt from the head porter, so I feel it's only right to return the gesture."

"Thanks." I felt a flush of pleasure. I remembered that Devlin had said that he would be going to Reading this morning to interview Richard Barrow. "Are you back in Oxford?"

"No, I'm still in Reading—I've just come from Joan Barrow's house, actually."

"Did you speak to Richard?" I asked eagerly.

"No. He gave me the slip," said Devlin, his voice thick with annoyance. "That man must have run from the police several times in the past—he's too practised at it. But I managed to pin his sister down. She didn't know everything—I think Richard was careful about what he told her—but she did confirm that he was at Wadsworth last Friday—the night of the murder—staying in the college guest room. He'd gone to Oxford hoping to persuade Barrow to pull him out of a tight spot."

"He owed money and was in debt," I guessed.

"Yes, a fair amount, I think," said Devlin dryly. "Our friend Richard is a bit of a wheeler-dealer and had got himself in with a bad crowd, making some big promises he couldn't keep. Now he owes money to some very bad people. And I've had some experience with these organised crime gangs he's involved with—they can be very unforgiving of those they think are trying to pull one over them."

"You mean he's on the run?"

"I wouldn't put it as dramatically as that—sounds like something out of a Hollywood film! But yes, I think he was getting desperate. He had no money, nowhere to go, and these gangs after him."

"And he thought Quentin Barrow would help him?"

"Apparently his brother had bailed him out before. But Barrow had warned Richard last time that he wasn't going to do it again and it seems like he stuck to his word—refused to help him this time. Joan told me they had a pretty heated discussion on Friday morning..."

"Heated enough that Richard decided the next best way to get the money was to kill his brother and get his share of the estate?"

"That's something I could find out from Richard Barrow himself—if I could interrogate him." Devlin sounded frustrated. "I'd like to know where he was at the time of the murder—Joan says he was in the guest room, but I don't know if she's lying to protect him or if Richard lied to her..."

"Quentin Barrow was quite a hypocrite, wasn't he?" I said in disgust. "Telling people he was against charitable giving and not helping the homeless because they deserved their lot—but then when it was his own brother, he wouldn't chuck him out on the street. He got him a guest room in college."

"I think that's why he wanted to keep it quiet. It would have been embarrassing for him to admit that he couldn't follow his own words. And since he knew that Peters the head porter was running this little scheme on the side..."

I remembered suddenly what I had been wanting to tell Devlin. Quickly, I recounted my idea about the hidden passageway out of the Cloisters.

"It would explain how Richard got out of the Cloisters so quickly, after the murder was committed, without anyone seeing him," I said excitedly.

Devlin sounded sceptical. "Secret passage? Gemma, this isn't some Gothic novel—"

"No, but this is Oxford," I insisted. "And hidden staircases and secret passageways are par for the course here in these ancient college buildings. You know that."

"Hmm..." Devlin still didn't sound convinced.

"We need to speak to Clyde Peters," I said. "He's the key to the whole thing. I'll bet he would know about any hidden passageways at Wadsworth—he's been the head porter there for years. And Glenda said that he told her he managed to get Richard out before the police arrived. I'd been wondering how he managed that. This would explain it. We just need to ask him. Have you tracked him down yet?"

"It was his day off yesterday but he wasn't at home. I left messages for him but he hasn't returned them yet. He should have been back in the Porter's Lodge at Wadsworth this morning, but he hasn't turned up, apparently. No one has any idea where he is."

I frowned. "I saw him on Wednesday night—the day before yesterday..."

"Where?"

"At Gees, when I was there with Lincoln..." I faltered slightly. "You know, when I told you what Glenda Bailey had found out from Clyde Peters... that was there. I saw them having dinner together."

"You didn't tell me you were there yourself as well." Devlin's voice was carefully neutral.

"No, well, I... I didn't get a chance. I just wanted to get you that information about Richard Barrow first... and then you had to dash off..."

I was stammering, embarrassed, defensive, and I was irritated with myself. Why should I have felt guilty about being on a date with another man? Like I told Cassie, it wasn't as if Devlin and I had actually made a commitment to each other yet. Still, I couldn't help the colour that crept to my cheeks and I was glad Devlin couldn't see me.

I cleared my throat and continued, as nonchalantly as possible, "So Clyde Peters was certainly fine on Wednesday night. Didn't anyone see him yesterday?"

"My sergeant is questioning some of his neighbours and colleagues now. It might be nothing; he might have gone away on a fishing trip or something and got held up coming back, although it's odd that he hasn't contacted the college to let them know. According to the college offices, he's incredibly conscientious—almost pedantic—and in all his forty years of duty at the college, he's only ever been late to work twice. Both times, it was due to things outside his control, like a traffic accident on the roads—but he always contacted them."

"You think something's happened to him," I said.

"I think Clyde Peters is in a position to know a lot about who was where on the night of the murder. Perhaps too much for his own safety."

"And... you don't think he might be the murderer himself?" I asked, voicing the thought that had been at the back of my mind. "I mean, we've all been focusing on everyone else, but Peters was there that night as well and nobody suspects him because he's the college porter. It was very convenient that he happened to discover Seth just at the moment when Seth was standing there holding the knife," I said bitterly. "If he was looking for a scapegoat and another suspect to distract the police, he practically had it handed to him on a plate..."

"Maybe." Devlin sounded sceptical again. "But a lot of things don't add up. For one thing, if Peters was really keen to hide his little guest room scam from the college authorities, the last thing he would want to do is bring attention to the fact that he was in the Cloisters at that time. Sooner or later, we would have double-checked why he was there and his lame excuse of making a college round wouldn't have really washed. The truth would come out very quickly. No, I think it would have been more in his interests—if he had committed the murder—to quietly return to the Porter's Lodge and wait until the murder was discovered by someone else, when he was a safe distance away from the whole thing.

"And besides," Devlin continued. "He has no motive. There's no reason why he would want Barrow dead."

"Maybe there's a motive we haven't discovered yet," I persisted. "Maybe there's some connection between him and Barrow going way back... They've both been at Wadsworth for a long time. Maybe... maybe... it's revenge! For something Barrow did to Peters, long ago."

"Yes, but why wait until now to get vengeance?"

I blew out a breath of frustration. "We seem to just keep going around in circles on this case!"

"Welcome to the real world of detective work," Devlin said with a dry laugh. "It's only in mystery novels that you get clues laid out for you to find and everything gets solved quickly with a nice ribbon on top."

There was a beep and Devlin said, "Hold on, I've

just had a message..." A long pause, then he returned to the line: "My sergeant has just informed me that he's picked up a lead. Clyde Peters was seen at his local pub late last night. I've got an interview set up with the landlord this afternoon... I've got to stop by the police station here in Reading first, but I'll catch the next train back to Oxford after that."

"Can I come?" I said eagerly.

Devlin made an exasperated noise. "Gemma. You know I'm not even supposed to be sharing the details of the investigation with you. I called you this morning as a special favour in return for yesterday, but don't start getting any ideas. No, this is a police interview and you can't come. You should know better than to even ask."

"Fine," I said, annoyed. "I suppose I'll have to wait to read about the arrest in the papers!"

Devlin chuckled. "You know what your problem is, Gemma? You don't like not being in control. You want to be involved in everything and you just can't bear it if you're not in the driver's seat. Look, you've been a big help and I appreciate it, but you've *got* to step back now and let the police do their job."

His laughter grated on my nerves and I hung up before I would say something I regretted.

CHAPTER TWENTY-SIX

The phone call with Devlin had made me late for work, but I was relieved to see that Cassie was already there when I arrived. She was showing Dora around the kitchen with a pride that was almost comical, given her complete inability to use any of the equipment she was talking about.

I was impressed with how quickly Dora took everything on board and instantly began working on the first batch of scones. An hour later the gorgeous smell of fresh baking was filling the kitchen and Cassie and I watched eagerly through the oven window as the little mounds of scone dough slowly rose, their tops smooth and golden brown, their sides beautifully scalloped. I could feel my mouth watering just looking at them, as the warm, buttery smell of baking filled my nostrils.

"They're not going to bake faster if you watch them, you know," came Dora's amused voice from behind us.

I turned to see her standing comfortably at the wooden table, her hands covered in flour, expertly kneading a huge slab of dough. Already, she looked so at home—as if she had always been there—and I felt a deep sense of happiness and relief at having found my baking chef at last.

As if reading my thoughts, Dora gave me a whimsical smile and said, "I'd forgotten how good it is to have something to do. I'm not made to be idle. Funny—when I was working at Wadsworth, I used to wish for the time when I could retire, but when I really stopped working, I found that I missed it terribly. I guess you get used to a routine."

Her mention of Wadsworth stirred something in my mind. "Dora..." I said, going across to her. "When you were working at the college, did you ever hear of any hidden passages or secret staircases?"

She looked surprised. "Secret staircases?"

I gave a sheepish smile. "I know, it sounds a bit silly. But I thought... well, a lot of Oxford colleges seem to have them... I just wondered if Wadsworth might have had one too."

She frowned. "Well, I don't know about secret passages, but there *was* an old staircase which led from the Porter's Lodge through the back of the tower and into the Cloisters behind it."

My pulse quickened. "I'd never heard of it. Is it still

in use?"

"No, it's been closed for years. In fact, I remember it being closed up about a year after I started working there. It had fallen into disrepair and it was too dangerous to use and not worth the expense of restoring. So they decided to close it up—didn't want the students finding it and having an accident, especially when they get a bit drunk and rowdy after a party."

I stared at her, my thoughts racing. "And who would have known about this staircase?"

She shrugged. "Some of the older members of the staff, I guess. The porters in the Lodge, old Clyde Peters, Darrel Wood, James Price... young Dave Malvern—Skinny Dave, we used to call him, all arms and legs he was—gosh, he'd be coming up for middle age now, fancy that—how time flies!" Her face broke into a soft smile of reminiscing. "He left to work for Oxford University Press... wonder how he's getting on? And some of the other older scouts, of course, such as my friend, Agnes... The newer members of the staff wouldn't know about it—it would have been boarded up and we didn't have much reason to mention it."

"So Clyde Peters would definitely have known about this staircase?"

Dora's face soured and she pursed her lips. "That old woman? Yes, I'm sure he would; he was a great one for always sticking his nose into everything and being a general busybody. Besides, the entrance to the staircase was behind a panel at the back of the porter's office in the Lodge."

I sank down on one of the chairs by the wooden table, my mind working furiously. According to everybody, Clyde Peters was a bit of an old gossip and probably inclined to talk and show off. I was willing to bet that he had told Richard Barrow about the hidden staircase—either earlier when he was showing the professor's younger brother the guest room or when he was helping Richard escape after the murder. Maybe he had even been in cahoots with Richard—perhaps the latter had offered to pay him a sum of money to help get rid of his brother...

Clyde Peters had all the answers. If only we could have found out where he was! Then I thought of Devlin and his interview with the pub landlord in Abingdon—the pub where the head porter had last been seen... I chafed at the thought of sitting here, waiting, waiting, while Devlin got crucial information about the case...

I sprang up from my chair. "Cassie, listen—do you think you can manage for a bit by yourself? I need to pop out to do something."

"Yeah, sure," said Cassie. "Now that Dora's here, I haven't really got anything to do in the kitchen anyway, so I'll be out with the customers." She looked at me curiously. "Where are you going?"

I hesitated. Cassie could be so volatile—and she was so emotionally involved in this case—that I wasn't sure how much I should tell her.

"Oh... just a possible lead on the case," I said lightly.

Cassie's eyes lit up. She followed me out of the tearoom and stood on the front step, rubbing her arms against the cold, watching me as I unlocked and mounted my bike.

"Is this a lead on the real murderer?" she asked.

"I'm not sure yet," I said cautiously.

"Gemma, we've *got* to get somewhere soon," she said. "Have you seen Seth lately? I went to see him last night—he's lost so much weight! I think he's getting depressed. I spent a couple of hours with him and he hardly said anything to me. And then he rushed me out, as if he had to go somewhere..."

"Well, maybe he *did* have to go somewhere."

She frowned. "Yes, but he was being really furtive about it. I mean, he wouldn't give me any details and that's not like him at all—if anything, he's usually trying to get me to go along to some obscure university society thing with him. I tried teasing him about it but he hardly responded. It was like he was afraid of letting me know what he was going to do. Gemma, we've been friends for yonks! Seth never keeps secrets from me!"

I gave Cassie a wry look. In fact, Seth had kept one very big secret from her for a very long time: he'd been secretly in love with her ever since the day they met. For someone who claimed to be an expert on romantic affairs, Cassie was pretty oblivious to what was going on right underneath her own nose.

Still, I could understand why Seth had never got the courage to confess his feelings. Cassie was beautiful and vivacious and had hordes of men eating out of her hands. It was easy to see why someone as diffident and studious as Seth would never have dared dream that he might have a chance with her.

"Cut him some slack," I said gently. "Seth's under a lot of strain at the moment. He's probably not himself."

Cassie sighed and stood watching, a troubled expression on her face, as I waved to her, then pushed off and cycled away.

***

Abingdon was an old market town to the south of Oxford, famous for Morris dancing and its quaint tradition of "bun throwing"—when the local dignitaries would throw buns into the assembled crowds from the roof of the County Hall Museum on specific days of celebration, such as royal marriages, coronations, and jubilees. Apparently the museum there had a collection of dried buns from throwings dating back to the 19th century. I shuddered to think of them.

I had been worried at first that I wouldn't be able to find the pub. Devlin hadn't mentioned the name, just that it was Clyde Peters's "local". Well, I might not have all the resources available to the police, but

I had other tricks up my sleeve. A quick call to Glenda Bailey and a few moments later I had the name of Clyde Peters's favourite pub: The Goose and Feather in Abingdon.

I saw the landlord as soon as I walked in. He was behind the bar, fiddling with one of the beer taps. He looked up as I approached him, a practised smile on his face.

"Drink or lunch?" he said.

I gave him a smile in return. "Neither, actually. I was hoping you might have a moment to chat."

"About what?"

"One of your regulars—Clyde Peters."

He raised his eyebrows. "You from the CID? I was told the detective would be in to see me this afternoon."

I looked at him, thinking quickly. Despite his hale and hearty appearance—the big paunch, beefy arms, and rosy-cheeked face—I could see the wary expression in his eyes as he assessed me. The image of the jolly bartender was deceptive; here was a careful, shrewd businessman who would never speak to me unless he thought I had some kind of authority. I hesitated, then made an impulsive decision.

"Yes, I work with Detective O'Connor." *It wasn't really a lie*, I thought. *I'm not trying to impersonate the police—it's not my fault if he assumes more than I meant.*

The landlord looked at me silently for a moment—

so long that I thought he was going to call me a liar—then he said, "Well, now, what d'you want to know?"

"Clyde Peters was in here last night?"

"Usual table there, in the corner." He nodded towards the far end of the pub.

"Was he alone?"

"He was when I saw him. But I had to pop out for a bit last night—problem at home with the Missus—so my barmaid, Jenny, took over for a while until I got back. I can call her, if you like."

"Please."

A young girl with wispy blonde hair and a mouth full of gum responded to his summons. She screwed up her face in an effort to remember.

"Dunno... it was real busy in here last night. I wasn't payin' much attention to the customers, if ya know what I mean. Just takin' orders and deliverin' drinks. Oh yeah, I think I remember old Clyde," she said, chewing the gum. "Over in the corner."

"Was he alone the whole night?" I asked again

She frowned. "Not sure. No... I think there might have been a chap with him at one point."

"Did you recognise him?"

She shook his head. "Dunno. Didn't get a proper look at him. Had his back to the room and was wearing a beanie and a coat."

"Do you know if he was a friend of Clyde Peters?" I asked, fishing desperately.

She shrugged. "Dunno. I was rushed off my feet last night and like I said, I wasn't payin' much attention to the customers—just the orders... I did hear him say somethin' when I stopped by to collect the empty glasses from their table."

"What?" I asked eagerly.

"Somethin' 'bout Oxford," she said.

Great. That was a big help. I resisted the urge to roll my eyes. "Like... as a tourist? Or did he sound like he lived there?"

She shrugged again. "Dunno. Something 'bout things lookin' different on Cornmarket. And he mentioned a college..."

"Clyde is the head porter at one of the Oxford colleges," the landlord put in helpfully. "He's worked there for years and met a lot of people in the course of his job."

"You think maybe this stranger used to work in Oxford—maybe even at the college—and he and Clyde were old friends?"

"Dunno." The girl shrugged and looked bored.

I sighed and gave up.

The landlord said, obviously trying to make up for his barmaid's lack of effort, "Or maybe this chap visited the college before when Clyde was workin' there? A porter would meet a lot of the visitors to a college."

I nodded and tried another tack. "Did you see if they left together?"

I thought the girl was going to say "Dunno" again and I had to restrain myself from shaking her—but she frowned and said, "No, this chap left first, I think.

Yeah, that's right—Clyde stayed on for another pint. Didn't leave until closin' time."

"Yes, I was back by then," the landlord chimed in. "I took that last order."

"Was he drunk when he left?"

"He had a couple—was a bit merry—but I wouldn't call him drunk." The landlord looked at me curiously. "Why all these questions? Is Clyde in some kind of trouble?"

"We're just gathering information at this point," I said, assuming my best police press-release voice. "We've been trying to locate Mr Peters to speak to him in connection to a case, but we haven't been able to locate him yet."

The landlord raised his eyebrows. "Have you tried his college—Wadsworth? Clyde practically lives there."

"Yes, we have, but we haven't been able to get hold of him there either." I leaned forwards. "So nothing strange or suspicious happened last night? Clyde didn't get into any fights or mention being worried or scared about anything...?"

"No." Both he and the barmaid shook their heads. "Can't help you there, sorry."

She left us and he began gathering some bottles together, while I stood at a loss. I was disappointed. I had to admit, I'd been hoping that the landlord would have some story of a violent fight between Clyde and some long-time enemy, or that he'd overhead a mysterious stranger making veiled threats at the head porter...

I smiled wryly to myself. Maybe Devlin was right—real life wasn't like mystery novels. Still, I wasn't ready to give up. The landlord had picked up a box and was descending a flight of rickety wooden stairs down into the basement below. I hurried after him and found myself in a snug little cellar.

"Do you know if Clyde Peters was in any kind of money trouble?"

"Him? Naw... he was a sly old fox. Always knew how to make a spare bob or two on the side. He did like a bit of a flutter, mind you."

"Betting? Horses?"

"Dogs. Greyhound track down in Cowley."

"And what about... um... ladyfriends? He was single, right?"

He started to answer but we were interrupted by Jenny the barmaid popping her head into the gap at the top of the stairs. "There's a gentleman here to see you," she called down. "Says he's a detective inspector from the CID."

My heart lurched. *Oh hell! That must be Devlin.* He'd come back to Oxford sooner than I expected. How was I going to explain my presence here to him?

I wondered frantically if there was any way I could run up the cellar stairs and slip out of the pub before Devlin saw me, but my hopes were dashed when I heard a step on the cellar stairs. A moment later, his lithe figure joined us in the small, cramped space. He was so tall that he had to stoop slightly and his cool blue eyes registered surprise when he saw me, though he masked it very well.

"Ah, Inspector—I was just talking to your partner here," said the landlord.

I held my breath, looking at Devlin, expecting him to expose me. Instead, to my surprise, he merely gave the landlord a nod and said:

"I apologise for my delay, sir. I was held up in Reading. But I'm glad that my *partner*—" he put a slight stress on the word and I flushed, "—was able to speak to you first."

"Well, we have pretty much told her everything we know," said the landlord. "I hope you're not going to make us repeat everything again. I've got a lot of things to get done before the lunch rush starts."

"No, we won't trouble you any more for now, sir," said Devlin, putting a proprietary hand under my elbow and hustling me up the cellar stairs. "I'll let you know if we need to ask any more questions."

We came out of the pub and stood in the weak winter sunshine together. It was promising to be a slightly warmer day today, with the sky a pale blue instead of the usual ominous grey. There was the first hint of spring in the air.

"Thanks for not exposing me in there," I said meekly.

Devlin gave me an annoyed look. "I could have you arrested for impersonating the police, Gemma."

I winced. "I know, I know... I'm sorry... I just... I just couldn't bear the thought of sitting around waiting... and I wanted to know what he had to say about Clyde Peters!"

Devlin looked as if he wanted to say something else, then held onto his temper with an effort. He ran a hand through his dark hair, causing an unruly lock to fall over his eyes, the way it used to when he was a student. My fingers itched to reach up and brush it away.

He took a deep breath, then let it out in a sigh. "So what did the landlord say?"

Quickly, I repeated what I had learned.

"Hmm... I wonder if this 'friend' that Peters was having a drink with was Richard Barrow," mused Devlin. "He would have visited Wadsworth years before—we know he came to Barrow for help before—perhaps he and Peters got friendly then. In fact, maybe he didn't give me the slip this morning; maybe Richard wasn't in Reading at all! He was here in Oxford last night, and is still here today."

"You know, I've been thinking..." I said excitedly. "Maybe it isn't one man. Maybe it's *two* men working together,". "Maybe Richard Barrow got the head porter involved in a plan to murder his brother, in return for a sum of money. And now Peters is running scared..."

"Yes, but—"

We were interrupted by the sound of a phone beeping. Devlin pulled out his mobile, glancing at the screen.

"It's my sergeant," he said, frowning. He listened

and I saw his face change. "Right. I'm on my way."

"What? What's happened?" I said, as he lowered the phone.

Devlin looked at me, his expression grim. "Clyde Peters's body has just been found in Jericho. Looks like he'd been hit on the back of the head and pushed into the canal."

CHAPTER TWENTY-SEVEN

The next morning, the whole tearoom was abuzz with the news of the second murder. The fuss from Barrow's death had barely settled down and here was a fresh killing already. The gossips were in overdrive, with Mabel Cooke leading the pack. She and the other Old Biddies had commandeered one of the tearoom's largest tables, with what looked like half the village gathered around them.

"I always knew that porter would come to a bad end," said Mabel smugly as she poured herself another cup of tea. "I knew it. I have an instinct for these things."

"Did he say anything when you were out at dinner together, Glenda?" asked one of the other villagers. "Like..." She dropped her voice to a theatrical whisper. "Did he mention being *in fear of his life*?"

Glenda screwed up her face, trying hard to remember something that could fit this dramatic scenario. She was enjoying all the attention she was getting—by virtue of her one brief dinner with Clyde Peters, she had become something of a local celebrity in Meadowford-on-Smythe—but even she couldn't stretch the truth to fit in with their histrionic imaginings.

She said regretfully, "No, he didn't. He seemed in very good spirits, actually."

"Well, what about gangs?" said another village resident, her mouth half full of buttered teacakes. "They say there are all sorts of organised crime groups from Eastern Europe these days. Those crooks from Albania—wasn't there an article about them in the papers?"

"I think it was one of the students at the college," said another villager darkly. "All these foreign students arriving at Oxford and you have no idea where they come from—maybe Clyde Peters saw them doing something they shouldn't and they killed him to stop him telling the college authorities!"

I smiled to myself as I passed their table, bearing a tray of tea and scones for the group of American tourists by the window. Hollywood directors should just come to Meadowford and mine the villagers' imaginations, if they need ideas for their next movies! I returned to the counter to find Cassie there and the smile faded from my own face as I saw the strained expression on hers. Her mind was obviously elsewhere as she stood staring into space, whilst a cup of hot chocolate cooled on the counter in front of her.

"You'd better take that over to the table before it turns into iced chocolate," I said.

She gave a start. "Oh. Sorry, Gemma..." She looked down in dismay at the mug on the counter. "I'll make a fresh cup."

She turned away but I stopped her with a gentle hand on her arm. "Cassie, are you all right?"

She gave me a troubled look. "I saw Seth this morning—I popped in to see him before coming in to work—and I caught him just as he was leaving his college rooms. He was heading to the police station."

"The police station?"

She nodded miserably. "They've called him in for questioning again, in connection with Clyde Peters's murder. I guess they want to check his alibi."

"Well, I wouldn't worry about it. I'm sure Seth had nothing to do with the porter's death."

Cassie didn't say anything for a moment, then she said in a rush, "Gemma, I'm worried about Seth."

"Well, we all are..." I trailed off and looked at her. "Do you mean something specific?"

Cassie hesitated. "He had a black eye this morning."

I frowned. "How did he get that?"

"That's just it! He wouldn't tell me! I mean, he said he tripped and banged his head against the side of the door and gave himself a black eye—"

"Well, I suppose that *could* have happened," I said doubtfully.

"Oh, Gemma, that's rubbish and you know it! Who gets a black eye from bumping into a door? It was obvious that he was lying! But he wouldn't tell me the real reason! And when I asked him where he went last night—you know, when he rushed me out of his room—he wouldn't tell me either."

"Cassie, what are you saying?"

She looked uncomfortable. "It's just that... Seth never used to be so secretive! He's hiding something, Gemma, I know it. And I thought—" She broke off.

"What?"

"Well..." She looked down, fidgeting with her apron. "I thought... Gemma, what if he's lying about other things too?"

"What do you mean?" I took a sharp intake of breath. "You can't possibly think... No, Cassie! You're not thinking that Seth might be involved in Professor Barrow's murder after all?"

She squirmed. "I don't know what to think! No... okay, I... I don't think he's involved—I mean, I can't imagine Seth hurting someone in a fight, never mind murdering someone! But it's just... I don't know... He's just been acting so odd lately!" She glanced around, then lowered her voice. "And you always think you know someone—but do you *really* know them? Do you really know what they're capable of?"

I reached out and caught her hand. "Cassie, we've known Seth since we were all eighteen together. He's like a brother. Whatever else he may be capable of, I'm sure he's not involved in a murder."

She nodded but didn't look convinced. And I had to admit, her words made me uneasy. I remembered my own doubts about Seth—I had purposefully pushed them out of my mind but now they came rushing back to haunt me. The memory of that dinner date with Devlin came back to me and what he had said about what people will do in the name of a cause. And that receptionist at the Domus Trust yesterday... she had said much the same thing... Since this case had begun, I had seen a whole new side to Seth and realised that I didn't know him as well as I thought.

Cassie and I didn't have much chance to chat again for the rest of the morning—the rest of the day, in fact. Saturday was one of our busiest days and we were flat out trying to cope with the groups of tourists that kept arriving, not to mention the locals who kept coming to join the Old Biddies' unofficial gossip centre. In fact, I reflected wryly that Clyde Peters's murder had probably brought me more local business than any advertising or marketing campaign might have done.

I had been a bit worried about Dora's ability to cope, given how new she was, but she had amazed me with her calm organisation and brisk efficiency. And a steady stream of scones, cakes, muffins, tarts, buns, and dainty finger sandwiches flowed out effortlessly from our kitchen. The tearoom was continually filled with the wonderful smell of baking, from the rich buttery fragrance of fresh pastry and the gorgeous smell of fresh bread to the delicate fragrance of cheesecakes and the spicy sweetness of cinnamon and chocolate. Every time the front door was opened, a mouth-watering gust of warm air wafted out onto the street and drew more hungry tourists to our door.

Still, despite the hectic day, I found my thoughts constantly drifting back to the mystery and especially what Cassie had said. I still couldn't believe that Seth could have anything to do with the murder but... I found myself wondering where he had been on Thursday night when he had got that mysterious black eye. And I couldn't help remembering the barmaid's words—that the "stranger" sitting with Clyde Peters the night he had been murdered was someone who had a connection with one of the Oxford colleges...

No. I'm letting Cassie's anxiety get to me. Resolutely, I pushed Seth from my mind and thought of the other possible suspects. Richard Barrow. The professor's younger brother was the strongest contender for the porter's killer. He had connections with Wadsworth too, he knew the porter, and he had no alibi for the night the porter was killed. Well, none that he had told anyone, at any rate, since Richard was still missing. He seemed to be in hiding—exactly what you'd expect from a man who had possibly committed two murders.

And what about Leila Gaber? Somehow, I was sure that she would have an alibi for Thursday night. Someone like Leila would always make sure that she had all the bases covered. But even if she did, I didn't know if her alibi would be worth much. With her manipulative charm, she probably had any number of people happy to lie for her. Besides, what would be her motive? Why would she want Clyde Peters dead? Perhaps... perhaps he knew that she had lied to the police? That she hadn't been in the library the whole time last Friday night, like she had said? And perhaps he had tried to blackmail her about it?

I thought back to what the pub landlord had said about Clyde Peters: "Always knew how to make a spare bob or two on the side..."—yes, I could easily see him in the role of a blackmailer. And just as easily, I could see that Leila Gaber wasn't the kind of woman to put up with extortion of any kind.

I got back home and my thoughts kept me occupied for the rest of the evening, which passed with nothing more eventful than Muesli deciding she was going to produce the biggest hairball in history and puke it all over my parents' cream carpet.

There was no word from Devlin; I knew this new murder must have put even more pressure on him to crack the case. I remembered the way he had looked the last time I saw him—the deep lines of fatigue around his nose and mouth—and I felt a wave of compassion for him. So although I was burning to know how the investigation was proceeding and if he had found any new leads, I restrained myself from calling him.

The next morning was Sunday and I remembered belatedly that my mother was returning from Indonesia that afternoon. I'd offered to go to the airport to pick them up, but had been indignantly rebuffed and told that they were going to finish their journey the way they had started. However, my mother had instructed me to pick them up from the bus station. So that afternoon, I found myself leaving the tearoom in the capable hands of Dora, Cassie, and the Old Biddies, and heading down to Gloucester Green. Just as I was crossing the piazza, I heard a voice calling my name.

"Gemma!"

I turned and found myself facing Lincoln Green.

"Hi, Lincoln," I said in surprise. "What are you doing here?"

"Picking up my mother and yours. I didn't realise you were coming too. My Mum sent me a message saying there was no one to meet them and insisted that I come."

Hmm. The mothers had known very well that I was coming to pick them up. I had a feeling that there was a bit of maternal matchmaking going on here. I suppressed a sigh.

"Actually, I've just had a text message from my Mum," Lincoln continued. "She said their flight had been delayed and they'd just missed the coach so they would have to wait half an hour for the next one.

So they're going to be back later than they thought."

I wondered if that was true. I wouldn't put it past my mother and Helen Green to manufacture some excuse, to force me and Lincoln to spend extra time together. They'd probably purposefully missed the coach and were now sitting languidly in some airport café, drinking tea and discussing what to name our firstborn child.

"Did everything turn out okay with Muesli in the end?" said Lincoln.

"What? Oh, oh yes... Yes, thank you, she was fine. The fire brigade arrived and started drilling holes everywhere and then the little minx just popped out of another vent." I rolled my eyes, then gave him an apologetic look. "I'm sorry it ruined the end of our evening."

"I'll say. She had the most dreadful timing," said Lincoln dryly.

I flushed as I realised what he was referring to. The memory of that interrupted "almost-kiss" hung between us. The embarrassed silence seemed to stretch interminably, then Lincoln said, "Er... fancy a coffee?"

I didn't really, but it would help to break the awkward atmosphere. Besides, there was nothing else I could do—there wasn't enough time to go back to the tearoom, which would be closing soon anyway, so I would have to kill an hour here in Gloucester Green somehow.

"Yeah, why not?" I smiled at Lincoln and started

to lead the way across the square.

As we were passing the cinema, I was pleased to see a familiar sight: a tall lanky man with fingerless gloves and a lanyard around his neck, holding a sheaf of magazines, with a smiling Staffie dog at his feet. I hurried over to greet them.

"Hi Ruby!" I bent down to pat the dog who was wagging her tail so hard, her bum was wriggling. She nosed my hands eagerly and I laughed.

"Sorry, girl, I don't have any chicken nuggets for you today. But I promise I'll bring some the next time I pass by."

"She'll never leave you alone again if you do that," said Owen, chuckling.

We each bought a copy of the *Big Issue* from him and he pocketed the change gratefully. Then he grinned at me and said, "Did you catch up with Jim in the end?"

"Oh, yeah… thanks. Yes, I found him down by the canal, although I have to say he wasn't very… um… chatty. He's not really the friendliest chap, is he?"

Owen guffawed. "'E's a miserable old git. Dunno 'ow 'e used to work in a porter's lodge, dealin' with visitors all day…"

I froze. "Jim used to work in an Oxford college? Which one?"

Owen shrugged. "Not sure. Reckon it was one of the reasons 'e came back 'ere, though, after 'e got off the drugs and got 'is act together. Me, I couldn't have done it—not with all the bad memories—but 'e seems to be managin' okay."

I stared at Owen. "What bad memories?"

"On account of the accident that killed 'is girlfriend," he said.

I remembered Seth mentioning that Jim had lost his family, but I hadn't been paying much attention to it at the time. Now, my heart skipped a beat as a terrible suspicion began to dawn on me.

"What happened to her?" I asked urgently.

Owen grimaced. "'It and run it was. Killed 'is girlfriend outright and they couldn't save the baby she was carryin' either."

"Did they catch the driver?"

"No, that was the worst part for Jim, I think. They never found the driver and made 'im pay. Some local drunk, probably, drivin' when 'e was over the limit. 'It 'is girlfriend just outside the train station—she'd come from Reading to see Jim and was just goin' back, you see. And what was even worse was that Jim couldn't even go to her funeral. She was married, you see—she was plannin' to leave 'er 'usband for Jim—but they were keepin' it quiet, like, until she told the 'usband. Well, after the accident, there was all this stuff in the papers about 'er bein' a lovin' wife and expectin' a new baby... Jim couldn't spoil 'er name and memory by tellin' everyone that she was leavin' her 'usband and the baby was 'is. But 'e couldn't handle it—lost 'is job, 'is house, started takin' pills... then 'e left Oxford."

"Oh my God..." I whispered, my thoughts reeling.

I remembered suddenly that conversation Lincoln and I had had with Clyde Peters on the night of the Oxford Society of Medicine dinner. The head porter had said then that Barrow wouldn't drive anymore after "a bad accident" and always requested a taxi...

"How do you know all this?" I said to Owen.

"Jim opened up to me once," said the homeless man. "I was takin' Ruby for a walk down by the canal and came across 'im under one of the bridges. We had a smoke together. Friday a week ago, it was, I think. 'E was in a strange mood that mornin'. Was really worked up about somethin' but when I asked 'im, 'e wouldn't tell me about it—just said that 'e had a drink with a friend from 'is old college the night before and that the chickens were comin' 'ome to roost." Owen shrugged. "Dunno what 'e meant by that."

Friday a week ago was the day of Professor Barrow's murder, I realised. What if Jim had had a drink the night before with Clyde Peters—the "friend from his old college"—who mentioned Barrow's drunk driving accident? The head porter liked to gossip and Leila Gaber's recent campaign might have brought the subject of the old professor's drinking problem to mind. Somehow, Jim must have put two and two together...

I thought of the expression Owen said Jim had used: "The chickens were coming home to roost"— yes, he had decided that it was time Barrow paid for what he had done...

My mind whirled as I suddenly remembered something else. Something Dora had said the day I asked her who could have known about the hidden staircase at Wadsworth. Clyde Peters, she had said, and some of the other porters who used to work at the college, including a James Price. James... Jim...

I walked away from the homeless man and his dog in a daze.

"What is it, Gemma?" said Lincoln, hurrying after me. "You've gone really pale. Are you all right?"

"Yes... Yes, I'm fine, Lincoln. I...I just realised something..." I stopped and turned around to face him. "I've been looking in the wrong direction—Jim is the murderer!"

CHAPTER TWENTY-EIGHT

"Jim? The tramp?" said Lincoln. "But I thought you said it couldn't be him because of the timeframe? There was only a six-minute gap in which the murder could have taken place and that was too short a time for Jim to make it from the Cloisters to the main gate—"

"But not if he knew about the secret staircase!" I cried. "He could have easily done the deed, escaped from the Cloisters, and got out, to be seen on the CCTV footage on the street across from the college gate at 12:23 a.m. All this time, I'd been thinking of Clyde Peters telling Richard Barrow about the hidden staircase but I hadn't thought of another person who could have known about the staircase as well—Clyde's old friend and colleague, James Price!"

Lincoln looked at me, completely lost.

I hurried to explain. "Clyde Peters was last seen in his local pub having a drink with an 'old friend'—someone who used to work in Oxford and had some connection to an Oxford college, according to the landlord and barmaid I spoke to. Dora mentioned some of the porters who used to work at the college and who would have known about the hidden staircase, before it was boarded up—amongst them, a James Price. I'm willing to bet that Jim was—is—James Price." I took a deep breath, gathering my thoughts. "And *he* murdered Barrow. Not to help the homeless or any other great cause—no, it was much more personal than that. I was right when I felt that this crime was about revenge and something that Barrow had done a long time ago. But I got it wrong. It wasn't something between him and Clyde Peters—it was between him and another porter at Wadsworth. A porter called James Price, whose pregnant girlfriend was killed in a hit-and-run accident many years ago. Barrow was the drunk driver."

"How can you know all that?"

"I don't," I admitted. "But I'm pretty certain I'm right... It all fits! Clyde Peters mentioned that Barrow stopped driving after a bad accident. He didn't say what kind of accident but with Barrow's reputation for drunken behaviour, I wouldn't be surprised... I'm going to ask Glenda!" I said suddenly. "Clyde Peters might have mentioned something to her during their dinner date. Let me ask her..."

I tried her phone but got no reply, so I rang the tearoom. Cassie answered.

"Hey, Cass, can you put Glenda on? I need to ask her something."

"You've just missed her," said Cassie. "She left a few minutes ago."

"Oh? I thought the Old Biddies said they were staying until the tearoom closed today."

"They were, but then Glenda got a phone call from some chap asking her to meet him."

"Some chap?"

"Yeah, apparently he knew something about Clyde Peters's murder, but he would only tell her in person. The Old Biddies all got really excited and rushed out."

"Who was he?"

"I don't know."

I was starting to have a bad feeling about this. "Glenda hasn't gone to meet him alone, has she?"

"Well, she was supposed to, but the other Old Biddies said they weren't missing out on the fun so they decided to all go, but the other three would follow her at a distance."

"Where have they gone? Do you know?"

"Jericho, down by the canal, I think. I heard them arguing about which bus would drop them closest to Canal Street."

"Okay, listen, Cassie: if they ring back, tell them that Glenda is in danger. That the man she's going to meet might be the murderer."

"What? But how do you—"

"I can't explain now," I said. "Just make sure Glenda knows that she mustn't meet him alone under any circumstances!"

I hung up before Cassie could reply, then tried Glenda's number again myself. It went to an answering service again. I tried the other Old Biddies but none of them were answering. I let out a sigh of frustration and looked up to see Lincoln standing patiently next to me, an expression of bewilderment on his face. Quickly, I told him about the situation.

"But... why do you think Glenda might be in danger?" said Lincoln. "Do you think this man who called her is Jim?"

"Yes," I said. "Don't ask me how—it's... it's a hunch, I guess. But I just feel... that there's something 'off' here..."

"But even if it *is* Jim, why would he want to harm her?"

"I... I can't explain!" I said helplessly. "Maybe he questioned Clyde Peters before he killed him and found out that the porter had been telling Glenda things... and he's not sure what she knows..." I paused as I suddenly remembered something. "Oh God! That time I went to see him by the canal, the Old Biddies were with me and they were being their usual nosy selves. I remember Jim yelling at Glenda, asking her why she was staring at him... I don't know—I mean, he doesn't sound like the most balanced character, does he? Maybe he got paranoid

291

that she's snooping around him and knows too much and might expose him..."

"Doesn't she have her friends with her?" said Lincoln.

I made an impatient gesture. "Yes, but what can they do? They're little old ladies. Besides, if they don't realise who he really is, they won't be on their guard..." I gripped my hands together, trying to quell a rising wave of panic. "We've got to warn them, especially Glenda, before she meets him. Oh God, I hope she doesn't get hurt. I'll never forgive myself—"

I whirled suddenly and started for the rear of the square.

"Wait! Gemma! Where are you going?" said Lincoln, hurrying to keep up with me.

"I'm going down to the canal," I said. "I'm going to look for the Old Biddies myself. They walk fairly slowly. I'm sure I can catch up with them if I run. It'll take me too long to get the car and drive up to Jericho, but there's a shortcut to the canal from the back of Gloucester Green—down Hythe Bridge Street. That's the way we went last time. I can search along the canal until I come to the stretch by Jericho and I might meet them there."

Lincoln put a hand on my arm. "Wait, Gemma... maybe you should call the police."

I started to disagree, thinking of the time wasted in explanations and proving that I wasn't a prank call—then I remembered Devlin.

"Yes! I must tell Devlin about this. He might be

able to find them faster."

My fingers fumbled as I dug out my phone and tried to dial the number. I had to force myself to stop and take a deep breath before continuing. I was relieved when Devlin answered on the first ring.

"Gemma? What's wrong?" he said as soon as he heard my voice. Devlin had always been able to pick up on my feelings instantly.

"It's Jim, Devlin!" I said, my words tumbling over themselves. "He's the murderer! He used to be a porter at Wadsworth... he worked with Clyde Peters... and his girlfriend... she was killed in a car accident... hit and run... and she was carrying Jim's baby... and he's been away from Oxford for years... but... but he came back... and he found out... I think Clyde Peters told him... about Barrow and the drunk driving and—"

"Whoa, slow down, Gemma," said Devlin. "How do you know all this?"

"I haven't got time to explain now," I rushed on. "Glenda Bailey might be in danger! Jim called her and asked her to meet him alone. I think he might have found out that she had dinner with Clyde Peters the night before he was killed... and maybe she knows too much—"

"Where is she meeting him?"

"Down by the canal, but I'm not sure which section. Maybe around Jericho. We can start searching from this end of the canal—we're in Gloucester Green now—but maybe you can—"

"We?"

"Me and Lincoln."

"Right." He paused and I knew that Devlin must have been jumping to conclusions. I wanted to explain but there was no time.

"Okay, you start from that end of the canal. I'm out of Oxford at the moment but I've got the car, so I'll start from the north end and work my way down," Devlin said briskly. "Listen, you told me you tracked Jim down by the canal a few days ago and spoke to him—where was that?"

"Um... by... by Frenchay Road Bridge," I said, remembering.

"Then I'll start there."

"Oh God, Devlin, what if he does something to Glenda—"

"He won't." His calm, authoritative voice was reassuring. "We'll find her first. Don't think about it, Gemma. Just focus on searching along the canal. Go now."

***

The light was fading rapidly, bathing everything in a grey gloom, and I found myself cursing the short winter days in England again. I jogged along the tow path, straining to look ahead. It was a completely different scene to when I visited only a few days ago: the canal was dark and murky, and the weeping willows looked sinister in the fading light, their trailing leaves hanging like ghoulish arms over the black water.

The tow path stretched empty ahead of us; in summer, this might have been a busy thoroughfare even at this time, but in the late afternoon on a chilly January evening, nobody wanted to be here on this damp muddy path by the canal. Even the most dedicated dog walkers and avid tourists were tucked up warmly indoors.

There was no sound except for my own harsh breathing and Lincoln's footsteps pounding behind me. The tow path was too narrow for the two of us to run side by side safely and I wondered if I should let him go ahead, although I was running as fast as I could and I didn't think he could go much faster in the dark either. The path was treacherous, wet, and slippery from the recent rain, and it would have been only too easy to slip and go over the bank into the icy water of the canal.

The branch of a hawthorn tree fell across my path, the leaves scraping across my cheek, and then a ramp loomed out of the darkness. It was the bridge over Isis Lock, empty now of all the tourists and families who had been taking photos and admiring the scene. I was up and over it in a flash, grabbing hold of the parapet to steady myself as I rounded the curve of the bridge and ran down the steep incline on the other side, Lincoln right behind me. I skidded slightly as I hit the tow path again and felt Lincoln's hand reach out to steady me.

"All right?" he asked.

"Yes," I panted. "Thanks."

I took off again at a quick jog. We raced past the Jericho boatyard and the tall blocks of the former ironworks foundry, barely discernible in the dark sky. Still we saw no one, and the canal boats moored along the banks had their windows and doors closed and shuttered against the cold, like dozens of blank eyes.

We came across a figure in a hoodie: a youth with his head down, nodding in time to music in his earphones, oblivious to the world. I thought of pausing to ask him if he had seen the Old Biddies, then I realised that he was facing the same way we were and going in the same direction. If we hadn't passed them, he wouldn't have either.

Darting around him, I ran on, pressing a hand to my side as a stitch began to bother me. My legs were starting to ache as well. I was in terrible shape. Working in a tearoom all day (and eating a lot of cakes and buns) obviously didn't do much for your athletic fitness. I wished now that I'd followed up my New Year's Resolution of regular jogging...

It was getting even darker now and I felt panic rise in my chest. Where were the Old Biddies? Why hadn't we seen them yet? How long had we been running? I knew that Frenchay Road Bridge was about thirty minutes from the start of the canal, at a comfortable walking pace, but we were now running as fast as we could. Surely we should have almost been there by now? The walk along the tow path had seemed so pleasant and easy that day in the sunshine—now, it seemed interminably long.

A humpbacked bridge loomed up suddenly out of the darkness. My heart gave a leap of hope, then I realised that it was the one before Frenchay Road Bridge.

"Almost there!" I gasped over my shoulder.

Lincoln didn't reply, although I could hear his footsteps behind me. I ducked under the bridge, passed through the darkness, and came out on the other side. The path had become more overgrown, with large puddles and muddy patches, and I had to concentrate harder to keep my footing.

Then I saw it—a large red brick structure in the distance, one side scrawled with graffiti. *Frenchay Road Bridge.* There was movement ahead of me, on the tow path by the bridge. It was hard to see in the gathering dark, but I thought I could make out two figures. Then as I got closer, I recognised one as Glenda. I felt relief wash through me. She was all right. I'd been panicking for nothing—

The figure next to her moved. He was much bigger and I caught a glimpse of reddish hair. *Jim.* Glenda looked tiny, like a child, standing next to him.

I opened my mouth to call to Glenda, but before I could say anything, Jim lunged towards her. I watched in horror as his hands came up round her shoulders and he grabbed her, shoving her towards the edge of the canal and the icy black water beneath.

CHAPTER TWENTY-NINE

"*Glenda!*" I screamed.

From the bushes at the side of the path ahead of me, three other small figures erupted: Mabel, Florence, and Ethel. They ran towards Jim and surrounded him, shouting and hitting him with their handbags. He faltered in surprise, but only for a moment. Then he swung around with an angry oath and cuffed one of the Old Biddies.

I gasped as I saw Ethel go flying, hitting the side of the bridge and crumpling to a heap on the ground. Florence gave a cry of alarm and ran to her side, whilst Mabel shrieked with anger and slapped ineffectually at Jim's shoulder. He ignored her, his hands still around Glenda's shoulders. She was flailing now, desperately trying to keep her balance on the edge of the bank. Any minute, she would go over.

"Glenda!" I cried, starting towards her.

Someone shoved me gently aside and then Lincoln overtook me, his longer legs closing the distance faster. But even as he passed me, I saw another figure race along the bridge above them.

Devlin!

He gave a yell as he looked over the bridge and saw Jim with Glenda, then my heart stopped as Devlin flung himself over the side the bridge. I thought for a moment that he would go into the canal, but he dropped onto the tow path, crashing into Jim.

The tramp let go of Glenda and reeled backwards, a stream of ugly curses spilling from his mouth. Glenda cried out, tottered slightly, then slipped on the bank and went down.

Mabel lunged for her and managed to grab an arm, holding on tightly as her own feet slipped in the mud. Then Lincoln was there. He reached down and grabbed Glenda's other arm, helping Mabel pull her out of the water.

I stood paralysed for a moment, the whole scene unfolding in front of me like a slow-motion nightmare, then I snapped out of it and ran to the water's edge. Glenda lay gasping and panting on the bank, her clothes sodden. Mabel was next to her, her usually formidable face grey with fright. They were both shivering.

"Are you all right?" I asked Glenda as Lincoln

quickly examined her for injuries.

Then a grunt and a cry of pain made us jerk our heads around. Two bodies hurtled across the tow path next to us.

Devlin and Jim, locked together in an ugly, vicious fight.

I heard the sickening crunch of bone on muscle, the harsh panting, as they wrestled and fought. Jim took a swing and I saw with a jolt of horror that he was holding a broken bottle in his hand. The jagged glass edge came perilously close to Devlin's face as he ducked just in time. He twisted and elbowed Jim in the stomach but the tramp seemed oblivious to the pain. He was fighting like a wild animal now, cursing and yelling, and lashing out in any way possible.

I gasped as I saw the broken bottle strike again, and this time it dealt a glancing blow to the side of Devlin's head. He staggered back and I saw blood. Jim took the opportunity to ram his head into Devlin's chest, taking them both to the edge of the bank.

"No!" I screamed.

Lincoln sprang up to help but it was too late. They struggled at the edge for a heart-stopping moment, then both fell into the canal.

There was a resounding splash and ripples spread out across the murky surface. Jim's head broke the water; he was at the edge, his elbows hooked on the bank, trying to haul himself out.

But there was no sign of Devlin.

My heart stopped.

Oh my God. No. No. No!

"Devlin! Devlin!" I cried, running to the edge where they had fallen in and peering desperately at the black water. Where was he?

Devlin's a strong swimmer, I thought desperately. *The canal isn't that deep. He should be fine.* Then I remembered that he had had a blow to the head. What if he had been knocked unconscious?

I was about to dive in myself when something broke the surface of the water in the middle of the canal. I sagged with relief. It was Devlin, his dark hair plastered to his head like a seal. He shook the water out of his eyes, then began swimming towards me. The next minute, he was there at the bank and Lincoln was reaching down a strong hand to help him out.

Devlin stumbled to his feet, coughing and dripping water, and stood up next to me. I flung myself at him, not caring about his wet clothes soaking into mine.

"Oh God... thank God you're safe..." I babbled. My cheeks were wet and I realised that I was crying.

"Hey... Hey, Gemma... It's all right... I'm fine," said Devlin gently, his arms around me. His hands gripped mine and I felt the strength in his warm fingers. The icy fear eased around my heart. He was all right. I hadn't lost him.

Next to us, Lincoln was helping Jim out of the canal. The fight seemed to have gone completely out of the red-haired tramp. Maybe the cold water had shocked him out of his berserker rage. He sat on the grass, wet and shivering, his expression dazed.

I suddenly remembered the Old Biddies and looked quickly around. Florence was kneeling next to Ethel. I ran over to join them.

"Ethel! Are you hurt?"

"I'm... I'm all right," the old librarian murmured. She tried to give me a brave smile. "Just slightly shaken up. I had the wind knocked out of me."

"I'll have a look at her," said Lincoln, appearing next to me and crouching beside Ethel.

Glenda and Mabel came slowly over to join us, their arms around each other. They were shivering and looked slightly shell-shocked. It hurt me to see Mabel, normally so loud and bossy, looking so pale and silent. I shrugged out of my coat and draped it around their shoulders. They clutched at it gratefully and huddled together.

"We need to call an ambulance," I said, fumbling in my pocket for my phone.

"There are reinforcements coming," Devlin spoke up. He grimaced and moved his right shoulder gingerly, dripping water as he walked over to me. "I radioed for backup before I came here. They should be here any moment."

I looked up and saw the blood pouring down one side of his face. "Oh my God, Devlin—you're bleeding!" I gasped.

He reached up and fingered his temple, wincing

slightly. "Must have been when he knocked me with that glass bottle. Caught me on the side of my head."

"It's bleeding a lot!" I said in consternation.

I turned to Lincoln, still tending to Ethel, and called to him. He came over and examined the wound with expert hands.

"It's not too bad," he said reassuringly. "Head wounds bleed like crazy but they usually look worse than they actually are." He dug into his pocket and pulled out a clean handkerchief, pressing it against the side of Devlin's head. "Here, hold this against the wound and apply pressure. That should help to stop the bleeding."

"Thanks," said Devlin, following Lincoln's instructions.

The brief wail of a siren told us that we were no longer alone. A minute later, the darkness was broken by the glare of headlights, followed by the whirling glow of red and blue. Police cars screeched to a halt on the bridge above us, and in a few moments officers were swarming the bank. An ambulance arrived. Car doors banged. Voices shouted. I felt slightly dazed myself as I was led up the embankment and onto the bridge. A paramedic came to fuss over me and I waved him away impatiently.

"No, no, I'm fine! It's the Old Bi—the old ladies you need to see to first. They've been hurt and are in shock. And Inspector O'Connor—he's had a bad cut to his head."

Then I remembered Jim and wondered if he had been injured in the fight too. I looked around for him—he seemed all right, sitting on the grass, his expression defeated. A police officer was standing next to him, giving him the official caution, but I didn't think Jim was taking in much of what was being said to him.

A stretcher went past me and I followed it to the ambulance, watching anxiously as Ethel and Glenda were lifted up.

"I'm fine," said Devlin irritably as a paramedic tried to persuade him to get in as well.

"You should go to the hospital," said Lincoln. "Get yourself checked out. You don't want to mess around with a head injury."

Devlin looked as if he was going to argue, then he ceded to Lincoln's advice. "Okay, but I'm not going in the ambulance. I've got my own car—"

"You're not driving in that condition," I said quickly. I held out my hand. "Give me your keys. I'll drive you. I would have followed the ambulance to the hospital anyway."

Devlin handed the keys reluctantly to me. Then I clapped a hand to my head as I remembered something and turned to Lincoln urgently.

"Oh, bloody hell—our mothers! They're probably stranded at Gloucester Green, wondering where we are!"

"I'll go back and fetch them now," said Lincoln. He grinned suddenly. "Don't worry—of all the excuses

305

there are, I think catching a murderer trumps the lot! I'm sure they'll be all agog when I tell them what's happened."

He left, and Devlin and I waited as Florence and Mabel were helped into the ambulance to join their friends.

"We'll be right behind you," I said, as I stood by the open back doors.

Mabel turned around and reached out to pat my hand. A flash of her old spirit showed in her face. "Don't worry about us, dear. We're tougher than you think."

Glenda's voice came muffled from one of the stretchers. "And I can't wait to tell everyone in the village that the handsome Detective O'Connor jumped off a bridge to save me!"

I laughed in spite of myself, feeling much better, and thinking that when I reached eighty, I hoped I would have half the spirit of the little Old Biddies.

CHAPTER THIRTY

"I still can't believe it." Seth shook his head. "Jim?"

I sank down into the armchair opposite him, grimacing slightly. My thighs were still reeling from the enforced workout along the canal yesterday and I winced as my sore muscles complained loudly.

"It wasn't because of the Domus Trust project, like we thought," I explained. "Although Jim did hate Barrow for his attitude towards the homeless. But he wouldn't have murdered him for that. It was much more personal. He found out that Barrow was the hit-and-run driver who had killed his girlfriend and unborn baby."

"But how did he find that out?"

"Clyde Peters. They worked together in the Porter's Lodge at Wadsworth College. Jim used to be a porter there as well. When he came back to Oxford, he decided to look up his old colleague again—it was easy because Peters was still the head porter at Wadsworth—and they met up for drinks the night before the murder. Peters was gossiping as usual and happened to mention Leila Gaber's campaign against Barrow and his drunken behaviour. He also mentioned that he once saw Barrow staggering into the college late at night many years ago, looking like death, very shaken up and reeking of alcohol. Peters had helped the drunk professor to his room and had heard him mumble something about an accident, although the next morning Barrow had denied everything. However, Peters noticed that Barrow sold his car soon after and from then on always insisted on taking a taxi everywhere he went."

"But how did he connect that with Jim's girlfriend?"

"He didn't," I said. "That's the whole point—otherwise he would have told Jim years ago. But Jim hadn't told anyone about his girlfriend; they kept the affair discreet because she was married. Of course, the papers did report the accident but they used the woman's married name and said she was a Reading housewife. Peters never suspected that Jim had any connection to the hit-and-run victim. And anyway, Jim went off the rails quite quickly after that—lost his job, left Oxford..."

"And meanwhile, Clyde Peters never said anything?"

"I think he was keeping it up his sleeve, as blackmail leverage, in case he ever needed Barrow's help with something. After all, the old professor had a powerful position on the college committee and that would give Peters some protection."

"So he kept it quiet all these years," said Seth thoughtfully. "Why suddenly tell Jim about it now?"

"I don't think he intended to tell Jim anything in particular—it just slipped out in conversation. I guess with him dead now, we'll never know. But I think he was just gossiping about Leila Gaber stirring things. Maybe he was wondering aloud if it was time he approached Barrow with this 'dirty secret', to ask for money in return for his silence... and of course, he wouldn't have known that it had personal meaning for Jim..."

"It must have been such a shock for Jim," said Seth.

I nodded. "Yeah, Owen mentioned that Jim was in a strange mood on Friday morning—that he was 'really worked up' about something. I think Jim must have carried the bitterness and anger in him for so many years and now suddenly, here was a chance to get closure. He probably became fixated on revenge. He remembered that Barrow had a habit of having a smoke in the Cloisters last thing at night—and he also knew about the secret staircase. It seemed like the perfect opportunity."

Seth frowned. "But why use Leila Gaber's dagger as the murder weapon?"

"I don't think he really planned it all out. Probably, he had some weapon of his own, but when he came through the Porter's Lodge that night, he must have seen the dagger sticking out of Leila Gaber's pigeonhole. He probably remembered Clyde Peters telling him about Leila's campaign against Barrow and thought that here was a chance to throw suspicion on someone else, someone known to be after Barrow." I gave Seth a rueful smile. "Of course, he didn't know that you had borrowed the dagger last and that suspicion would be thrown on you instead."

Seth leaned forwards and took his glasses off, rubbing the bridge of his nose tiredly. "The whole thing is like a terrible nightmare. When Devlin called this morning and told me that I was cleared of all charges, I almost couldn't believe it. In fact, I still can't believe it's all over!"

"Seth..." I hesitated. "Now that it *is* all over, can you tell me the truth about something?"

He looked puzzled. "Yes, of course."

"How did you get that black eye?"

"Oh, this..." He fingered his left eye socket self-consciously. The skin around it was an ugly mottled mix of purple, mauve, and brown. "Um... it's nothing, really."

"If it's nothing, why couldn't you tell Cassie about it?" I gave him a stern look. "She didn't believe that cock and bull story you spun her about walking into a door."

Seth looked down, his cheeks reddening. "Well, I

couldn't tell *her* the truth... it would have been too embarrassing."

I looked at him quizzically.

He took a deep breath, then said in a rush, "I got the black eye from my personal trainer. I had a session with him on Thursday night—the night Clyde Peters was murdered. We were doing some boxing and I didn't duck in time."

"Your personal trainer? Since when do you have a personal trainer?"

"Since a month ago. I thought... well, I thought maybe if I could... you know... beef myself up a bit..." Seth's voice sank so low, I had to strain to hear him, "... Cassie might... um... notice me a bit more."

I stared at him, torn between the urge to laugh and the urge to whack his head in exasperation. "Seth, Cassie does notice you!"

"Yes, but not like... Not as a man," Seth mumbled, still not meeting my eyes.

I opened my mouth, then shut it again. I didn't know what to say.

Finally, I said gently, "Maybe you should just tell Cassie how you feel—"

"No," said Seth quickly. "I can't. It would be so humiliating. I know she won't feel the same way and then—"

"But you *don't* know," I said. I thought of Cassie's recent distress and that awkward moment when she had nearly flung herself into Seth's arms when he was released from the police station. I had a feeling that my best friend didn't know her own feelings either. "I think... I think you might be surprised if you spoke to her..."

Seth gave me a despairing look. "I can't, Gemma. It's hard enough now, trying to hide my feelings, but it would be even more awkward if she knew... It could destroy our friendship. Please... don't say anything to her."

I sighed. He was right. In fact, it was awkward enough already for me, stuck in the middle, but if Seth declared his feelings and Cassie didn't return them, it would put a terrible strain over everything. Our trio would probably never be the same again.

"All right. But I still think you should tell her." I glanced at my watch. Cassie taught a few classes at the dance studio in Meadowford-on-Smythe as a supplementary income earner and tonight was one of them. "She'll be finishing her class now—she should be joining us soon."

Seth pushed his glasses up his nose in that familiar gesture and gave me a smile. "I'm really looking forward to this party."

So was I. Somehow, at the eleventh hour, the housing project for the homeless had been approved. Seth had been ecstatic—almost as happy as hearing that he had been released from all charges. The Domus Trust was holding a small drinks party to celebrate, and Cassie and I were invited as Seth's guests. The Georgian building housing the charity's offices looked very different to how I remembered when we arrived there half an hour later. It was lit up with disco lights and filled with the buzz of laughter and excited conversation. Someone had even rigged up a sound system and cleared a space in the middle of the office for those who wanted to dance.

"Eh, now... nice to see you here, miss!"

I turned and smiled in delight as I recognised Owen, looking smarter than I'd ever seen him. My gaze dropped automatically to his feet, expecting to see a doggie smile.

He laughed. "No, Ruby's not with me tonight. Dogs aren't allowed 'ere in the office. She's with a friend."

"Oh, in that case, you'll have to give Ruby her present for me," I said, pulling a large rawhide bone wrapped with a red ribbon out of the gift bag I was carrying.

Owen's face split into a grin. "Oh! Ta! Very kind of you, miss... Ruby girl will love that." His grin widened. "I've got good news to tell you too—they've approved pets at this development and I've bagged a ground-floor unit. Me and Ruby are goin' to 'ave our own 'ome!"

"I know—Seth told me," I said, smiling warmly. "I'm so happy for you, Owen! I thought it wasn't going to happen. The last I heard, the project seemed to be in trouble. When I spoke to the receptionist here, she told me that the Wadsworth college committee had been swayed by Professor Barrow's views and were refusing to give approval—"

"Yeah, but the new 'Ead of the Ethnoarchaeology Department worked 'er magic," said Owen with grin and a jerk of his head across the room.

I followed the direction of his gesture and as the crowds parted, I saw a vivacious, attractive woman, clad in a glittering jewelled kaftan, standing across the room from me. Her head was thrown back in laughter, her generous mouth smiling widely and her mane of dark hair flowing down her back. And all around her was an eager congregation, laughing with her, listening to her every word, basking in her charm as a flower basks in the warmth of the sun.

"Leila Gaber!" I said in surprise. "What is she doing here?"

"She's been amazin', Dr Gaber," said Owen. "Talked to the college committee, she did, and I don't know 'ow she did it, but she got them to approve the project within an 'our. And she put in a good word for those of us with pets too—said she's got two kitties of 'er own and they're like 'er family. That's 'ow they agreed to let us 'ave pets at the development."

I was wrong about Leila Gaber, I thought. It seemed that she could use her manipulative charm for more than just her own ends. Across the room, the beautiful Egyptian woman turned her head and our eyes met. There was a pause of a second, then she gave that Mona Lisa smile of hers and raised her glass to me. I smiled back and saluted her with my own glass.

Then I turned back to the man beside me. "Hey,

Owen—I've brought something for you too."

"Eh?"

I put my hand into the bag again and drew out a large cardboard box. Owen's eyes widened in surprise and delight as I handed him the gift. "It's sort of a house-warming present."

"Cor! For me?" He turned the box over, staring at the picture of the sleek coffee machine.

"I remembered you saying how much you love your coffee," I said with a smile. "Well, now you can make your own... in your own home."

He seemed speechless for a moment. "This... it's wonderful... wonderful..." He looked back up at me and blinked rapidly. "Thank you, miss... it's real kind of you."

"You're welcome. And please call me Gemma."

"I'll look forward to makin' you a cuppa when you come to visit Ruby and me, Gemma," he said with a nod and a smile.

The music in the room changed suddenly and I heard the distinctive opening piano flourish of ABBA's "Dancing Queen". Several people rushed into the empty space in the middle of the floor and began swaying and spinning, singing loudly with the song. I laughed as Owen grabbed my hand and urged me to join the crowd.

From the corner of my eye, I saw Cassie standing at the edge of the dance floor, tapping her foot eagerly in time to the music. Seth was standing next to her, looking from her to the dance floor and then back again wistfully. I saw him hesitate, make as if to speak to her, then waver and turn away.

Argh! I wanted to march over and shake him. Then suddenly I saw him swing back and lean close to Cassie, saying something in her ear. She turned to him, a smile lighting up her face. The two of them joined the crowd of dancers. They didn't touch and Seth shuffled self-consciously next to Cassie, but something in the way they moved together made me smile. Rome wasn't built in a day, I reminded myself. But I had a feeling that the first stones had been laid in place...

***

A couple of nights later, I found myself at a very different sort of evening: this time at my parents' house, with Helen Green, her husband Charles, and Lincoln as the guests of honour for dinner. The table was laid with the best china and gleaming with silverware and crystal glasses, and my mother had pulled out all the stops with the food. Although I noticed, as we sat down, that many of the dishes had a distinctly odd appearance and smell. I yelped as I took a bite of the orange-coloured roast chicken and found my mouth on fire.

"Water!" I gasped, grabbing my glass and gulping down the cooling liquid.

"I think you've used far too much *sambal oelek*, dear," said Helen, eyeing the chicken disapprovingly.

"Nonsense," my mother said. "It was only a bit in the marinade."

I spluttered and took a shuddering breath and said to my mother, "What have you put on the roast chicken?"

"Oh, darling, it's the most wonderful traditional Indonesian hot sauce, made with chili peppers, ginger, garlic, shrimp paste, fish sauce, shallots, lime juice, palm sugar, and lots of vinegar. Isn't it marvellous?" She picked up a bowl and thrust it towards me. "I've put some on the Brussels sprouts too. Here, try some."

"Er... I'll... I'll help myself later," I said.

"Have some tamarind roast potatoes, then," said my mother. "Or how about some *gado-gado* green salad?"

I looked around the table in despair. Wasn't there any *normal* English food?

"Mother, I thought we were having a traditional British roast?"

"Well, you see, darling, Helen and I had such *interesting* food in Indonesia, we decided that we simply had to get more adventurous in the kitchen! And you know that there is Dutch-Indo fusion cuisine—from the time when Indonesia was a Dutch colony—so we decided: why not British-Indo cuisine?" My mother beamed at me and Helen nodded in agreement.

"Lincoln, you haven't had any yet! Here you go, have some *sambal* Brussels sprouts..." My mother started heaping green vegetables covered in hot sauce on his plate.

"Er... thank you, Aunt Evelyn... no, no... that's... that's quite enough..." Lincoln said desperately.

I saw his eyes bulge and tears spring to his eyes as he took his first bite but, ever the gentleman, he ate a few mouthfuls valiantly under his mother's proud eye. The two fathers watched us apprehensively, like condemned prisoners who knew their turn was next. Somehow, we got through the rest of the meal by eating as sparingly as possible and drinking copious amounts of water. Finally, we were released from the dining table and escaped gratefully to the living room.

"I'm afraid I've only got normal tea and coffee," said my mother and there was an audible sigh of relief around the room.

"It's a shame we didn't bring back any *kopi luwak*," said Helen. "You would have loved that."

"What's *kopi luwak*?" said Lincoln.

"It's a type of traditional Indonesian coffee and it's one of the most expensive coffees in the world!" said my mother excitedly. "It's made from coffee beans which have been eaten by a type of Asian cat-like creature called a civet and then passed through their stomachs and defaecated. Oh, don't worry—they clean the beans before roasting them," she said, seeing my expression. "We tried some, Helen and I— it's really lovely—much less bitter than ordinary coffee. It's the enzymes from the civet's bowels, you see, that do that. But we forgot to bring some home."

Thank God for small mercies. I was pretty sure I could happily go through life without experiencing coffee made from beans pooed out by some weird Indonesian cat.

As my mother and Helen went off to make the tea and coffee, and my father and Charles became engrossed in a discussion of the next Parliamentary election, Lincoln came over and sat down on the sofa next to me. I hadn't seen him since the fiasco by the canal and I thanked him again now for coming with me.

"I checked at the hospital and it seems that the Old Biddies came through fine," he commented.

"Yes, thank goodness! Ethel in particular—it was a miracle that she didn't break any bones when she hit the side of the bridge—and I was sure Glenda would develop hypothermia or something... but they all seemed to be all right. They were treated for shock and kept in overnight, but insisted on going home the next morning." I shook my head and chuckled wryly. "In fact, they rang me to make sure they had the biggest table reserved when the tearoom re-opened on Tuesday because they'd already organised for all their friends in the village to come and hear their story of how they captured the deadly 'Wadsworth Cloisters Murderer.' It was absolute mayhem. Even a few reporters turned up. I was run off my feet catering to them all."

"Sounds like some kind of senior citizen press

conference," Lincoln laughed.

I rolled my eyes. "I have a feeling the Old Biddies are going to live off the celebrity of this murder for a long time."

"Well, I have to admit—that day by the canal was probably the most exciting day I've ever had," said Lincoln, his eyes twinkling. "And I'm including the day we had three cardiac arrests, an acute renal failure, and a patient come out of a sixteen-year coma on the ICU ward."

I laughed. "It was a bit much for me too. I don't know how Devlin does his job—he seems to take it all in his stride."

"Yes, danger and excitement seem to follow Devlin O'Connor around," said Lincoln. His eyes met mine. "It's hard to compete with that."

My heart gave an uncomfortable stutter. "Lincoln..." I started to say.

"It's okay," he said, holding a hand up and giving me a rueful smile. "You don't need to say anything. I knew the minute I saw your face."

"My... my face?"

"When you thought Devlin had gone under in the canal. You looked as if your world had ended." Lincoln's smile turned wistful. "Maybe one day I'll meet someone who can look like that for me."

I squirmed, feeling terrible. "Lincoln—"

He waved his hand. "It's okay, Gemma. Honestly. I'll admit that I'm disappointed but you haven't broken my heart or anything. And in the meantime..." He held his hand out to me with a smile. "I hope we can remain friends?"

I felt a rush of affection for him. Putting my hand in his, I returned the smile. "Yes. Friends. Very good friends."

"*Meorrw!*" came a plaintive little voice next to us.

We looked down to see Muesli rubbing herself against a corner of the sofa.

"Hey, Muesli, want to come up and say hello to Lincoln?" I said, patting the empty space on the sofa next to us.

The little tabby cat eyed Lincoln suspiciously, then came closer and sniffed his ankle.

"*Meorrw!*" she said. She gave me a disgruntled look, as if to say, "*Not this one. I want the other one!*" then turned and stalked off.

I smiled wryly to myself. I hated to admit it but, as usual, Muesli was going to get her own way.

EPILOGUE

The air was crisp and cold, and the moon bright in the starlit sky as I stepped out of the Jaguar XK whilst Devlin held the door. He shut the door behind me, then put a gentle hand under my elbow as he walked me up the front steps of my parents' house. A sense of déjà vu swept over me. I had been here a little over a week ago—coming back after a romantic dinner, with a different man by my side...

"Would you like to come in for a drink?" I said softly. I felt suddenly shy and couldn't look Devlin in the eye.

He raised a teasing eyebrow. "I think it was hard enough for your mother watching me pick you up for dinner. I don't think she could cope with a nightcap as well."

"They're not in," I said. "My parents have gone out for dinner with friends. In any case..." I stood up a bit taller. "My mother will just have to get used to it."

A slow smile spread across Devlin's face. "That's

not what you would have said eight years ago."

"I've changed since then."

"Yes. I'd noticed." Something in the way he said that made my pulse quicken.

I let us into the house and we stood facing each other in the darkened hallway. My heart was pounding. It had been a wonderful, magical night— the night I had been dreaming of ever since Devlin came back into my life: the romantic candle-lit dinner, the warm conversation and easy laughter across the table, and the sense that we were slowly, slowly, finding each other again. There was just one thing left to make this night perfect.

A kiss. Our first kiss. Again.

Devlin came closer and I felt his arms slide around me. I caught my breath, my pulse racing now like a wild thing. I was very conscious of the clean, male scent of him, the way his body felt, hard and warm against mine, and the look in his blue eyes—a look that caught me and held me captive. My lips parted. He lowered his head. I held my breath, waiting, yearning—

"*Meorr-eeoorrw!*"

Devlin faltered, but I reached out and yanked his head down to mine. This time, I wasn't going to let Muesli ruin the moment.

Our lips met. Softly and tentatively at first, then bolder, deeper, more urgent. It was everything I had dreamt of and more. I didn't want the kiss to end. Then, somehow through the haze of passion and

323

longing, I became aware of the persistent cries at our feet.

"*Meorrw... meeeeorrw... meeeeorrw-orrw...*"

Finally, we could ignore it no longer. We broke apart and glanced down. Muesli was sitting next to Devlin's legs, looking up at us, her little tabby face indignant.

"*Meorrw!*" she said again and raised up slightly on her haunches.

Devlin chuckled. "I think she doesn't like being left out."

He bent down and scooped the little cat up in his arms, then drew me close again. Muesli looked up from where she was wedged snugly between us, a complacent expression on her face as she began to purr loudly. She was happy now.

I scowled at her. "This isn't a threesome, Muesli."

"*Meorrw?*" she said, giving me a challenging look which clearly said: "Oh, yeah?"

FINIS

THE OXFORD TEAROOM MYSTERIES

A Scone To Die For (Book 1)

Tea with Milk and Murder (Book 2)

Two Down, Bun To Go (Book 3)

Till Death Do Us Tart (Book 4)

Muffins and Mourning Tea (Book 5)

Four Puddings and a Funeral (Book 6)

Another One Bites the Crust (Book 7)

Apple Strudel Alibi (Book 8)

The Dough Must Go On (Book 9)

The Mousse Wonderful Time of Year (Book 10)

All-Butter ShortDead (Prequel)

For other books by H.Y. Hanna,
please visit her website:
www.hyhanna.com

GLOSSARY OF BRITISH TERMS

At loggerheads – in a violent disagreement over something, usually when neither side will give in

Bin (Dustbin) – container for rubbish *(American: trashcan)*

Biscuits – small, hard, baked product, either savoury or sweet *(American: cookies. What is called a "biscuit" in the U.S. is more similar to the English scone)*

Bloody – very common adjective used as an intensifier for both positive and negative qualities (e.g. "bloody awful" and "bloody wonderful"), often used to express shock or disbelief ("Bloody Hell!")

Bollocks! – an expression of dismissive contempt or disagreement, same as "Rubbish!"

Bob ("spare a bob or two") – a pound; (historically, a bob was slang for a shilling but inflation has raised its value!)

Bugbear – something that is a source of obsessive anxiety or irritation, a thorn in your side

Bugger! – an exclamation of annoyance

Bum – the behind *(American: butt)*

Carpark – a place to park vehicles *(American: parking lot)*

Cheers – in everyday conversation, a casual way to say "thank you", also often used in farewell

Chum – close friend *(American: buddy)*

Chuck – throw

Cuppa – slang term for "a cup of tea"

Flat-out – very busy, doing something as fast and as hard as you can

Flutter – a small bet or wager, eg. "have a flutter on the horses"

(to) Fob someone off – to appease someone by evasion or deceit

(to be) Having you on – to delude or dupe you, to pretend something is true when it is not, usually as a tease or a joke

Git – a despicable person

(to) Give a toss – to care

Go down a treat – be very well received

Hobnob – a type of traditional British oat biscuit, often dunked in tea. Also used as a verb – to "hobnob with someone" meaning to hang out / spend time in a friendly manner (usually used in the context of being with celebrities or other rich/power/famous personalities)

Lie-in – when you remain in bed, lazing around, even after you're awake, often done as a special treat on weekends *(American: sleep-in)*

Knackered – very tired, exhausted (can also mean "broken" when applied to a machine or object); comes from the phrase "ready for the knacker's yard"—where old horses were slaughtered and the by-products sent for rendering, different from a slaughterhouse where animals are killed for human consumption)

Plonker – an annoying idiot

Prat – idiot, often a superior, condescending one

Porter – usually a person hired to help carry luggage, however at Oxford, they have a special meaning (see *Special terms used in Oxford University* below)

Pudding – in the U.K., this refers to both "dessert" in general or a specific type of soft, jelly-like dessert, depending on the context.

Queue – an orderly line of people waiting for something *(American: line)*

Row – an argument

Sodding – am adjective used as an intensifier, usually in a negative context

(to be) Stuffed – to be in deep trouble (milder form of the F-word version)

Ta – slang for "thank you", more often used in the north of England

Torchlight – light from a torch, a portable battery-powered electric lamp. *(American: flashlight. NOTE – different from the American usage of "torch" which is a blowlamp*

Tosser – a despicable person

Tuck into – to eat with great enthusiasm

Yonks – a very long time, "ages"

SPECIAL TERMS USED IN OXFORD UNIVERSITY:

College - one of thirty or so institutions that make up the University; all students and academic staff have to be affiliated with a college and most of your life revolves around your own college: studying, dining, socialising. You are, in effect, a member of a College much more than a member of the University. College loyalties can be fierce and there is often friendly rivalry between nearby colleges. The colleges also compete with each other in various University sporting events.

Don / Fellow – a member of the academic staff / governing body of a college *(equivalent to "faculty member" in the U.S.)* – basically refers to a college's tutors. "Don" comes from the Latin, *dominus*— meaning lord, master.

Fresher – a new student who has just started his first term of study; usually referring to First Year undergraduates but can also be used for graduate students.

High Table – refers to both the table and the actual dinner for the dons of a college and their guests. Often situated at one end of the dining hall.

Porter(s) – a team of college staff who provide a

variety of services, including controlling entry to the college, providing security to students and other members of college, sorting mail, and maintenance and repairs to college property.

Porter's Lodge – a room next to the college gates which holds the porters' offices and also the "pigeonholes"—cubby holes where the internal University mail is placed and notes for students can be left by their friends.

Quad – short for quadrangle: a square or rectangular courtyard inside a college; walking on the grass is usually not allowed.

S.C.R. – the Senior Common Room, for the Fellows

CHELSEA BUN RECIPE

First created in the 18th century at Bun House in Chelsea, London, these delicious buns were a favourite with the Hanoverian royal family. They have a distinctive square spiral shape and are made with a rich yeast dough, flavoured with mixed spices or cinnamon, and lemon zest. Inside the swirls, the bun contains a mixture of brown sugar, butter and dried fruit such as currants, raisins, cranberries and sultanas. An iconic product in British baking, Chelsea buns are a bit similar to the more well-known cinnamon roll.

INGREDIENTS:

- 500g (4 cups & 2.5 level tablespoons) plain white flour (plus extra for dusting / kneading)
    -
- 250ml (1 cup & 1 tablespoon) milk
- 5g (1.5 teaspoons instant) quick yeast
- 50g (3.5 tablespoons) unsalted butter
- 60g (1/4 cup) caster sugar
- 1 egg, lightly beaten
- Zest of 1 lemon
- 1 tsp mixed spice OR cinnamon
- 1 tsp salt
- Vegetable oil for greasing

For the filling:
- 30g (2 tablespoons) butter (very softened / slightly melted)
- 75g Demerara sugar
- Dried fruit (as much or as little as you fancy): 100g dried sultanas (golden raisins) / 100g dried cranberries / 100g seedless raisins (100g = ½ cup packed)

For the glaze:
- 2 tbsp caster sugar
- 1 tbsp milk
- OR
- 2 tbsp citrus juice
- 90g (2/3 cup & 1 tablespoon) sifted icing sugar.

INSTRUCTIONS:

1)   Sift the flour into a large mixing bowl and combine with the sugar, salt, yeast and mixed spice or cinnamon, plus the lemon zest – mix well so that the spices and zest are evenly distributed in the flour.

2)   Melt the butter and add the milk, warming the mixture until it is about 40°C / 105°F.

3)   Make a well in the centre of the flour mixture and pour in the warm milk & butter mixture, as well as the beaten egg.

4)   Stir and mix to combine the contents of the bowl, until it forms a wet dough and comes away from the sides of the bowl (you may need to add a little more flour)

5)   Tip the dough out onto a well-floured clean surface and knead lightly for 5 minutes, until the dough is smooth and elastic. Add more flour if necessary so that the dough no longer feels sticky. *(You may prefer to use the dough hook on your standing mixer for 5 minutes, which is easier than kneading by hand.)*

6)   Lightly grease the mixing bowl with some vegetable oil, then return the dough to the bowl and cover with a damp tea towel. Leave it in a warm, draught-free place and allow the dough to rise, until it has doubled in size (about 60 minutes). *** If the milk is not warm enough, the dough may need longer to rise—leave it until it has doubled in size.*

7)   Tip the dough back out onto the work surface and knead briefly, then roll it out into a large rectangle that's about 20cm x 30cm (8in x 12in). You will have to use your fingers to stretch the dough, to coax it into a rectangular shape. Make sure the

longer side is facing you.

8)   Brush the surface of the dough with the melted butter and then scatter the Demerara sugar and dried fruit evenly across the surface.

9)   Using your thumb, press down the edge of the long surface nearest to you, so that it "sticks" to the table – then take hold of the other end and roll the dough up towards you, into a tight cylinder. It's important that the dough is rolled as tight as possible.

10)   Using a sharp knife, cut the roll up into slices, each one about 4cm (1½in) thick.

11)   Lay the slices (cut side up) on a lightly greased baking tray, making sure that they're about 1cm apart. This is important so that they stick together as they bake and when pulled apart, produces that characteristic "square" shape of a Chelsea bun.

12)   Cover with a tea towel and let them rest again for about 30mins.

13)   Meanwhile,   preheat   the   oven   to 200C/400F/gas mark six.

14)   Bake for about 20 – 25 minutes, until the buns have risen and are golden-brown. Check at around the 15 minute mark to make sure the fruit isn't

burning – if so, cover the buns with a piece of foil.

15)   While the buns are baking, make the glaze by heating the milk and caster sugar in a saucepan until boiling, then reduce the heat and simmer for 2-3 minutes. (Alternatively, you can also make a glaze by combining citrus juice and icing sugar)

16)   When the buns are removed from the oven, brush immediately with the glaze, then set aside to cool on a wire rack. Once cool, tear them gently apart.

Enjoy!

ABOUT THE AUTHOR

USA Today bestselling author H.Y. Hanna writes British cosy mysteries filled with humour, quirky characters, intriguing whodunits—and cats with big personalities! Set in Oxford and the beautiful English Cotswolds, her books include the Oxford Tearoom Mysteries, the 'Bewitched by Chocolate' Mysteries and the English Cottage Garden Mysteries. After graduating from Oxford University, Hsin-Yi tried her hand at a variety of jobs: advertising exec, model, English teacher, dog trainer, marketing manager, educational book rep... before returning to her first love: writing. She worked as a freelance writer for several years and has won awards for her novels, poetry, short stories and journalism.

A globe-trotter all her life, Hsin-Yi has lived in a variety of cultures, from Dubai to Auckland, London to New Jersey, but is now happily settled in Perth, Western Australia, with her husband and a rescue kitty named Muesli. You can learn more about her and her books at: **www.hyhanna.com**

Sign up to her newsletter to be notified of new releases, exclusive giveaways and other book news! Go to: **www.hyhanna.com/newsletter**

ACKNOWLEDGMENTS

I owe a huge debt of thanks to the many members of my fantastic team: first, to my beta readers: Basma Alwesh, Rebecca Wilkinson, Jenn Roseton and Melanie G. Howe for their tireless enthusiasm and for always finding time to squeeze me into their busy lives; thank you also to my proofreaders, Connie Leap, Adriann Harris, Deanna Stevens and Katja Bishop for their eagle eyes in checking the manuscript and for doing such a great job at such short notice!

A long overdue thanks to my editor, Chandler Groover, for being so great to work with and so patient with all my questions and accommodating of my production schedule—as well as being so game, no matter which new book (and genre) I throw at him!

A special thank you goes to the talented Kim McMahan Davis of _Cinnamon and Sugar... and a Little Bit of Murder_ blog, for acting as my "baking consulant" and helping me test the Chelsea bun recipe.

And of course, to my wonderful husband for his encouragement and support, his patience with me and everything he does to help me achieve my dream. He is one man in a million.

Made in the USA
Monee, IL
05 April 2023

31391730R00201